# A Deal with Her Father

by

Caitlyn Callery

This is a work of fiction. Names, characters, places, and incidents are either the product of the author's imagination or are used fictitiously, and any resemblance to actual persons living or dead, business establishments, events, or locales, is entirely coincidental.

**A Deal with Her Father**

COPYRIGHT © 2024 by Hilary Mackelden

Cover Art by *Tina Lynn Stout*

The Wild Rose Press, Inc.
PO Box 708
Adams Basin, NY 14410-0708
Visit us at www.thewildrosepress.com

Publishing History
First Edition, 2025
Trade Paperback ISBN 978-1-5092-6064-5
Digital ISBN 978-1-5092-6065-2

Published in the United States of America

## Dedication

To Nanna Jo,
with grateful thanks for her memories

## Other Books from Caitlyn Callery

# Chapter One

*Fieldhurst, Sussex, 1926*

Reggie Chilvers threw her pen onto the desk in frustration. A jagged-edged circle of black ink spread across the pink blotting paper, while the numbers she had written so neatly in the ledger seemed to taunt her, as if they knew, by refusing to tally, they'd force her to go out where the public would see her.

Usually, Sally Ann would fetch the receipts from the shop, bringing them back to where Reggie sat, hidden from view in her tiny, windowless office. But Sally Ann had gone out to an appointment and wasn't likely to be back before the tea shop closed for the evening. Reggie couldn't wait for her: she had to be home on time or there would be questions asked and trouble brewed.

Perhaps, if she walked down the short staff hallway and stood behind the door at the end, she could catch Elsie's eye and still keep out of sight of most of the patrons. But if the waitress was serving a customer, or rearranging the display of cakes, or, most likely, daydreaming about her new gentleman friend, Reggie would be left waving at her like an idiot and getting nowhere.

There was no choice. She sighed and pushed herself upright, paused for a few seconds to stretch her spine and legs after so long hunched over the desk, then made her way to the front of the shop.

Her heels clicked against the red tiled floor of the corridor, past the kitchen where Sally Ann made the cakes and sandwiches each day, and where the tea was brewed, along with the occasional cup of coffee. The *very* occasional cup of coffee. The beverage wasn't popular with the residents of Fieldhurst, Reggie knew, since she was in charge of ordering stock that needed replenishing. She couldn't remember the last time she had ordered coffee beans, and the gleaming grinder on the kitchen counter was so seldom used it hadn't even been switched on today. It probably wouldn't be tomorrow, either. Coffee was just not something the rural English drank.

Which was neither here nor there. Right now, Reggie needed the receipts from this afternoon, not the statistics on coffee drinking.

She reached the door to the front of the shop and peered through the gap between the hinges, heartened to see nobody sitting at any of the tables in the main serving area. That was good, because it meant there would be nobody here who was likely to recognize her and tell her father what she was doing.

The tea shop was darker than the serving corridor, by design. The corridor was for workers who needed to see what they were doing and where they were going, whereas Sally Ann had wanted the tea shop itself to have an atmosphere of calm, somewhere her customers could relax and not be made too aware of the passage of time. So she had told Reggie when she first showed her around. Consequently, the only light came from the windows at the shop front, although if it got too dark outside, there were electric lights that could be switched on. The walls were a shade of dark blue-green, almost the color of the sea on a cloudy day, and the wall at the very back was covered with a dark green wallpaper, on which were painted large flowers and decorative leaves. The dark wood floor matched the dark wood tables and chairs. Tea was served from beautifully painted China pots into matching cups, through gold colored strainers, and the food was presented on gold-rimmed China plates. If Reggie didn't work here, albeit on an unpaid basis, she would, doubtless, have patronized the place. It was a constant source of surprise to her that her friends and family had not yet discovered it.

Having made sure the tables around the main floor of the shop were empty, she turned back toward the counter, and was dismayed to see there was one table occupied. A man sat at the very back of the shop, at the only table that was actually on the path between her and Elsie.

Reggie pursed her lips and thought a very bad word. It was just her luck, although she didn't think she knew him, so it should be all right.

He looked to be in his mid-twenties and, although he was sitting slightly hunched so she couldn't be certain, she thought he was tall. She based her supposition on the fact that he seemed to take up a lot of space at the table, and his arms, resting on the French-polished wooden tabletop, were long. His hair was dark and waxed down fashionably, any curls or waves ruthlessly tamed. His suit was well made, contouring his broad shoulders beautifully. It looked new, too, which was unusual for one of the tea shop patrons. Most of the men they served here were either office clerks and shop workers, who came in on Fridays with their wage packets to treat themselves, or else they were bank managers and solicitors, taking time from their desks to escort their wives on market day. All of them wore suits that were cheap, and usually at least a year old. For most, money was tight; you could see them mentally calculating what they could afford to buy in here, before they ordered.

This man didn't look as if he'd have any trouble paying for anything on the menu.

She could only see his face in profile, but from that she surmised he might be what her sister called a sheikh, a label Florence and her friends had given every good-looking man since they'd seen the Rudolph Valentino film last year.

Reggie shook her head, annoyed with herself. What did it matter if this man was good-looking or not? She rolled her eyes, pushed him from her thoughts, and started toward the counter.

She was halfway across the floor when he clicked his fingers at her. Reggie stiffened, unsure whether to be concerned or insulted.

"I'd like more tea, please," he said. His voice was deep and low, and might have been pleasant, in the right circumstances. "And a slice of Madeira, if there's any left."

*Do I look like a waitress?* She didn't wear the uniform Elsie wore: the black dress, white apron and cap. Why would this man think she could be commanded to fetch and carry for him? At the click of his fingers, no less!

Reggie pasted on a bright smile, turned to him, and said, "I'm sorry, sir. I don't serve in the shop."

"Oh," he answered. "Then, could you pass my order on, please?"

She blinked, slowly. Most customers went to the counter to order what they wanted. They wouldn't dream of sitting imperiously, ordering the staff about as if they were at the Ritz. He wasn't even looking at her anymore. He'd dismissed her from his mind and gone back to reading the book on the table in front of him, clearly expecting her to jump to it and do his bidding.

Reggie took a deep breath and clenched her jaw. In the back of her mind, she heard a voice telling her not to say anything, that Sally Ann would be angry if she upset a customer. But this man had clicked his fingers at her. Then dismissed her! This was one customer who, in Reggie's opinion, needed upsetting. He needed putting in his place. If he never returned to the shop afterward, well, he would be doing them a service.

So, in a quiet voice that anyone who knew her would be wary of, she said, "Do I look like a telegram boy?"

He looked up, eyebrows raised, dark brown eyes rounded in surprise. "Excuse me?"

Her smile was patronizing. "You need to go to the counter," she said, enunciating every syllable, as if she thought he was slow-topped. "Elsie will be happy to serve you there." Then, with her chin defiantly high, Reggie moved away from him and went to the counter herself.

\*\*\*\*

Harry Pearson was not in the best of moods. The bank manager, Hugh Burgess, had just refused to lend him the money to start his business. Since he and Hugh were old school friends, Harry had been particularly irked at his refusal, although he should have expected it. Every other bank manager in the area had turned him down, too. Somehow, though, Hugh's refusal had rankled the most of all of them.

On top of that, Harry's legs were more sore today than they had been for weeks, probably thanks to all the activity he'd demanded from them of late. And now, this woman had refused to serve him! What sort of establishment was this? A place where the staff could say what they liked to customers with impunity, or so it seemed.

Well, he would show her! He didn't need her, or anybody else, waiting on him.

He took his sticks from where they rested against the nearby wall and braced himself to stand. This was always the worst part of any maneuver, the first seconds when he put weight on his legs, and they objected. From the knees down, they were stiff and uncompromising and constantly threatened either to turn to jelly and leave him in a crumpled heap, or to lock, forcing him to stand still for long enough that he felt ridiculous.

His sore and limited legs were the reason he had asked for waitress service today. Movement was difficult; carrying a cup of tea without spilling it was nigh on impossible.

But, he thought now, why should he have to justify asking for help? Even if he wasn't battle-scarred and broken, was it too much to ask that he be brought a cup of tea? His coin paid the insolent woman's wages, after all. And it wasn't as if the tea shop was busy. Harry was the only customer in here. He ought to ask for the manager and complain about her rudeness!

Although, if he did that, Harry knew the consequences could be dire for her, and he didn't want to be the cause of anyone losing their job over something so trivial. Harry knew, only too well, how it felt to be unemployed and hopeless. He wouldn't wish it on anybody.

In his own case, of course, it wasn't the end of the world. Unlike many, including, he suspected, this woman, Harry was fortunate; his family could afford to care for and keep him, whether he worked or not.

Which wasn't the point. He *wanted* to work, to *be* something, *do* something other than sit all day, being pampered. It was why he was so desperate to start his business, and why the rejections by all the banks had hurt him so much.

Thankfully, if a little surprisingly, those refusals had not spelled the end of his dream. He had one more meeting this evening, one last chance to finance everything.

He pulled his watch from his pocket and checked it for the fiftieth time since he had come in here. Another hour before he needed to be there. He didn't want to be too early. It wouldn't do to appear too eager. Which meant he needed to buy another cup of tea, so he could stay here a little longer.

On that thought, he braced himself to stand, then hesitated. He didn't relish the thought of limping to the counter. Not while she was there. He imagined the horror on her face when she saw his disabilities, the regret at refusing him, and the pity in her eyes for a man whose future was ended before it had properly begun.

Horror, regret, and pity. Those were the usual reactions. They were also the last things Harry wanted. He especially didn't want them from yet another beautiful young woman. He'd already had more than enough of that, thank you very much.

This woman was beautiful, no arguing that. Not in

the conventional way: her face was too square and her mouth too small and thin to be magazine-beautiful. But she had the most stunning eyes. They were blue, with a hint of gray, the color of sea mist on a summer's day.

He shivered at the memory of them. Like the mist they had reminded him of, the ice in those eyes had dropped the temperature considerably.

She was tall for a woman, about five feet eight inches, though her slender frame made her seem even taller. She wore her light brown hair in a fashionable bob, her fringe held back from her face with a silver clip, an amethyst set into it which perfectly matched the shade of her long, drop-waisted dress. Harry blinked, then frowned. He was no expert on ladies' fashion, but he thought the dress looked more expensive than he would expect a shopgirl to wear. Especially for work.

It was probably as well he'd decided not to complain about her attitude to the manager. Looking at the way she was dressed, that position was, most likely, hers. Since he did not wish to be summarily evicted, embarrassed and left looking for somewhere to wait for the time of his appointment, he could swallow her insult. Besides, for all he knew, she had worked her way up to her position from being a waitress, putting in long hours to gain her promotions. She wouldn't want to do the job of someone further down the pecking order from her, any more than Harry would have done, in her place.

All of which was unimportant, he thought, crossly. What was important was that he wanted a cup of tea and a slice of Madeira. Since those things wouldn't appear on his table by magic, he'd have to fetch them himself. Somehow.

He pressed his hands down on the handles of his

sticks and pushed himself to standing. His legs complained at the movement, shooting darts of pain through him and refusing to propel him forward. He waited, but their stiffness didn't abate; he had truly overdone it today. Perhaps he should not have started the morning by practicing driving for more than two hours, changing gears and braking until he knew he could handle the little Austin smoothly, come what may. He'd only stalled it once all day and was especially proud that he'd got it going again single-handedly.

He grimaced. Not starting a car without help wasn't any great feat. That he thought it was, even for an instant, heated his anger. His father's attitude to his injuries was clearly rubbing off on Harry, and that was unacceptable.

Although, even he could admit that two hours of driving, then walking from the car to the bank at one end of the High Street, then to this tea shop at the other end, was too much for him to have done in one day.

Now he was paying for it, because his legs refused to propel him the short distance to the counter. "For the love of all that's holy!" he muttered. "All I want is tea and cake. Is that too much to ask for?"

Elsie looked up from her discussion with the woman-who-wasn't-a-waitress and smiled at him. "Right you are, sir," she called, cheerfully. "Coming up in a jiffy."

The younger woman turned, her expression one of disdain, which softened when she saw the sticks in his hands. She looked away again, the sort of head-turn people did when they wanted you to think they hadn't noticed your disability, and they wouldn't dream of staring, curiously. It made him angrier than ever. He clenched his jaw, his mouth pulled tight.

"Sit down, sir," insisted Elsie. "I'll bring it over to you."

Harry longed to say it was all right, he'd come and get it, but he knew he couldn't. Shamed, and trying not to look too relieved, he sat back down.

\*\*\*\*

Reggie felt a pang of conscience. She'd thought the man imperious and lazy when he asked her to wait on him. Now she could clearly see his very good reason for not serving himself. If she had known he walked with sticks…

*But I didn't*, she told herself, silently, while Elsie made him a fresh pot of tea. *I couldn't have. And, besides, it doesn't change the fact that he was rude to me.* She did not take kindly to being summoned by the click of fingers and ordered to do something.

Of course, she had also been rude in return. It was one thing to point out she wasn't a waitress, although she could have done even that in a gentler, more polite way. But to refuse to pass on his order, the remark about not being a telegram boy… She felt her cheeks heating and knew it was shame that made her blush. She ought to apologize to him. Or would that make it worse?

He must shoulder some of the blame, surely? His attitude… What was it about men? Why did they have to be so domineering? Just like her father, this man clearly expected his life to be made easier by the women around him, women who—he seemed to think—existed only to do his bidding. No doubt he would also say a woman should only live as the men in her life saw fit. Regardless of her own wants and desires.

That was unfair. The stranger may have assumed she was there to serve him but that was not to say he agreed with her father that a woman was not truly a person in her own right. She should not assume that he believed that, as a man, he was entitled to dictate her entire future. Although, if he didn't think those things, it would set him apart from every other man Reggie had ever met.

Elsie took the man his tea and cake and collected his money. Meanwhile, Reggie headed back to her office to enter the amounts on the receipts into her calculations, and determined to put the customer out of her mind.

That was easier said than done. She sat at her desk and found herself thinking about him again. He had looked striking in profile, whilst sitting down, but, when he had stood up and faced them, Reggie had had to admit he'd been more handsome than she could have imagined. His eyes were so dark they seemed almost black, glinting chips of coal above his well-defined cheekbones. He had a straight, narrow nose and a mouth that turned up slightly at the ends, as if he was always ready to smile. She'd also been correct in thinking he was tall: even with legs that couldn't straighten completely and shoulders rounded from leaning on sticks, he was still almost six feet tall. Reggie was used to being as tall as, or even taller than, most men of her acquaintance. To find one she would have to look up at was—pleasing.

Not that she was ever likely to be close enough to look up at him. In fact, she doubted she would ever see him again. Reggie didn't think he was a regular customer, for Elsie had not greeted him like one. In which case, he would drink his tea, leave the shop, and probably never return. For some reason, she found that regrettable.

She huffed, annoyed with herself. "Stop lollygagging, girl, and get on with your work," she muttered, and she attacked the receipts with gusto.

\*\*\*\*

Harry left the tea shop and walked back along the street to where he had parked the car. His thighs hurt and his back ached with the effort. He'd wanted to prove to himself that he could walk the High Street just like everyone else, but it had been foolish to try. He'd probably pay dearly for it over the next few days.

All he wanted now was to go home, have a warm bath, then sink into his armchair, the fire in the grate warming his tortured muscles while he read his book or listened to the radio. Before he could do that, though, he had one more port of call.

William Chilvers was his last hope of raising the money he needed to start his company. The local businessman had a reputation for taking calculated risks, something which had made him very wealthy and had earned him a great deal of respect amongst the business community. That his main business was a direct rival to Harry's father's shop was, to Harry's way of thinking, a bonus. The older Pearson had refused to help Harry in any way, not just financially, but practically, too. He hadn't even been willing to give Harry a job in his offices, as if he thought shattered knees and broken tibias and ankles affected a man's ability to think. He'd decided Harry was now useless, and nothing would change his mind. If his main rival felt differently, Father would be furious. And it would serve him right.

Grinning wickedly at that thought, Harry drove toward the edge of Fieldhurst, where Chilvers lived in a large, Edwardian house at the end of a long, tarmacadamed driveway. A well-manicured lawn sat in front of the house, surrounded by beautifully pruned bushes and colorful flower beds, even now in late February when the night frosts were still a danger and the spring flowers had not yet dared show their heads. Wide windows stood either side of an arched porchway and a dark wood door on the ground floor. Four stone steps led up to the porch. On the upper floor was a balcony with a waist-high balustrade, and two enormous, gabled windows. The size of the house was intimidating, and Harry swallowed hard, before talking sternly to himself.

"The worst he can do is say no," he murmured. "And you've had that happen before. Too many times."

He climbed out of his car, struggled up the steps, and tugged at the bell pull. A maid in a black dress covered by a white apron showed him into a large hall with a high ceiling and a black-and-white checkered floor. A wide staircase rose from the center of the hall, with corridors on both sides of it, leading to the back of the house. At the top, the staircase branched into two landings that, Harry assumed, led to bedrooms.

Several doors lined the ground floor corridors, and it was through one of these Harry was taken, into a parlor.

"Mr. Chilvers will be along presently, sir," said the maid. She curtsied and left.

Although the parlor was not over-large, its high ceiling and wide windows made it seem spacious. The well-polished parquet floor was covered in the center of the room by a deep pile rug in several shades of light green, all of which were echoed in the curtains tied back from the windows, and the pelmet above them, as well as in the cushions on the caramel brown-and-cream sofa, and the matching wing-backed chairs either side of the cream tiled fireplace. A bureau stood in one corner, its dark wood gleaming, and an octagonal table sat in another, on top of which was a lamp with a light green Tiffany lampshade. A cream dado rail ran around the room, separating the lower wall, painted in soft caramel, from the cream of the higher wall. Above the mantelpiece hung a framed painting in the style of Constable. Altogether, the room held an atmosphere of understated elegance.

The door behind Harry opened and Chilvers strode in. A tall, thin man in his late forties, everything about him seemed long. His legs, torso, fingers, even his nose seemed stretched. He wore a dark suit which fitted too well to be off the peg, with a pristine white shirt, a perfect collar, and a plain, blue tie. A gold tiepin glinted at Harry. His only other adornment was the thick gold wedding band on his finger. Iron gray hair was cropped military short, and he had shrewd gray eyes. He gestured that Harry should sit and offered him a drink before sitting himself and crossing one leg over the other.

"What can I do for you, sir?" he asked. Clearly, he had no desire for small talk. Harry was grateful. He, too, would rather get down to business.

"I'm looking for investors," said Harry, relieved his nerves did not sound in his voice.

He spent the next half an hour outlining his dream of a delivery service for the Fieldhurst area.

"Delivering what?"

"Anything and everything." Harry sat forward and watched Chilvers closely. "You own a department store. You know you need to retrieve goods from suppliers so you can sell them. In your case, your business is large enough to warrant a van of your own, which means that collecting your goods from your suppliers and passing them on to your customers, is not too much of a challenge. But consider the greengrocer, the haberdasher, and the pharmacist, among others. They must also get their goods from their suppliers to their customers, via their shops.

"The goods they sell come from the suppliers into Tunbridge Wells by train in the first instance, just as yours do, and the retailers have to go there to get them from the station yard. But, unlike you, they don't have their own dedicated delivery vans, which means they must make special trips to collect their goods in their private cars, which won't hold nearly so much. Of course, they could use a national carrier like Pickford's, but that can be expensive, and unless you are using them regularly, Pickford's will fit you in to suit themselves, rather than to meet your exact needs. As a local deliverer, I can provide a service at a reasonable rate, far more quickly, and with the needs of my clients at the heart of it. I can also provide local businesses with an extra service by delivering to their customers." He pulled out the papers showing his vision in detail, complete with costs and earning potential.

"Who would drive this van?" asked Chilvers. He glanced at the walking sticks stacked beside Harry.

Harry took a deep breath. Here it came. The point where, in every previous interview, things fell apart. "Me," he said.

In every bank he'd approached, the manager's face had blanched at that. Even Hugh, who knew Harry well, had refused to believe him capable of driving. However, rather than say so and risk being thought rude, every single one of them had made excuses about times being hard and the bank cutting back on lending.

Which was kinder than Harry's own father had been.

"Don't be ridiculous," the old man had scoffed when Harry had told him his plans. "You can't drive a heavy vehicle, not with those legs. I'm not altogether happy with you driving the Austin, let alone a goods van. And don't look so affronted, you know it's the truth. What's more, it's your own fault. You didn't have to run off to those damned trenches and get yourself blown up, did you? If you'd not been such a hothead, if you'd waited till you were of age to join up, well, then the war would have been over, and you would still be whole. We all have to learn to live with the consequences of our actions, lad, and this is the consequence of yours."

Harry had gritted his teeth and said nothing. It wasn't worth it. As far as his father was concerned, Harry had been disobedient and reckless, and his punishment was to sit in a chair for the rest of his life, his body turning to mush as his brain atrophied.

So now, bracing himself for the same reaction from Chilvers, Harry looked the older man in the eye, defiantly.

Chilvers studied him for a long moment. He sipped his drink. "I take it you can drive?"

"I can." He'd practiced for at least an hour, sometimes two, every day for weeks. His reactions grew quicker with each time. He had never had much trouble operating the pedals in his car, because his thigh muscles, which did the bulk of that work, were undamaged and strong. Lifting and carrying the goods wouldn't be too much of a problem either, if he used a sack trolley.

"Yesterday," he told Chilvers, "I drove to Lewes

and back. I'm as safe and as competent as any other driver." He leaned forward again, to emphasize his point. "I can't stand up for long, that's true. And I need the sticks when I walk. But driving, that's something I can do. There's no pain. No awkwardness."

"In a car." Chilvers nodded his agreement. "I can see that might be all right. But a wagon?" He raised an eyebrow in disbelief.

"I can handle it."

There was a long silence. Chilvers was clearly thinking about all Harry had said, which made him more hopeful than he'd been at any of his other meetings. Harry longed to say more, to give the man information, facts and figures that would sway him, but he sensed to do so would be a mistake. If he looked too desperate, Chilvers would refuse him. So Harry bit the tip of his tongue behind his closed lips and forced himself to sit still.

"All right," said Chilvers, at last. "I'll front you the money for a van, a workshop, and a storage shed, along with the other costs of starting up."

Harry was elated. For the first time since the bomb had exploded, collapsing the front-line trench and burying him, he saw a way through to a future he chose, a future where he was useful and independent, not sitting at home being treated like a child.

"But I do have a condition," continued Chilvers. "Something you must do for me in return."

Harry's heart stuttered and the bubble of joy within him burst. He should have known it wouldn't be that easy. "What would that be?" he asked, with trepidation.

"My eldest daughter, Regina. She's a bit, ah, headstrong. Somewhat…defiant. Case in point, she's twenty-one in a few weeks and still not married, or engaged. She doesn't even have a steady beau, for goodness' sake, though she's comely enough. The girl's got it into her head that she's not going to marry, if you can believe that." He chuckled. "Wants to be independent, if you please." He shook his head. "She doesn't know when she's well off, if you ask me."

Harry sipped his drink and said nothing. He had an idea of what Chilvers wanted, but he refused to jump to conclusions. He would let the man call his terms before he responded.

"I blame the war," said Chilvers. "It gave women all kinds of silly ideas, what with them replacing the men in the workforce and all that. Not that Regina worked then, of course. She was only thirteen when the whole thing ended. But she saw her mother doing her bit, and other women, of course, and now she thinks she should be allowed to do the same. I've told her, that was then, in an emergency. This is now, when there are men here to do the work. I've pointed out the men need the jobs, and she doesn't. But it's all to no avail. Damned girl will not listen to me."

After being turned away from several jobs himself, thanks to his injuries, Harry had more than a little sympathy for the woman's point of view. If she wanted to work, and was capable of doing so, why shouldn't she? At least until she married, anyway.

"Thing is, when she comes of age," said her father, "she'll come into an inheritance from her grandfather. She plans to use it to leave home. Lord knows what she thinks she'll do then, but what can you expect? Women think with their hearts, not their brains. Which is why we must rein them in. Protect them from themselves."

"What do you want me to do?" asked Harry. If Regina Chilvers was going to be in possession of the funds to take her life into her own hands, he didn't see what he, her father, or anyone else could do to stop her. "You can't think I can change her mind, if you can't. I don't even know her."

"You will." Chilvers grinned. It reminded Harry of a picture of a shark he'd seen in a periodical. "I want you to marry her."

"What?" Harry sat upright. His drink sloshed over the side of his glass, covering his fingers and dripping onto his trousers. He put the glass down, took out his handkerchief and wiped away the spillage, then looked hard at Chilvers, searching for a sign that this was a prank.

The man's face was serious. "I want you to marry my daughter," he repeated.

"That isn't funny." Harry was growing angry. He knew, as well as anyone, that he didn't appeal to young ladies, unless they were at their last prayers. It didn't sound as if Regina Chilvers was anywhere near there. This man was either making fun of his lack of prospects in the marriage market or he was deluded.

Harry didn't think the man was deluded.

"Didn't mean it to be," Chilvers answered Harry's statement. "I am in earnest."

Harry took a moment to clarify his thoughts. Then, he took a deep breath and said, "I am very sorry, sir. Sorrier than you can imagine, since my answer will, presumably, cut me off from the money I was hoping to borrow from you. I am flattered that you think me worthy of your daughter. But I cannot, in good conscience, marry her."

"Have you met her?" asked Chilvers. He stood and went to the drinks cabinet, poured himself another shot, then held up the bottle, offering to refill Harry's glass. Harry shook his head. The last thing he needed was to dull his wits with alcohol. He had a feeling Chilvers would pounce on the slightest weakness.

"I have not met her," he answered. "That is one of my objections. I do not know the woman, and she does not know me. You can't really expect us to enter into a permanent state such as marriage when, to my knowledge, we have never even clapped eyes on each other."

"People do such things all the time." Chilvers sounded matter-of-fact. He sipped his drink, put one hand in the hip pocket of his trousers, and levelled a steady gaze on Harry.

"People may do as they will. I won't marry a woman I don't know. Before I even considered marriage to anyone, I would need to know that I cared for her, at the least, and that she cared for me. That is non-negotiable. So, if your offer of a loan is contingent on that marriage taking place, I must apologize for wasting your time."

*And say goodbye to my dreams for the foreseeable future.* Defeat tasted bitter on his tongue. He put down his glass, grabbed his sticks, and began to rise.

Chilvers watched him for a moment, then nodded. "Your scruples do you credit. I can see the validity of your arguments. Sit down, man."

Harry eyed him carefully for several seconds, then sank back to his chair.

"All right," conceded Chilvers. "I won't insist on marriage. I can see that might be a rather drastic solution to the problem, at this stage." He sat down. "But you could court her."

Harry closed his eyes for a moment, then re-opened them and looked, as steadily as he could, into Chilvers' eyes. They seemed shuttered. They certainly gave away nothing of the man's thoughts or emotions. Harry bet he would be a hell of a poker player.

"I think you should know, sir, ladies are not interested in being courted by me. They want somebody who can take them dancing—"

"Regina doesn't go dancing."

"What I mean is, I'm not exactly…" He waved his hand in front of him, at a loss for how to describe what he was.

Chilvers put down his glass, sat forward and rested his elbows on his knees, so that his hands dangled loosely in front of him. "Look. Regina drives me to distraction. She's so full of wanting to be… Well, to tell the truth, I don't know what she wants to be. But…" He sat back again, resting his arms on the chair arms. "She needs a beau. Somebody who can, at least, make her *think* of husbands and babies and running a household, before she wastes her money building herself a life she will come to regret. Before she ends up cutting herself off from family and friends and any hope of a decently happy future, she needs to know something of what she might be throwing away. Is that so much for a father to want for his daughter?"

"No. It isn't." Harry could agree that much. Any father would want to protect his daughter's interests to that degree.

"So, here's the deal. I will front you the money you need. In return, you court my daughter. And, before she reaches her majority and gets her hands on the money she needs to fund a lifestyle she will one day rue, you get her to change her mind about leaving home the moment she can do so. Make her stop and think a little, so she will give herself the time she needs to weigh all her options."

Harry thought about it. That did not sound like such a terrible thing to ask.

"You make her think a little deeper about her future. That's all I ask. Give her enough pause for thought that she doesn't leave home and accept some unsuitable position. If, by the time her birthday comes, she has decided to, at least, delay her plans, I will consider you've fulfilled your end of our bargain."

Harry nodded at what seemed a much more reasonable proposition than the original.

"You're a charming lad," continued Chilvers. "Intelligent, go-getting. Just the type of man she would go for, if she was going to go for anyone. In short, I have every confidence you can do this."

"All I could hope to do is my best, sir," replied Harry. He would not promise what he could not deliver.

"That's all I ask." Chilvers smiled and picked up his drink again. "There are six weeks until her birthday. Time enough to persuade her that settling down is a good option, I would think."

Harry rested his elbow on the arm of the chair and massaged his forehead with his fingers. This was a tall order. A young woman who didn't want a beau at all would certainly not be impressed by him. Besides, it didn't seem right to shatter her dreams and thwart her ambition. Wasn't that what people had been doing to Harry for the last eight years?

Although that wasn't what her father wanted to do.

He wanted to give her the chance to consider more options than the narrow ones she currently had. Was that such a bad thing?

And yet…something didn't feel right. He couldn't put his finger on it. Chilvers sounded sincere, and his words were those of a concerned father. There was nothing to object to in what he said. And yet…

Harry should say no. He opened his mouth to say no. But then, a little voice in the back of his head cried, "Wait!"

Chilvers wasn't asking him to marry his daughter. Not anymore. He wasn't proposing anything irreversible. All he wanted Harry to do was court her. Make her question her desire for an independent, husband-free life, make her stay with her family for longer than she originally planned.

Six weeks. Until her birthday. Was that so hard to do? Once her birthday had come and gone, provided Regina had not yet left the family home and struck out on her own, Harry would have fulfilled his task. And he'd have the money to start his business.

He'd have that anyway, just by agreeing to try. If the woman refused to fall in with her father's plans, provided Harry could truthfully say he had done his best…

"I should add," said Chilvers, with another of his shark smiles, "if you fail, if she's not amenable to rethinking her options by her birthday, or if she's still determined to leave home then, the loan I make you now will become instantly repayable. In full."

Harry gulped. It was almost as if Chilvers had read his mind, and was tightening every screw, sealing every escape hatch.

He considered the deal the man wanted him to make.

It did not seem a fair one, by any stretch of the imagination. But, Harry could see, it was the only one he was going to get. If he succeeded, he'd have his business, a sweetheart, and the gratitude of a powerful man who could be a great help to him. If he failed...

If he failed, if Regina was not persuadable, Harry could lose everything.

But if he didn't try...well, then he definitely would lose everything. He was out of options. Nobody else was willing to give him a chance. His business, his dream, his entire future rested on Chilvers giving him this loan. And all he had to do in return was squire a woman about for six weeks and make her reconsider her plans.

On top of his own considerations, he should think of her, what this deal would mean to her, both in the short term and in the long run. In the short term, she might see it in a dim light, but, looking at it from a longer perspective, he'd be doing her a favor. Wouldn't he?

Of course, he would. A woman on her own would struggle, even with an inheritance to cushion her. She'd be much better off staying here, with her family. Where she would be safe. And she'd then have the time to fine-tune her plans, allowing her to have what she wanted in a way that was better for her.

She would be safe and secure, and yet still free to pursue her dreams. Harry would have his business. Chilvers would be happy. In the long run, everyone would win.

"All right," he said. "I'll do it."

They shook hands and Chilvers poured fresh drinks to toast their new partnership.

The door opened and a woman walked in. She glanced at Chilvers, then at Harry.

"I'm sorry," she said. "I didn't realize you were—" She stopped speaking and stared at Harry, her eyes wide with shock and recognition. Harry stared back, disbelief catching his breath.

Chilvers looked pleased with himself. "Pearson, may I introduce my daughter, Regina? Regina, this is Mr. Harry Pearson, a business colleague of mine."

Harry's heart sank. The lady he'd just agreed to court was the supercilious woman from the tea shop.

## Chapter Two

Reggie stood and stared at the man struggling to get to his feet to greet her. She wondered now if he had been sent to the tea shop to spy on her, and she had fallen into his trap when she came out of her office to pick up those wretched receipts. It wouldn't be the first time her father had employed what he called his "agents" to gather information for him. Doing so allowed him to make his decisions from a position of knowledge, and had contributed to his success as a businessman. The "agents" allowed him to swoop in and grab deals before anyone else could, and to undermine his rivals' effectiveness.

Was he now employing the same tactics to keep family members in line?

If he was, it was too late to avoid it. All she could do now was brazen it out. To be honest, Father looked far too happy to have discovered she had defied his edict, and that gave her hope. Perhaps he didn't realize she and this man had already crossed paths, didn't know she was on to him.

On that thought, she pasted a bright smile onto her face, stepped forward with her hand outstretched and said, "How do you do, Mr. Pearson. It's a pleasure to meet you."

His eyebrows raised slightly and she widened her eyes, silently pleading with him to take the hint and pretend they'd never seen each other before. It was in his best interests, as well as hers, surely? If Father had sent him to spy on her, he wouldn't have wanted him to get caught by her. And, on the off chance that Father hadn't sent him, well, then, it wouldn't do to give her secret away.

After the briefest of hesitations, Mr. Pearson smiled and took her hand. A strange heat seemed to transfer itself from his hand to hers at the contact. It made her fingers tingle, in the way they had when she'd touched an electric fence once. It shocked her, but not badly; stung, but it wasn't wholly unpleasant. The look of surprise on his face suggested he had felt it, too.

"Charmed to meet you, Miss Chilvers," he said.

She withdrew her hand as quickly as she could without alerting her father, who was, thankfully, standing with his back to them, poking at the coals to make the fire flare. Having done that, he stood straight. "Another drink, Pearson?"

"No more for me, sir." Mr. Pearson turned to Father as he continued, "I don't want to see double on the road and crash my car. It's not as if I can walk home if I do." He winked at Reggie. She felt the heat of her blush at the gesture.

She hadn't really taken notice in the tea shop earlier, but he had a wonderful voice. There was a deep timbre to it, and yet it held a softness that made it sound as if it was coated in honey. His smile lit up his face, too, making it impossible to deny how handsome he was.

*Handsome is as handsome does.* The thought acted like a splash of cold water, pulling her back to the here and now before she could make a complete noodle of herself.

"Your timing is perfect, actually, Regina," said her father, moving away from the decanters. He had the most guilty of his innocent looks on his face as he pushed his hands deeper into his trouser pockets and tried to seem nonchalant. "I have to fetch...papers. From my study. I left them there. Would you mind entertaining Mr. Pearson for a few minutes while I'm gone?"

All Reggie's suspicions came roaring back. She frowned at her father, then at Mr. Pearson. The younger man's expression put her at ease somewhat, because he seemed surprised, astonished even, by her father's request. She didn't think Douglas Fairbanks Jr. himself could have pulled off that look unless it was genuine. Whatever Father had in mind, then, he hadn't taken Mr. Pearson into his confidence.

"I was just—" said Mr. Pearson, pointing to the door.

At the same instant, Reggie said, "I only came in for—"

They both stopped talking and each waited for the other one to go on. Father moved with alacrity toward the door.

Reggie knew there was no use fighting. Father was determined to leave her here, alone with this man, and neither of them could stop him. Mr. Pearson couldn't leave without giving his proper farewells to Father, and she couldn't walk away and abandon the poor man. Not without being incredibly rude. She had been abominably rude to him once today already, and despite that, he hadn't betrayed her. Under the circumstances, it ill behooved her to insult him again.

"I don't mind," she said, pushing down the resigned sigh. "Please, sit down, Mr. Pearson."

Father almost ran from the room, shutting the door firmly behind him, raising both her hackles and her misgivings. Usually, Father was incredibly Victorian in his attitude toward his daughters. They were *never* allowed to stay in a room with a man they weren't related to, especially with the door shut and no chaperone in attendance to keep things aboveboard. What on earth was he up to?

Mr. Pearson's sticks thudded on the carpet as he returned to his chair and sat down again, heavily. She wondered if his obvious difficulties with mobility explained her father's sudden laxity. Did he truly think a man with damaged legs posed no threat to his daughter's virtue? If he did, he was not just unkind, he was positively stupid. To her, it was all too obvious that those walking sticks did not reduce this man's virility in the slightest.

She and Mr. Pearson sat in the room. A silence grew between them. It lasted just long enough to be awkward, before Reggie said, "I apologize for my rudeness earlier. I should not have spoken to you as I did. And I should not have refused to serve you, or at least to ask Elsie to do so. I didn't realize at the time that you…" She stopped talking. What more could she say that wouldn't insult the man more than she already had? She glanced at his legs, then looked away, guiltily.

He shrugged his shoulders, nonchalantly. "Most people don't notice when I am sitting down."

That much, she thought, must be true. His legs weren't deformed, at least, not enough to be obvious through his trousers. His feet were flat, planted firmly on the floor, and there was nothing about his shoes that gave away his infirmity—no excess heels, no calipers on show. To all intents and purposes, Mr. Pearson looked exactly what he was, a handsome young man who happened to have called on her father.

He didn't seem put out by her awkwardness, either. He was probably used to it, she reflected with some shame. She had seen the way people treated those who'd been marked by the war. People, most of whom were old enough and intelligent enough to know better, stared at the scarred and the disfigured in horrified fascination, sometimes openly, sometimes with an attempt at subtlety. If they had to move past the veterans, they often tried to leave room, as if getting too close might contaminate them and make them social pariahs, too. Reggie had always despised people who did such things, and yet, here she was, doing something similar herself. The man's opinion of her must be at rock bottom, for he must have noticed her awkwardness, surely?

A moment later, he proved that he had when, his tone strangely emotionless, he said, "In case you were wondering, Miss Chilvers, I would far rather people just asked me about my legs. I always answer truthfully, and then nobody need be awkward going forward."

She nodded. "Something which cannot be said when people only stare, I assume?"

He grinned. "Worse are the people who try not to stare. Or try to look as if they're not staring, while they do just that. They think they are being discreet, that I won't notice them watching me as long as they turn their heads just so, and look at me from the corners of their eyes. But I will notice them. I do." He sighed and shook his head. "But even those people are not as bad as the worst kind of all. They're the ones who do look at me. The ones who look me in the face, their expressions full of pity." He grimaced and she saw the contempt for those people in his clenched jaw, and the icy glint in his eyes. "People like that assume I can do nothing for myself. Most of them don't even talk to me directly. Instead, they talk to whoever is with me." He mimicked a kindly-meaning but insensitive lady. "Would he like a cup of tea, do you think? Is he allowed one, or should I fix some cordial for him?"

Shock made a laugh explode from Reggie. Her face heated with shame at her reaction. "I'm sorry."

"Don't be. It's good to know you see the absurdity in their behavior. As if they truly believe my damaged legs must take away the functioning of my brain." He grinned. "That's what I like about children, you know. Children don't beat about the bush. They're curious, but they're honest with it, and they come right out and ask."

Reggie nodded and smiled, sheepishly. "Point taken." She gestured toward his legs. "Are they—your injuries—from the war?"

That was the first explanation that came to mind. Just eight years after the Great War ended, many men still bore the scars of it. Although, looking at Mr. Pearson now, she wondered if she had been too hasty in her assumption. Was he old enough to have fought? He looked to be in his mid-twenties: he still had the boyish bloom of youth on his skin. His face was well defined, but there was a softness about his jaw that indicated full adulthood was still not upon him. Had she told him he looked older than he was, and insulted him again?

Then again, he might not take umbrage at that at all. He might be pleased. After all, she knew from her sister Florence's misadventures, some people *wanted* to be thought of as older than they were. In Florence's case, it opened the doors to clubs and other entertainments her sister had no business going to. Perhaps Mr. Pearson was able to benefit in similar ways.

"They are."

*What were? Oh, yes. His injuries. From the war.* Reggie noticed he answered her question with no hint of bitterness or anger in his tone. He seemed quite resigned to his limitations.

She relaxed a little.

He looked down at his legs then, his smile rueful. "It was my own fault, really. As my father tells me regularly, and I have to confess he is right. I shouldn't have got myself into the mess in the first place."

"That's a bit harsh." His father sounded unacceptably unsympathetic, and rather heartless, considering his son had been injured whilst doing his duty to his country. He ought to be a source of pride to his father, not an object of his ire.

"Not a bit of it," Mr. Pearson answered. "He's correct. I was an idiot. Rushed down to the recruiting office as soon as I could get away to do it. I thought, like so many others did, that battle would be all glory, honor, and making a man of me."

"But it wasn't."

"No." He lowered his gaze and studied the rug in the middle of the floor.

Reggie knew, instinctively, he would not answer any more questions on his wounds today. So she changed the subject. "I should thank you," she said. "For not telling my father you saw me in the tea shop. It would have caused a deal of trouble if you had said anything, and I…well, thank you."

He gave her a fleeting frown, then nodded. "He

doesn't know that you work there?"

Reggie cleared her throat and looked to the fireplace, where the flames licked cheerfully at the coals Father had shoveled on and poked into the most efficient positions. Their warmth filled the room. The pine cones between the coals sent a sweet perfume into the air, to mix with that of the beeswax used to polish the wood furniture and the lingering sweetness of Father's cigars.

She thought of what she had just confessed, that she worked in the tea shop without her father's blessing. Most people would be appalled that she'd gone behind his back. They would be horrified to learn he had forbidden her to do it, but that she had taken up her position anyway. Well-bred young ladies, most people thought, should obey their parents and be respectful of them and their wishes. She waited for Mr. Pearson's censure of her actions.

Instead, he chuckled. "I can see where it might be awkward between you. Given his views of a woman's place, and the idea of her working outside the home. I only met him today for the first time, and I already know that much about him." He laughed again. "Although, I think his attitude is only for women in his own family. I assume he doesn't object to employing others? The secretary I made my appointment with was most definitely a woman. As is your maid."

"There is a certain double standard in his attitude," she agreed. She had thought such a thing before, but never voiced it aloud, for fear that if she pointed out his hypocrisy, Father would answer by sacking poor Miss Buck, the excellent secretary in question. But while Reggie had thought such things herself, she had never expected a man to agree with her. It made her reassess her opinions of the male sex. Perhaps they weren't all as bad as her father, after all.

"He will not learn of your activities from me," promised Mr. Pearson.

Reggie nodded her appreciation. "What brings you to see Father today?"

"He is investing in my business idea."

"Oh. Good. I hope it's successful."

"Thank you," he answered. "So do I."

"I'm sure it will be."

Inwardly, Reggie winced. Could this conversation be any more stilted? She had been brought up to be an asset to her father, engaging perfect strangers in charming conversation at dinner parties and cocktail evenings. She could put people at ease, and talk to them like old friends. Yet here she was with this man, making trite remarks that meant nothing, and struggling to do that. For pity's sake! They would be discussing the weather next.

They sat for another fifteen minutes, trying, and failing, to think of interesting things to talk about. She offered him a drink. He refused. She asked him if he would like tea instead. He said no, because he really did have to leave, he explained, although it had been nice to meet her properly and he had enjoyed their chat.

Of all the things he had said to her today, that sentence was the one she believed the least.

Finally, he stood again and she accompanied him to the front door. She caught the slightest hint of his cologne—a clean, pine scent that was outdoorsy and active. She thought it suited him. His activities may have been curtailed by that terrible war, but inside, she suspected, he was still full of energy and vitality. He would probably pour all of it into his business now. It wouldn't surprise her if she was looking at a tycoon in the making.

She waved him off. He waved back, before he climbed into his car and backed down the drive to the road, then drove away. Part of her was grateful he had gone and the awkward interaction between them had ended. Although, perversely, she wished their time together could have been longer. Why that should be was a complete mystery to her. It had been agonizing, not something to savor. She thanked God it was finished and over with. And since she would probably never see him again, or at least, only fleetingly, she didn't have to dwell on it.

Blowing out a huge sigh of relief, she went in search of a cup of tea before she changed for dinner. She felt she had earned it.

\*\*\*\*

Harry drove away from the Chilvers' home, grateful the long day was coming to an end. He drove slowly, keenly aware his legs would not respond quickly enough should he need to brake suddenly. His knees were stinging. There was a dull ache in his ankles and in the joints of his toes that made him want to groan loudly and try to move them into a more comfortable position, although he knew, from experience, there wasn't one. His back ached, and his wrists hurt from the pressure that went through them when he leaned on his sticks. All he wished to do now was to get home, soak in a warm bath, and then sit in his armchair next to the comforting fire.

Not that he would ever admit such a thing to anybody. Pride was a powerful emotion. On many an occasion, it kept him upright and walking in a straight line for longer than he would have thought possible, and it dictated all his actions and reactions, especially around his family. Never, not for one minute, would he allow his parents to think he had overdone it. Even when he had.

It had been a long and tiring day, yes, but it had also been a good one, on the whole. He sped up slightly to overtake the omnibus, packed with homecoming office workers, then slowed again as he drove into Fieldhurst High Street. It was twilight now, the sky not quite as blue as it had been, but not the navy-black of full night, either, and the evening held a gloom that was only fractionally dispelled by the yellow beams of Harry's car lights.

The pavements were empty now. The shops were all closed. Some of them were in complete darkness, while others were lit by display lights that allowed casual passersby to see their wares. A translucent yellow blind had been lowered at the window of the menswear shop. A metal grille protected the windows and doors of the jeweler's. The bank and the tea shop were both in absolute darkness.

Three young men in cheap suits waited at a bus stop. They laughed at each other's comments as they stood, hands in pockets, hats jauntily angled on their heads, the way they had probably seen some film star wearing his. Harry smiled as he drove by, then forgot them as he thought back over his time at the Chilvers' home.

He had been shocked when Regina walked into the room, he could not deny it. He had almost thrown in the towel there and then, convinced he wouldn't even get her to speak civilly to him, let alone allow him to befriend her and then court her. At that moment, he had all but kissed the loan from her father goodbye.

The assignment Chilvers had given him sounded

tough enough as it was, and a little unfair, if Harry was honest. Manipulating a woman into changing her mind, so she would give up her dream of the future, didn't sit well with Harry, and he had regretted agreeing to do it almost the minute he had said yes. When he'd discovered the lady he was supposed to woo out of her independence was, in fact, the Ice Princess from the tea shop, he thought himself doomed. Like his legs, he had thought, this was all his own fault. He only had himself to blame. He had braced himself for a deserved comeuppance.

Except, it hadn't come. The woman in the parlor had been completely different to the one who had put him so firmly in his place in the tea shop. The woman in the tea shop had been curt, to the point of rudeness. She'd been unsympathetic and humorless and had left Harry feeling as if he were a nuisance, a burden she wished not to carry. The woman in the parlor had been pleasant and polite and welcoming, everything she should be.

Better still, his legs did not seem to horrify her the way they had horrified so many other women over the last eight years. He'd had, as he had told her, condescension and humiliation thrust at him, along with looks of abject pity. He had also faced openly expressed disgust. Some people acted as if his appearance in public was an affront to their sensibilities and should not be permitted.

He hadn't felt anything like that from Regina Chilvers. Oh, she'd been awkward at first, unsure what to do or say, but he thought that was because she didn't wish to offend him rather than anything else. And when he had told her, as gently and politely as he knew how, the way he preferred people to react, she had listened, and she had not disappointed. She'd made him feel like an ordinary man again, after so many others had led him to believe he looked like a freak, grotesque and unbearable to behold. Something like the actor, Lon Chaney, when he'd played Quasimodo.

Harry was not the only unlovable creature in the room this evening, though. William Chilvers had left him cold, his predatory manner a complete contrast to his daughter's unforced pleasantness. The man was a classic bully. That much had been clear to Harry. The man was used to getting his way, and he didn't take it kindly if he was thwarted. Ruthless in matters of business, he must have been awful as a father. No wonder his daughter wanted to strike out on her own and free herself from the power he had over her. Anybody would.

As for Harry, he felt he had held his own with Chilvers. He wasn't too bruised by their encounter, although that may have been because he'd built up a certain immunity to big, bluff bullies over the years. Harry's own father was cut from the same cloth. Harry and his siblings had learned early that it was Walter Pearson's way or the highway. He controlled everything and brooked no argument.

The one time Harry had rebelled and been successful at doing so, he had come to regret it. That had been back in 1917. Walter had been furious with Harry for signing up to the army. He'd tried to have him returned home forthwith. In all fairness to his father, Harry knew he should have been sent home, with a flea in his ear, because he had lied about his age to the recruiting sergeant. With hindsight, Harry realized the sergeant had known full well that Harry was not eighteen, as he claimed, but a mere fifteen years old. That was why he had been so quick to spirit the eager boy away, before his parents got wind of what he had done and came looking for him.

Walter had fumed and seethed, threatened legal action against the recruiting office and all who worked within, the army, the government, and anyone else he could think of, but in the end, even Walter Pearson could not fight the British Army and win.

He held his grudge, though. When Harry's broken body had been stretchered back to England after his first, and only, foray into action, Walter had let him know he would get no sympathy from him. He told his wayward son it was his own fault, and that he considered it a self-inflicted injury. He forbade Harry's mother to fuss over him. That part, Harry had to admit, he didn't really mind. He didn't need the pity and cossetting she would give him, if she were given free rein.

In fact, Harry didn't object too strongly to his father's lack of sympathy, either. It was expected, and he could live with it. No. The thing that had upset Harry most was the way the old man had written him off. Not caring was one thing. Deciding that Harry was now too useless for anything was quite another. And, having made that decision, Walter refused to budge. From the moment he'd seen Harry's broken body in the infirmary, Walter had decided there was no role his crippled son might be able to play, ever again. He had completely written Harry off, and for that, Harry didn't think he would ever forgive him.

At least William Chilvers had not done that to him. He had asked pertinent questions, understandable questions. He hadn't assumed Harry's injuries left him on life's scrap heap. The man had taken him on his merits and dealt with him accordingly. Lord above! he hadn't even balked at the idea of Harry wooing his daughter. Many fathers would have. But then, courting Regina Chilvers wasn't the same thing as courting anybody else would have been. William Chilvers wanted to bring Regina into line, and Harry was someone who could be coerced into accepting that job.

When William spoke of his daughter, Harry had pictured a chit of a girl, barely out of school, flighty and flirty, with not a thought in her head except whether she should wear her red silk scarf tonight or her blue one. For a man like Harry, who had long ago accepted that he would never marry because no woman would have him, spending time in the company of a pretty hooey-noodle was likely to be a pleasant interlude. Through her, and the deal he'd struck with her father, Harry would be closely associated with one of the wealthiest, most successful, and most respected businessmen in Sussex. Chilvers' investment in Harry and his business would attract other businessmen, and that would mean the future of his company was assured.

When measured against the rewards, a few weeks of vacuous conversation seemed a small price to pay.

But Regina Chilvers was no hooey-noodle. She was an intelligent, quick-witted woman who knew exactly what she wanted from life. She had a wry sense of humor and a compassion that came through in the way she had listened, truly listened, to Harry today. She clearly liked her independence, and why not? More and more women were using their brains these days, working for their living. At least until they got married.

Marriage was something these women seemed to be delaying, as well. Whereas, in the last century, a woman of good family was usually married by her twentieth birthday, often to a man her parents had picked for her, women since the Great War chose for themselves, and many waited until they were in their late twenties, or even their early thirties, before they tied the knot.

Of course, the shortage of young men might have played as big a part in the rise in the average age of brides as a woman's longing for independence. So many men had died in the War, there were nowhere near enough to go around.

Which was probably another reason Chilvers had chosen Harry for his dirty work. He had clearly seen Harry was unlikely to marry, for even the most desperate of brides did not want a broken husband. That left Harry free to court an unenthusiastic woman, and romancing Regina would not deprive any other, more willing brides of a potential groom. Harry felt a sharp stab of regret in the vicinity of his heart. It was lowering, to say the least, to realize one was only useful because one was not fit for the purpose.

His complete lack of credibility as a romance partner, combined with Regina's intelligence, meant Harry would need to be careful going forward. The woman would, doubtless, be suspicious of him and his motives from the start. She would see through any insincerity in a heartbeat. If she so much as sniffed a conspiracy against her, all Harry's efforts would be for nought.

Therefore, if he wanted to succeed at this and keep his own dream alive, he would have to be smart about it.

Harry shuddered. This, what he was doing, went against every ounce of integrity he possessed. But he had no choice. And, he reminded himself, it wasn't forever. Once he had persuaded William Chilvers of his success with Regina, and thereby secured a payback period of a reasonable length for his loan, Harry could let the woman go back to the life she truly wanted, with nothing more than a short delay.

He drove along the road to his parents' home. A large red brick house, built in the mid-Victorian era, it had leadlight windows and an array of chimneys, and a painted oak door flanked by tall, red-leafed bushes his mother was extremely proud of, having grown them from seedlings. The graveled area in front of the house was large enough to comfortably park all six of the cars the family owned, with room to spare. A small lawn lay to one side of the gravel, an ornate bird bath in its center, and a row of trees shielded the house from the prying eyes of passersby.

To one side of the house, a suite of ground floor rooms had been adapted for Harry's use, so he did not have to negotiate the stairs. They gave him a relative amount of privacy, for which he was grateful. There he had his own bedroom and bathroom, and a sitting room where he could receive his visitors. Not that he had ever had any visitors of his own, but it was good to know the opportunity was there, should it ever be needed.

His wheels crunched across the drive. He parked next to his father's Bentley, then made his way, wearily, to his rooms, still thinking about Regina, feeling like the biggest cad in England but unable to do anything about it. He had agreed to the terms of the loan, and he must fulfill his side of the bargain. The trick would be in doing so without destroying the young lady, and without having her hate him too badly when all was done and dusted.

Throughout the welcome soak in his bath, he

pondered the problem. He hardly heard any of his family's dinnertime chatter, nor did he really taste the food he was served, so wrapped up was he in his dilemma. After dinner, the family dispersed, and he went back to his room, where he sat in his chair, feet up on the custom-made pouffe, a book open on his lap, with not a single word of it read.

Eventually, it came to him. He didn't have to court Regina Chilvers at all. He just had to seem to do so to William Chilvers' satisfaction. That was not the same thing at all. What William saw need not be what was actually happening. If Harry cultivated a *friendship* with Regina, spent a great deal of time with her, and if her father saw her enjoying his company, perhaps it would be enough. As long as he came up with some ruse whereby she did not move out of her father's home until after her birthday had passed, Chilvers could not say Harry had failed.

*In other words,* said the little voice inside his head, *you will deceive him.*

"He deserves it," he muttered, aloud. "He shouldn't be trying to dictate her life."

*He is her father,* insisted the voice.

"This is the twentieth century, not the Middle Ages. A woman isn't her father's chattel any more. Some women are able to vote. Nancy Astor even sits in the House of Commons! If she can do that, surely Regina Chilvers can be permitted to decide her own fate."

*You're deceiving him, and you'll deceive her.* The voice was quiet and effective.

Harry reached for the whisky on the table at his side, took a healthy swallow, and tried to wash away the dissent.

It didn't work.

"Be quiet," he ordered the voice. He thought he heard a derisory sniff, which he ignored. "If I do it," he said, "I can make sure she gets to choose what she wants at the end of it. If I don't do it, he'll just find someone else, and they won't take her wishes into account."

*If you say so.*

Harry swore. It didn't matter how much whisky he drank tonight. He wasn't going to be able to drown that annoying little voice inside him.

"I'm doing this," he said, in a tone of no surrender. "I said I would, so I will. But I'll do it my way. And that is all-she-wrote. I refuse to listen to you anymore."

The voice didn't answer. Which made him feel worse than if it had harangued him, and left him second guessing himself, right up until he finally fell asleep that night.

And dreamed of Regina Chilvers.

Chapter Three

Harry waited three days before he went to the tea shop again. He sat in the same spot as before, ordered a generous slice of Victoria sponge and a cup of tea, then relaxed, savoring each bite of the light-as-air cake. They didn't have cake at home, as a rule. Father called it an indulgence, something for special occasions, although Harry suspected the real reason was that their cook was not a great cake maker, and Walter Pearson did not want to admit that. Mrs. Bell was very good at dinners and cooked breakfasts, and she could certainly manage stodgy puddings such as Jam Roly Poly. But melt-in-the-mouth biscuits and fluffy sponges? For those Harry would have to come here.

It was the middle of the day, and the tea shop was full. Every table was taken, and the waitress was rushed off her feet trying to prepare each order, as well as bagging cakes, pastries, breads, and the like, for those who wanted something to take home. Harry finished the tea in his pot but he didn't have the heart to ask the waitress to bring him another one just yet. So he waited, chewed slowly on his cake, pretended he still had a drink, and watched people come and go, while he kept one eye on the door to the back of the shop, where only staff were permitted. He willed Regina to come out, but she didn't.

A buxom blonde in a cream skirt and blouse, white apron tied at her waist and a white voile cap covering most of her hair, appeared at the staff door. She had a smudge of flour on one of her pink cheeks, and eyes that crinkled, as if she smiled a lot. She looked around the tea shop with satisfaction before heading to the counter and collecting the receipts. She exchanged a few words with the waitress, who nodded at whatever she had said, then served yet another customer. Watching the woman collect the bills disappointed Harry, for if she was doing it, it was likely Regina would not leave her lair today.

The blonde, who he assumed was Sally Ann, the shop owner, shut the till and moved away from the counter, clutching the precious receipts.

Harry thought quickly. He had made sure not to contact Regina straight after their introduction. He'd known, somehow, that if he was too eager to see her again, she would smell a rat and keep her distance. But at the same time, he only had six weeks to persuade her father he was doing his job, and that meant he needed to get to know her better, and soon. How was he to do that if she didn't make an appearance?

He couldn't sit here all day, taking up a much-needed table, either. Sooner or later, the staff would become suspicious of him. They might even ask him to leave, considering how busy they were.

Which meant there was only one thing he could do. As Sally Ann passed his table, he held out his hand to grab her attention and said, "Excuse me?"

The blonde stopped and gave him the bright smile one only saw when a retailer encountered a client. Briefly, Harry wondered whether there was a special training program that taught them how to do that. If there was, he thought, he would need to enroll in it before he started touting for business himself. He shook away the absurd thought and concentrated on this conversation.

"Can I help you, sir?" Sally Ann's voice held a soft Sussex burr. It was warm and welcoming and suited her.

"I was wondering if Miss Chilvers is working today?"

The smile slipped and her eyes narrowed. "You must be mistaken, sir," she said, the warm burr of a moment ago replaced by crisp ice. "I don't have anybody by that name on my payroll."

"I am a friend of hers," he told her. Which was stretching the truth a little, he knew. "We have met in here before." He gave her a meaningful look. "Without her father's knowledge, obviously."

"I am very busy, sir," she said. "If you've finished…"

"Could you please ask Miss Chilvers if she would share a pot of tea with Harry Pearson?"

Sally Ann pursed her lips. He was losing this.

"Elsie will tell you, we have spoken to each other in here before," he tried. *When she put me in my place and refused to help me.* Surreptitiously, he crossed his fingers and hoped for the best.

Sally Ann's eyes flickered over to the counter. Elsie served her customers, who stretched in a long line through the shop and out of the door. A strand of hair had escaped the waitress's cap and now hung down the side of her face, dark threaded through with gray. Her eyes looked tired, but her smile stayed in place.

"Please?" Harry said, softly, pulling Sally Ann's attention back to him. "I simply want to buy her a cup of tea. Whatever else she does while she is here is none of my business, and not something I will ever mention to anybody else."

A long moment passed. She studied him closely. Then she sniffed. "I need to go back to the office, sir, if you'll excuse me. But if I should happen to find somebody who is *not* on my payroll, I will mention you to them. Should it be that person knows you and wishes to speak with you, I shall send them out here to do so. But I offer no guarantee that any such person exists, or if they did, that they would want to come out here to see you. I don't hold out a lot of hope for you. There might not be anybody back there at all. And I have to say there shouldn't be anybody who isn't on my payroll. Employees are the only people who are permitted back there, and I am telling you, quite categorically, I do not have any Miss Chilvers on my payroll. All I can do is look for your friend. On the off chance that she's wandered through there by mistake. Do you understand?"

"Perfectly."

Sally Ann gave him one more uncertain look, then bustled away and disappeared into the staff area of the tea shop.

Two minutes later, Regina appeared round the door. Her eyes roved over the crowd, cautiously, for a few seconds, before she relaxed and came fully out onto the shop floor. Today, she wore a calico dress in a muted peach, with a repeating pattern of large flowers in bright peach and fresh springtime green, and some smaller flowers in a dark chocolate color, their tips a mix of bright orange and creamy yellow. Harry thought those might actually be stylized nuts, but he wasn't *au fait* enough with women's fashion to know for sure. The neck of the dress had a collar reminiscent of a man's shirt, and a row of buttons led from the collar to the dropped waist, below which were sharply creased box pleats. A long chain of jade-green beads matched the color of the cloche hat which she wore pulled low, hiding all her hair. The way it sat on her head made him think it had been pulled on in a hurry. She pulled on cream-colored gloves as she crossed the floor to him, and what looked like a thick, black coat was tucked into the curve of her elbow. Clearly, she wanted any casual observer to see her as a customer, someone who would be wearing outdoor clothes, not somebody who had settled in for a day of work.

Harry made to stand but she gestured that he should not. She sat across the table.

"What are you doing here?" she whispered.

"Drinking tea and eating cake."

"That's not what I meant, and you know it. Why did you ask for me?"

He shrugged his shoulders. "I hoped you would share a pot of tea with me."

"Did you, now?" She didn't sound impressed. "I am supposed to be working."

Harry grinned. "Are you? Truly? Because your boss denies that you are on her payroll."

Regina colored, a becoming shade of dark pink. It made her eyes shine. Today they were more blue than gray, and he could see tiny flecks of silver and navy in them. Her lashes were long and dark, too dark for her coloring, which made him wonder if they'd been enhanced. He knew his sister did something to make her lashes stand out. She said it improved the shape of her eyes. Their father complained she was a hussy, but Dorothy took little notice of his opinion. From what he knew of Regina, he would bet her father's objections would fall on deaf ears too.

"I am not on her payroll," she said now, in answer to his comment. He frowned and she chuckled. The smile lit her entire face and made his day seem brighter somehow. "To be on the payroll I need to be paid. I am not."

"You work for no pay?" That didn't sound right.

"I do."

"But…why?"

She batted her eyes and looked wonderfully innocent. "I am a dutiful daughter, Mr. Pearson. Obedient to my father at all times."

Harry snorted.

"For now, anyway. Until my birthday, when I shall reach my majority, I have no choice but to be so. I am under his control and at his command."

*Of course you are. That is why he is so worried about losing you.*

"He has forbidden me to take a paid position," she continued. "And since, if I go against him while he's still my legal guardian, he could make life less than pleasant for me, the sensible course of action is to do as he says." Her grin grew wicked. "However, he said nothing about my taking an unpaid position. So I work for Sally Ann on a voluntary basis."

"How pedantic of you." His lips twitched at the clever way she had thwarted her father by sticking to the letter of his law but reinterpreting the spirit of it.

\*\*\*\*

Reggie relaxed a little. Her first instinct, when Sally Ann had told her Harry was in the tea shop and asking for her, was to panic. What did he want? Why was he here? Had her father sent him?

Then she reminded herself he'd been here earlier in the week, before he met with her father. Not only that, he had said nothing to her father about her working here, when he'd had the chance. But did that mean she could trust him?

"Want me to get rid of him?" offered Sally Ann.

Reggie shook her head. "No. It's all right. I'll go and see what he wants." But just in case he wasn't the only person in the shop who knew her and her father, she decided to take precautions. "If I wear my hat and carry my coat, it'll look like I am a customer. Can't be in trouble for being a customer." She winked at Sally Ann. "I'll even buy a pot of tea."

Sally Ann nodded. "Your decision. But if you need me, you holler. I'll be out in a second, and he will rue the day." Reggie knew she meant it, too. If Harry *was* playing the smart aleck, he would come to regret it, and quickly.

"Thank you," said Reggie. She pushed her hat onto her head as firmly as she could without pins. It would mess up her hair, she knew, having it that firmly in place, but she could always fix her bob when she came back into the office, when he had gone. Then she picked up her coat and bag, held her gloves in one hand, and headed out into the shop.

A cursory glance had told her she knew nobody else in here. That never ceased to amaze her. She had been born and grown up in Fieldhurst, and had thought she knew everyone. But never, not once, had she encountered any of her crowd in here. The place was often packed to the rafters, with not one familiar face. Which was quite humbling, really. It made her think her world must be incredibly narrow.

She sat at the table with Harry and talked. He didn't seem to have any ulterior motives for calling her to join him. He was relaxed and at ease, and seemed to enjoy their verbal sparring as much as she was doing.

He had seemed outraged at the idea of her working for no pay. Which, on its own, made him an improvement on her father, who thought that was the only way a woman *should* work. And, he had seemed to appreciate the moral twists and turns she had done, so that she could obey her father yet do what she wished, too.

Now, she blinked, exaggeratedly, as she explained how working for no pay was exactly what her father wished her to do. "Father appreciates my working as a volunteer," she said, "or so he tells me."

Harry nodded, sagely. "I can see he would be appreciative."

"He is. He is proud of me for 'making better the lives of all those I help,' " she continued, quoting her father when she had first told him she would be volunteering her time to a worthwhile cause. He had been pleased with her for doing such a wonderful thing, believing his daughter's good deeds would be bound to improve his own standing within the community. Of course, he hadn't been interested enough to ask *which* worthwhile cause she had chosen. Just as well, really. She liked not having to lie outright to him.

Harry laughed. "Tell me, is Sally Ann a widow, or an orphan?"

"Neither." Reggie grinned, thoroughly enjoying this to and fro with him. "She is an army. The clue is in her name. Father is over the moon when I tell him I am going to help Sally Ann."

He nodded, sagely, but his eyes glittered, mischievously. Who would have thought such dark brown eyes could hold so much light within them? They positively sparkled with it. "Bangs a nifty tambourine, does she?" he asked.

"Indubitably."

Harry nodded and grabbed his sticks. "Glad to hear it. But I'm sure that even the estimable General Booth never begrudged his troops a cup of tea and a short rest. My treat."

He made to stand and she reached out, putting her hand on his arm to stay him. Even through his clothes, and her gloves, she felt the stunning warmth of his skin, the jump of surprised muscle, the twitch of a nerve.

Nonplussed, she withdrew her hand again, quickly.

"I will get them," she argued.

"No, I insist. I'm not the kind of man who takes a lady to tea and then expects her to pay for it."

"You didn't 'take' me to tea, or anywhere else. But if it makes you feel better, you pay. I will simply fetch the food."

Harry gave her a ten shilling note and she joined Elsie's queue, which had diminished a little, now that the lunchtime rush was almost over. Elsie glanced at Harry, then winked at Reggie and gave her what the waitress probably thought was a subtle thumbs up. Part of Reggie wanted to argue, to deny whatever idea Elsie might be getting about Harry and her. Another part, the sensible, rational part, said that arguing and denying would just ensure Elsie's beliefs would be further entrenched. Wasn't it Shakespeare who said, 'The lady doth protest too much'?

So she said nothing as Elsie prepared a tray, filling

it with a pretty blue teapot, a matching milk jug, and a bowl of sugar lumps. The sugar tongs sported handles that also matched the teapot, as well as the two cups and saucers and the cake plates onto which she had dished up two slices of cake. Sally Ann had been determined the shop would be known for its elegance and refinement. She wanted people to feel they were getting a treat when they came here.

"He's a looker," murmured Elsie, in a near-whisper so the other customers wouldn't hear her. She nodded and gave another of her not-very-subtle winks, then put Harry's change onto the tray.

"Thank you." Reggie knew she would get the third degree about him. There would be no avoiding it. But that was for later. She picked up the tray and walked away.

Reggie transferred the tea stuff from the tray onto the table, put the tray on a spare chair, then sat and stirred the tea that was brewing in the pot. "Milk in first?" she asked Harry. "Or last?"

"First, please."

She poured the tea, handed him his cup, then sipped her own before using her fork to cut a sliver of her cake.

He did the same. "I begin to worry that, if I make a regular habit of visiting this place, I will probably grow so round I will be like Tweedledum and Tweedledee."

"Which one?" she asked, as if the idea was not absurd but very likely to happen.

****

Harry pretended to ponder the ridiculous question. He'd started this thread of the conversation for a reason, but now that he had, he felt awkward and discomfited, as if he was in a sea made of honey that sucked him down even as it held him fast. He should have thought about what he wanted to say a little more. Prepared something.

It was too late now. He had jumped in, both feet first, and all he could do now was go with it, and hope he reached solid ground soon. "Both," he answered her question. "Together. Sally Ann's cakes are disquietingly difficult to resist once you have come in here and tried one."

"True. But you can't blame Sally Ann for your lack of resistance. Nobody has ever been forced to come in here at gunpoint." She took another dainty bite of her own cake and put it into her mouth without leaving so much as a crumb on her lips. Had he thought those lips thin when he first saw her? He'd been wrong. They were not plump, or pouty, but they weren't thin, either. They were…just right.

"You chose to come in, you know."

It took him a moment to work his way back into the conversation and make sense of her words. *Forced in. At gunpoint. Chose to come in.* Right.

It was the opening he needed to get the conversation back on track. "I did," he admitted. "Because I wanted to see you."

She paled and the smile dropped away.

"I enjoyed our conversation the other evening. I hoped we could be friends."

"Friends?" She did not sound particularly eager.

"Is there something wrong in that?"

She shrugged her shoulders. "I dare say not."

Less sure of himself than he had been a minute or so ago, he decided he had better move on before he lost her completely. "I was wondering, as a friend…if you are not on the payroll here, are your hours more flexible than, say, Elsie's?"

"I come and go at my own convenience, if that's what you're asking. That's what volunteers do."

And what he had hoped she would say. He took a deep breath. Here went nothing, he told himself. Aloud, he said, "so, if I offered to take you for a drive, you would be able to say yes?"

"Well." She drew the word out to three syllables. "My time is, of course, my own, but I should tell you, Mr. Pearson, I am not now, nor will I ever be, interested in courting you." She sipped her tea in a manner that suggested that was the final word on the subject.

Harry disagreed. There were many more words to be said. "I didn't ask to court you," he pointed out. "I asked if you would like to go for a drive. In my car. As it is a lovely day, and we are friends, and I thought you would enjoy it. I am a perfectly safe driver, my legs notwithstanding."

Regina's cheeks colored. "I am sorry. I shouldn't assume..."

Harry waved his hand. "It's of no consequence. A misunderstanding, that's all."

She lowered her eyes and Harry watched her face. The color in her cheeks subsided as her embarrassment dissipated. He sipped at his cooling tea and willed her to say yes. It really was the most beautiful day, one of the nicest days of the year so far. True, it hadn't been a particularly cold or wet winter, but it hadn't been invitingly warm over the last few months, either. Now they were in the first days of March, and the sun had warmed the land enough that they could sit on a picnic blanket and enjoy a little time outside. Today, there was even enough heat to tan skin, if one was not careful. The sky was a deep blue, the tiniest wisps of pure white cloud floating in it, and the air outside had a golden brightness that made him glad of the brim of his hat to shield his eyes.

A minute passed. She didn't answer. Two minutes. Still nothing.

She was going to turn him down. He knew she was. Although, why she would hesitate before she did so puzzled him. Regina Chilvers did not strike him as a woman who would beat about the bush. If she was going to say no, she would say no and have done with it.

He longed to say something else. Anything else. Something to break the silence, perhaps to persuade her to accept. He forced himself not to. His father had taught all his sons that silence was a powerful tool. If one used it correctly, one could snatch victory where none had been certain.

And so it proved. Finally, Regina smiled. "Why not?" she said.

Harry pressed his lips together to prevent the victorious grin. He wanted to punch the air and holler triumphantly. Which would be conduct unbecoming, at the very least, and would do absolutely nothing to further his cause at all.

His cause. His business. The deal. The sour taste those reminders left on his tongue threatened to spoil the afternoon before it could even start.

*I haven't asked her for a date. Just a drive. I'm not courting her here.* If he told himself that often enough, he might persuade himself it was true.

He stacked his plate onto hers and put his cup and saucer on top of them both, just to busy his hands. The gold-and-onyx ring his grandfather had given him to mark the end of his convalescence gleamed on the third finger of his right hand. The old man had died last year, and Harry missed him tremendously. He'd been the only one to stand up for Harry on his return from the Front. When Walter Pearson harangued Harry for his stupidity, Grandfather had succinctly reminded him of some of the more idiotic things Walter had done in his own youth. Grandfather had never dismissed Harry as useless, and had berated Walter for doing so, which had given Harry's confidence a huge boost. In fact, it was probably true to say that, without his grandfather, Harry probably would never have dared even to dream of building his own company.

And, which was more, he thought, with a hint of sourness, Grandfather would have loaned him the money to get that company started. *If only...*

Harry thought then of something their nanny had been fond of saying, whenever any of her little charges spoke of "if only."

*If ifs and ands were pots and pans, we'd have no need of tinkers.*

The thought, after all these years, of Hetty Wright, the nanny who'd brought all the Pearson children up, made him want to smile. The woman had had corkscrew curls that constantly threatened to break free from her starched cap, and a stern glare that promised retribution for misdemeanors, but which was, in fact, the biggest lie of all.

*"You have to do what's right, Master Harry,"* she had told him, her Sussex accent contorting her vowels. *"Course, what's right for one i'n't right for all, so as long as it don't hurt nobody else, and don't land you in prison, you do what's best for you."*

She was a wise woman, was Hetty Wright, he thought now, as he escorted Regina out of the shop.

\*\*\*\*

Half an hour after leaving the shop, Reggie sat beside Harry on the front bench of his car as he motored across the Ashdown Forest. The softly undulating land around them was an array of colors—the yellows and greens of new grasses and ferns crisscrossed by the deep yellow scars of bridleways and footpaths, the dark greens of gorse bushes, already dotted with their bright yellow flowers that made the air smell of burnt coconut. There was the hazy violet of the first bluebells, growing in clusters in the shade of the birch trees, which grew in clumps, their silver trunks tall and almost unnaturally straight. Other trees dotted the landscape: many different varieties of pine and fir, an occasional oak, hazel, and chestnut, and alder trees near to where the ponds glittered, silver streaked with gold in the bright sunlight.

The road wound across the forest, a narrow, gray ribbon that twisted and turned this way and that. Now and again, the sheep and cows that grazed on the grassland wandered onto the road, then stood as if, having got themselves there, they were now unsure how to get back. Harry sounded his horn. They bleated and lowed their disapproval at him. But they did, at least, move out of the way.

They drove for several miles and didn't see another car. Occasionally, they saw an intrepid walker—a shepherd following his flock over the landscape, and a couple of hikers in plus fours and shooting jackets, their backpacks weighing them down as they tramped over the land. They waved at Harry and Reggie, and they waved back.

Finally, they stopped near the windmill at Nutley. The land their parking spot overlooked sloped sharply away from the road before turning up again, creating a V-shaped valley between two hillocks. A line of trees was silhouetted on the top of the farthest hillock. A herd of deer meandered across the land, stopping here and there to graze.

"Would you care for a walk, milady?" Harry asked.

She looked dubiously at his legs. The ground was rough and uneven.

"I can walk short distances," he assured her. "Even over this sort of terrain, if I'm careful. I'm not saying I can hike from here to Brighton, but a few hundred yards won't kill me." He lifted his chin and held her gaze. Though he smiled, there was a defiance to it. If she refused, and he thought it was for his sake, he would be hurt and angry.

"A walk would be lovely," she said.

He climbed from the car and moved round to open her door for her, then offered her his arm. She took it, and they walked together over the sandstone path. After a few rain-free days the path was hard and dry, although it was also unevenly rutted by the hooves of the animals who had used it, and the shapes carved into it by the relentless elements. Its soft, white chalky dust floated in the air, and coated their shoes.

The forest, and the South Downs beyond, stretched away from them, the landscape changing from the bright colors of their immediate surroundings, through a series of muted greens and browns, to the purples, lilacs, and indigos of the horizon. Here and there, a farmhouse stood out, red and brown against the green and blue of the land. Livestock dotted meadows, and bright green shoots showed where early crops grew in regimented fields. Balls of steam rose from a train that travelled through the countryside.

"It is beautiful here," Reggie murmured.

"Scotland in the South."

"Excuse me?"

He grinned. "Scotland in the South. I heard somebody call it that. Sums it up perfectly, wouldn't you say?"

"I don't know. I've never been to Scotland." Although she had seen pictures, and she could see why a comparison might be drawn.

Harry's eyes widened and his mouth formed a horrified O. "Never been to Scotland?" he spluttered. "Never been to Scotland? Milady, you have not lived!"

She grinned. "It's nice there, then?"

Now, he looked even more appalled. "*Nice*? No. It's not *nice*. *Nice* is a cup of tea to refresh you. Or a pleasingly comfortable piece of furniture. Scotland is more than *nice*. Scotland is…" Harry struggled for a moment, as if he searched for the right words. "Breathtaking. Yes, that's it. Breathtaking. You pass through the Highlands, and the road goes between two mountains—craggy rocks and green slopes with the clouds hanging around them—and alongside, the lochs, blue and inviting, and you think there could never be any better sight than this. Then you drive around another corner, between two more mountains, and pow! There is. It's magnificent and majestic, and… I don't have the words to do justice to it."

"What you said sounds wonderful."

"Everyone should see it for themselves." He winked. "It's not something you forget."

"And this…" she gestured at the landscape around her, "this reminds you of it?"

He nodded. "To an extent. It wasn't my phrase, remember. I was quoting someone else. To be fair, he was trying to market the place. I believe he has a hotel near here, and he dreams of tourists filling his rooms and making his fortune."

"Do you think that will ever happen?"

"No reason why it shouldn't. It is beautiful here. And Ashdown Forest—the whole of Sussex, for that matter—is far easier to get to than Fort William in Scotland."

"Unless you live in Glasgow," she pointed out pertly.

Harry laughed. "Touché, Regina. Do you mind if I call you Regina? 'Milady' always sounds so formal."

She swatted his shoulder. "Formal, and incorrect. Call me Reggie. Everybody does. Except for my father."

"Reggie," he agreed. "It suits you."

"Does it?" She raised her eyebrows, surprised. "In what way?"

"In lots of ways. It's no-nonsense and succinct, and it has a hint of…"

"If you say masculinity, I will crown you." Her father had said that. It was the reason he refused to use the nickname.

"You're my daughter, not my son," he had objected. "Have some decorum." Which, of course, had made her encourage the use of the name even more.

"I wasn't going to say any such thing," said Harry, consigning Father's opinions to the recesses of memory, where it belonged. "Of course, I would say that Regina suits you, too. That draws attention to the fact that you are tall and proud, and carry yourself like a queen."

Reggie laughed. "You do have a flair for the absurd, Mr. Pearson."

"Nothing absurd about it," he insisted. "And it's Harry."

"I beg to differ. It is very absurd." She glanced at him before adding, "Harry."

He grinned like a buffoon. "I just remembered," he said, pointing over his shoulder toward their car, "our cook packed me a hamper. Would you care to share it with me?"

Suspicion wiped the smile from her face, and she looked at him through narrowed eyes. His cook packed him a hamper? Had he been that certain she would agree to his impromptu drive into the countryside? She wasn't sure she appreciated that. It made her feel as if her acquiescence was taken for granted. As if she, a mere woman, would fall in with his plans without demur.

"A hamper?" she asked, coolly.

Harry nodded. "She often packs me one," he replied. "She worries I'll find myself in the outer reaches of East Grinstead and be lost for days. She needs to know I have enough supplies to guarantee my survival until the rescue team can flush me out."

"You are so full of applesauce, Harry Pearson," said Reggie, but she couldn't help the smile at his nonsense.

"It's not applesauce," he answered, affronted. "I promise you, every word is true."

"Of course it is."

He affected an expression of injured innocence. "I'll have you know that our Mrs. Bell prepares hampers for everybody, at the slightest excuse. She's one of those people who thinks if she doesn't feed us enough at luncheon to keep the British Army marching, then we will never make it home to dinner, because we will have starved and fallen into a ditch somewhere, too weak to climb out of it again."

"I see." Reggie sighed, exaggeratedly. "Well, we wouldn't want to upset your Mrs. Bell, would we? We'd better see if we can put a dent in her banquet of delights, hadn't we?"

She took his arm again, and they made their way back to his car.

Chapter Four

They pulled a large picnic rug from the boot of his car and spread it over a patch of grass away from the dusty trail, then settled onto it. Reggie automatically took the role of "mother," handing out plates and cutlery before offering him a selection of chicken slices, ham, hard-boiled eggs, bread and cheese. She poured him a glass of crisp, cold lime cordial. Only when he had taken his plateful from her did she start to serve herself.

The irony was not lost on her. "We are born into our roles, it seems." She laughed. "No matter how we kick against them and try to break free of them." He frowned, puzzled, and she gestured at her plate. "It's always the woman who dishes up the food and pours the tea. Or, in this case, the lime cordial."

"Ah. My apologies."

She waved away his words. "That's not what I meant. I wasn't criticizing you. If anything, I was criticizing myself. I tell myself daily that I am an independent spirit. That being a woman does not mean I can't do exactly the same as a man, and that I am going to prove it. I will not do what is expected of me, unless I wish to, of course. And yet…" She shrugged and nibbled on a piece of chicken. "Not that it really matters, I suppose." It was only a plateful of picnic food, after all.

"It matters to you, I can see that." Harry's voice was quiet, filled with understanding. It encouraged her to go on.

"Women's right to be independent and the right to be equal to their brothers—those rights have been hard fought for. Oh, not by me. But by others, people I admire. Women who gave a lot, suffered, died even, so that women like me could be free to choose what we wanted. I don't want to let them down."

"Is that what you think you would be doing? By serving food?"

"Not by that precisely, no. But…"

"The automatic assumption of the role?"

"Yes!" Reggie grinned broadly. Harry got what she had been trying to say. He understood. There was hope.

"So, you don't want to work to be like a man, *per se*…?"

"I want to be *free* to work. I want to be able to choose it, if it's what I wish."

"You want to be *more* than a man."

"No. Not *more*. The same."

Harry's grin did not reach his eyes. "It's not the same. You choosing to work if you want to is one thing, and you should be able to. But men, as a rule, don't *choose* to work. They must do it. Or their families will starve."

Reggie stopped chewing her food and stared at him, astonished. She had never thought of it like that before. But, she could not deny, he had a point. One she would need to ponder.

"What about other things?" he asked, now. "Do other things diminish your rights? Things like marriage, having children?"

They were back on more solid ground now. "Marriage and children are not, in themselves, the problem," she told him, in the same way she had told her brother, James, and Father, when she could get them to listen. "They are laudable ambitions. As long as they are entered willingly, and are what both want."

"But they are not for you?"

Reggie smiled. This might be the first time in her life that a man showed interest in her opinion. Genuine interest, that was, not an indulgent pat on the head, as her father had been wont to offer when she had first espoused her beliefs. Not the vacant smile James offered, the smile that said he thought she was foolish but he couldn't be bothered to argue with her. And not the angry demands for it to stop that Father yelled at her these days, now he had realized it wasn't just a phase she would grow out of.

Harry asked questions. He was interested in her replies. He wanted to know. So, she would be truthful with him. She owed him that, at least.

"It isn't that marriage in itself is not to be borne," she explained. "If I found the right man for me, and we both entered into a mutually beneficial agreement, then I would consider it. But I am nothing if not pragmatic, and I know the chances of that happening for me are minimal. So, why dwell on it and wish for something I can never have? Surely, I'm much better off finding something that not only makes me as happy, if not happier, than marriage to the right man would, but which is within the bounds of possibility for me to achieve."

Harry frowned and ate the egg he had just bitten into before he answered her. "Something you could never have?" he asked. "That seems presumptuous."

Reggie shook her head and smiled. "It's the war," she said. "It changed things for all of us." She turned and stared across the land. The grasses swayed on the gentle breeze. Leaves on the trees whispered secrets to each other. She could see the fluttering shadow as the sails of the nearby windmill turned, although the windmill itself was hidden by the woods surrounding it. A hawk hovered in the blue sky, head bowed forward as it studied the land, looking for the slightest movement to betray its next meal.

"When I was at school," she continued, "my teacher, Miss Howe, called us all together. I was fifteen years old, full of hope and promise. The war was finally over, and things were, I thought, looking up. Then, Miss Howe spoke to us. She felt it was her duty to make us aware of how life had changed for us."

She sipped daintily at her cordial and thought back to that day. There had been twenty girls in the room. Not all of them were Reggie's age. Some were as young as twelve years old, barely out of their nurseries, too young to be gathered to hear the teacher's bleak forecast of their futures.

"Miss Howe told us, in no uncertain terms, that the war had changed everything for everybody. Thanks to what it had done, she said, only one in ten of us girls would ever be able to marry."

Reggie shook her head, remembering the horrified gasp that statement had sent through the room. For most of those girls, marriage had been their lifelong destination. It had never occurred to them that it might not happen.

"She said it was a statistical fact. And, as we all know from our mathematics lessons, one cannot argue with statistical facts."

"Surely the prospects of marriage are not as

prescriptive as the angles on an isosceles triangle," Harry argued. "The one is unanswerable and it could never change. The other…"

"In this case, they are the same thing."

"But—"

"The war, Harry. It all comes down to the war. You men had all gone marching off, you see, and so many had been killed, and now there weren't enough to go around. Miss Howe, who, incidentally, was a spinster herself because her young man was killed at the Somme, estimated that there was so few men left, nine out of ten of us would never marry."

"Nine out of ten?" Harry's eyes were round with shock.

Reggie nodded. "Nine out of ten."

The trenches had been unimaginable carnage. The men in them, men like Harry, had known that, of course. They had suffered in them, and watched their friends suffer. They'd seen other men shot and blown up, or succumb to disease and cold, or fall victim to mustard gas. Some had lived but lost their minds, coming home empty shells, helpless as new born babes.

Some of the survivors, like Harry, had kept their wits but lost full use of their bodies. Those men doubtless counted themselves the lucky ones.

But even the lucky ones had known how horrific war was, and the price it exacted from everyone it touched.

For girls like Reggie, it had taken the quiet, matter-of-fact words of a teacher to bring that reality home.

"You are an attractive woman," Harry said now. "There is no reason you couldn't—"

"There is every reason," Reggie snapped at him, which was unfair. She knew he wasn't arguing because he thought she was wrong. After all, he had seen for himself the damage the Great War had done. He was simply saying she didn't need to despair over it.

What he didn't know was that Reggie wasn't despairing.

"There is every reason," she said again, calmer this time. "You see, when Miss Howe told us the facts, I did not go away and cry about them like some of the girls did. Instead, I decided, there and then, that I would be one of the nine."

Harry frowned. "You decided? Why would you decide such a thing?"

Reggie took a long drink of her cordial, then pressed her handkerchief to her lips before she answered him. Her reasoning had been sound in 1920, and it was, she thought, still sound now. It was based on logic and fact, with no emotion clouding it, and that had enabled her to make her decision easily.

"If there was such an abundance of young ladies," she told him," and a dearth of young men, then it stood to reason that only the best-looking, most charming, and most presentable females would be snapped up. I have always known I am none of those things."

"I beg to differ."

"Thank you. But you saying so does not make it so. I am, and always have been, aware of my own…shall we call them flaws? My father would call them that."

"Your father does not speak for everybody. He cannot know there isn't someone out there, waiting just for you." Harry's lips thinned and there was a glint in his eye that she thought of as mutinous. It made her like him even more.

"My father does know me, though. He knows all that

I am." She counted her points out on her fingers as she made them. "He knows I am plain to look at. Yes, I am," she insisted as Harry opened his mouth to argue. "There is no sense denying it. My chin is too square, my lips too thin, my nose too long. I take after my grandfather in looks. On him, the face was well suited. But it is not a feminine face."

Harry rolled his eyes and shook his head, but she pressed on, not permitting him to say anything in return.

"I am also plain speaking. I always have been so. I've never dressed things in pretty words and lacy euphemisms. I like my own way. In disagreements and debates, I don't give quarter, and that upsets and offends people. I don't court the good opinions of those I don't like. I can be cold, and unforgiving."

"I have not found you so," he insisted, but she knew he was lying. Had she not put him firmly in his place when he had asked her to serve him at the tea shop?

"With you, I have been on my best behavior," she said. "But that's of no consequence. Even if I was the most beautiful, charming, and irresistible female in the British Isles, I still would be one of the nine. Because, you see, I am not in the least domesticated. I'm certainly not maternal. I have never fawned over a baby in my life. While my friends coo at them and long to cuddle them, I am afraid I do not. I would much rather be independent and free than a wife and mother. I am meant to be a working woman, making my own way in the world. So why would I take up a man when they are scarce, and somebody else could have him? Somebody who actually wants him?"

There was a moment of silence. She chewed on a piece of bread and butter and watched the herd of deer in the distance.

Harry looked thoughtful for some moments. Finally, he sighed. "Well," he said, "that was candid."

She inclined her head. At least he knew where she stood now.

\*\*\*\*

Harry took a deep breath and pushed down the panic welling up inside him. She didn't want to marry. Didn't want to be courted. Of all the things that could possibly scupper his plans, this was one he hadn't even contemplated.

Because all women wished to marry and have children, eventually, didn't they? Even those who hoped for some independence in their lives. They might hope to spend a year or two at university, or time in an office, earning their own pin money. But they didn't see those things as something that would take up the whole of their lives.

Except, apparently, this one did.

Which did not bode well for Harry at all. How could he possibly hope to court a woman who genuinely did not wish to be courted? Lord Almighty! He might as well have agreed to court a woman who wanted to enter a convent! He would stand about as much chance of success.

Surely, William Chilvers did not know his daughter's feelings on the subject. He could not know how deeply held her beliefs were or he would not have drawn Harry into a situation where he could not possibly win.

Then again, perhaps Chilvers did know but chose not to believe his daughter. The man clearly had a low opinion of women, so perhaps he did not take Reggie seriously.

In his mind's eye, Harry watched his dreams implode. He took a sausage roll from the hamper and bit into it. It tasted like dry ash and took an eternity to chew. When he finally swallowed, he brushed the fallen crumbs of flaked pastry from his lapels and tried not to look as miserable as he felt.

He must have failed, because she narrowed her eyes at him, suspiciously.

"You do believe me, I assume?" she said.

Harry took a long swallow of his cordial, until he thought his mouth was moist enough for words to form, and not sound labored. "Why would I not?" he asked. Inside, he cringed. Nothing shouted guilt louder then answering a question with a question. "You have said so. Told me your feelings. I'm not about to call you a liar."

"No, but…" She bit her lip, cutting off what she had been about to say. Harry ate the rest of the sausage roll, chewing it as slowly as he could, so that he didn't have to say anything more just yet. He had a feeling that if he tried to fill the silence, he would merely incriminate himself.

"Why did you invite me to come here with you today?" she asked.

If that question wasn't an ambush, he didn't know what was. "It's a nice day," he said, as nonchalantly as he could manage. "I wanted to drive out, but I didn't want to do it alone. I thought…" He shrugged his shoulders. If he said too much, she would figure him out, and she would be off like a greyhound from the traps. Reggie Chilvers was not stupid. She would recognize any rambling by him now as a sign of subterfuge. The only chance Harry had of salvaging anything was to persuade her he genuinely wanted nothing more than friendship.

His conscience pricked, causing a sharp pain in his chest, just behind his breastbone. He tried not to brace himself against it too openly.

Reggie watched him, closely, for perhaps half a minute. It felt like a month. He reached for the bottle of cordial and topped up his cup, then held the bottle up, silently offering to fill hers. She shook her head, then pursed her lips. Harry's throat was dry again. So dry he didn't trust himself to speak at all.

"My father put you up to this, didn't he?" She asked the question in a flat, I-already-know-the-answer tone.

"Excuse me?" Harry tried to seem innocent, but not so innocent his guilt would be clear. This served him right, he thought. He should have known better than to try to manipulate her, to thwart her dreams. What was that old saying about doing unto others as you would be done by?

"My father," she repeated. "Did he make you court me?"

There are moments in a life, Harry thought, when you stand at a crossroads, and the way you move on will significantly alter everything. This was one of those moments. If he turned right and said yes, admitted everything to her, then the road would take him one way. It would be a rocky road, one where he would never reach the destination he wanted. There would be no business owned by him. No loan from her father. And, saddest of all, no friendship with this woman whose company he already enjoyed far more than he had expected.

If he turned left and lied to her now, telling her he

didn't know what she meant, then the road would be completely different. She would believe him— perhaps—and their friendship would survive, at least for now. His dreams would limp on, still alive for the time being, although battered.

But lies had a way of catching a person out. Sooner or later, Reggie would discover the truth, and all Harry would be doing was delaying the inevitable.

So Harry turned neither to the right or to the left. Instead, he crossed the junction and moved on along the road ahead. What he said wasn't exactly a lie, but it wasn't exactly the truth, either.

"I choose my own companions for social occasions," he said. He pictured himself crossing his fingers, although he couldn't physically do so at this moment, because she would see.

It was the truth, though carelessly packed, and with no care for its condition. And it didn't answer her question. What it did do was make his stomach churn, and it coated his tongue with something very bitter indeed.

Reggie fidgeted. She folded her long legs to the side of her, and tucked them against her bottom. The peach dress moved slightly, its hem rising to just above her knee, showing off a little more of her leg. Harry cleared his throat and tried not to ogle her, although looking away and ignoring the sight would be impossible.

So now he was not only a lying cad, but a lecherous peeping Tom, too. Could this day get any worse?

"I have offended you," she said quietly. She lowered her gaze and looked chastened.

Harry could not have that. Not when she was the one, if she did but know it, who had the right to be offended, while he had no right to it at all.

"I'm not offended," he said. "But I am intrigued. Why would you think such a thing?" *What gave me away?*

Reggie sighed and reached for another piece of chicken. She wrapped it in her linen napkin and nibbled daintily at it between sentences. "You would not have been the first person I had offended with my 'forthright opinions' and 'flawed logic.' "

"Let me guess. Those are your father's words." Harry was coming to dislike William Chilvers a great deal. How could he be so dismissive of this woman? Why was he not proud of her? She was everything a man should be proud of. Intelligent, ambitious, and despite what she seemed to think, beautiful, to boot. If her father could look at her and see nought but her flaws, he was a man to be pitied.

Reggie grinned. "His words," she confirmed. "He is, shall we say, a man who is very set in his opinions. He believes, fervently, that a woman's place is in the home, and *only* in the home."

She took another bite of chicken, then licked her lips. Harry watched the tip of her tongue run across her bottom lip and felt its effects in the tightening of his thighs, and the not-unpleasant ache in his lower belly.

"Many men feel the same," he answered. To his own ears, his voice sounded strained.

"Are you one of them, Mr. Pearson?" A direct question. One that required a direct answer. An answer he would give her, just as soon as his brain moved out of his lower regions and back into its correct position.

"Harry," he said. "Call me Harry." He smiled at her. "And no. Not necessarily."

Reggie frowned at that, as if she didn't understand.

He went on, "I believe a woman's place is where she is happy to be. Just the same as a man's place is where he is happy to be." He was a little surprised, and very relieved, to find that those words conveyed his true feelings. Now, if he could make her happy to be where he needed her to be, at least for a short time...

Her face relaxed into an easy smile. "As you say, Harry." She wrapped up the food they hadn't eaten and started to pack it into the picnic hamper. "I am happy when I am working. I wish to earn my own living. I have wished that since I was first able to contemplate my future."

"Then you should do it." Under his napkin, Harry crossed his fingers. Although, he told himself, it wasn't a lie. Because, all other things being equal, he did agree with what he had said. And he had no doubt she would get what she wanted from life, in the end.

That did not make him feel better.

"Although," he continued, "you'll not get far at earning a living if you work for no pay."

She laughed. "*Touché.*" She picked at the edge of the blanket while she spoke. "Sally Ann doesn't give me money, that's true. But the experience I am gaining there, and the character she will give me at the end of it, are worth a fortune."

"Is that the kind of work you wish to do?" he asked. "Accounts?"

"I don't know. I suppose I'd like to try several different things and find the best fit for me. Does that make sense?"

"Perfectly."

Her answer gave Harry an idea. He could give this

woman the work experiences she wanted, fulfil his deal with her father, and walk away at the end, knowing he hadn't hurt her at all. In fact, he would have helped her in her quest by building her skills set as she tried various different things. It was, in fact, a way for everyone to get what they wished for. He wondered why it had taken so long to come up with it.

"Would you like to sample another aspect of working life?" he asked her. "On the days when you aren't in the tea shop?"

Reggie frowned, puzzled.

"I am building," he explained, "from the ground up, a delivery company. I'll be delivering to the businesses around here, and then delivering goods from those businesses to their customers. Eventually, I would like to have a passenger coach company as well, but one thing at a time."

She nodded. "This is the company you want my father to invest in?"

"It is. And he has agreed to do so, which means I now have the funds to get started. So, why don't you join me as I find a warehouse, and a garage, and everything else I'm going to need?"

"Me? I know nothing about business premises."

"Neither do I. Not really. Although I'm sure we will both learn quickly enough." *Please say yes.* "If you come with me, you can learn another aspect of business life. Add another string to your bow, so to speak." *And I won't feel as if I am taking away the things you want.*

The smile she gave him was radiant. "When do we start?" she asked.

Chapter Five

They began the very next day. Harry picked up Reggie in his Austin and drove her to the nearby town of Tunbridge Wells. This was the nearest town with a large rail depot, and would, therefore, be where the goods he dealt with were most likely to arrive. A warehouse here would be perfect.

He soon realized that a warehouse here was well out of his budget. Tunbridge Wells was a medium-sized town with a thriving business community, reflected in the fact that it had not one but two rail stations to serve it. Although not as fashionable as it had been in its eighteenth-century heyday, it was still a sought-after place, both for people to live and for tourists to visit. Especially popular among visitors were the Pantiles, an upmarket shopping area where exclusive shops nestled under a colonnaded walkway. The Chalybeate Spring was there, the well of water that had given the town its name and original popularity. Even today, people queued up to take a cup of the waters, although Harry was bemused that anyone would want to: the water was an off-putting rusty red, and it had a strange flavor with a strong, metallic aftertaste that had made him scrunch his face in disgust on the one occasion he had tried it. He knew it was rumored to have health-giving properties, but he thought one would have to be desperate to endure that taste more than once.

Surprisingly, the railway station used by most passengers, the Tunbridge Wells Central Station, was not the nearest one to the Pantiles. That station was perfectly placed for most of the town's amenities, though, being at the top of the busy High Street. It, and its surroundings, were ideal for shoppers and other visitors to Tunbridge Wells, but it was not what Harry was looking for. He was far more interested in Tunbridge Wells West Station.

There were some passenger trains coming into this station too, but most of the traffic here was made up of goods trains and freight. That it was a busy hub was obvious, because it had five separate rail lines leading into it, as opposed to the two at Tunbridge Wells Central.

The station itself was imposing, built to give a good first impression of the town. A large building with red brick walls and a three-story clock tower, it boasted ornate arched windows and doors, complete with a liveried doorman. There were Corinthian arches and marbled ticket halls. To the northeast, one of the rail lines headed through a tunnel toward Tunbridge Wells Central. To the southwest, the engine sheds were full of life, with the huffs and puffs of the idling engines, the smell of steam and coal, tar and oil, and the soot which sharpened the taste of the air and smudged itself onto skin and clothing.

Men shouted at each other, ordering wagons this way and that, while donkeys brayed and cattle lowed as they awaited transportation. Small children in clothes that didn't fit them darted around, hoping to make pennies carrying bags, while cars and charabancs idled in the road, waiting for new passengers.

"It's busier than I thought," said Reggie, raising her voice to be heard over the din.

"I'm told a hundred trains a day come through here," he replied.

She nodded. "Where would you be? Your warehouse, I mean."

Harry laughed. "If I had my way, I would be right here, in the thick of it. But there aren't many properties to be had this close to the station, and absolutely none of them are in my price range."

Reggie nodded and skimmed through the pamphlet she had picked up when they'd gone inside the station. They had hoped there would be someone in there who could answer Harry's questions and point him in the direction of suitable warehouses to let. What they found was a supercilious ticket clerk, who sniffed and said he did not deal with traders, nor any aspect of that part of the railway. Harry had wanted to draw himself up to his full height—something he rarely did these days, and demand, "Do you know who I am?" the way his father would have done. He'd refrained from doing it, knowing his satisfaction in it would be too brief to matter, if it came at all.

The doorman had been more respectful to Reggie, recognizing her for the lady she was. Then again, how could he have missed her quality? Today, she was dressed in a dark green skirt that sat scandalously above her knee, and a long jacket in a green-and-white houndstooth. It had huge pockets in the same fabric as the skirt, a plain green collar, and a wide silk ribbon tied into a bow at her throat. She wore it with cream gloves and a deep red cloche hat that matched her clutch bag. Harry suspected she had tried to look businesslike, but there was no mistaking her for anything but a lady. While Harry had been dismissed as unworthy by the ticket clerk, Reggie was treated to smiles and bows from the doorman, who handed her a pamphlet she might find interesting. He explained that it told, in a nutshell, everything she would need to know about the station and the railway company that owned it.

"The station has been called the Saint Pancras of the Weald," she read now.

"Fancy names don't hide shoddy service," answered Harry. He made an effort to smile, and to dispel the desire to pout like a child denied jelly for tea.

Reggie chuckled. "Your man wasn't as polite as he might have been," she acknowledged.

"All he had to do was answer my question and keep his opinion of me out of it."

"The doorman was nice, though."

Harry gave her a sidelong look, which made her laugh again. Her laughter was charming, a melodic sound that made him think of the little silver bells his mother hung at Christmas. He rolled his eyes at his own absurdity.

She went back to reading her pamphlet and followed him to the engine sheds.

"It says here, Buffalo Bill brought his Wild West show through this station," she announced as he approached the shed and peered into it, hoping to find someone who could help him.

"Really?" he asked, only half listening.

"Really." She looked up and around her, as if searching for some landmark. "He drove the Deadwood stage right out of the train, through the goods yard, and up to the common."

"Good for him." It was difficult for Harry to muster enthusiasm for something that must have happened years ago and which had no bearing on his quest today.

"Hmm." She grinned at him. "You, Harry Pearson, are travelling in the footprints of elite and noteworthy company."

"Only if I can find somewhere to store the blasted goods after they have left the train," he said.

"You will." She sounded absolutely sure. "Your warehouse is there. We just haven't found it yet."

Reggie pushed the pamphlet into her bag and threaded her arm through his.

They returned to Tunbridge Wells and resumed their search the next day. And the next. They spoke to various people, some eager to help, others completely indifferent to them. They looked at warehouses, both occupied and empty. Some were well kept and tidy, their floors even, their walls smooth and sturdy. Others were dirty, their surfaces covered in grease and Lord alone knew what else. They soon learned that the prices were very much the prices, and there would be no negotiating. Either you could and would pay, or you did without. Harry's heart sank when he realized this. He knew he could not pay what they asked, and that was that.

On the fourth day of their search, having looked at properties scattered all around the town, they drove home. He was feeling demoralized now. It had seemed so simple at the start. Get somebody to back him financially, set up the company, make a fortune. He hadn't factored in that property prices in a thriving, bustling town would be so high. At this rate, he would have to find a warehouse in Fieldhurst and transport the goods away from Tunbridge Wells before storing them. It wasn't ideal, as he would need to spend more money hauling them, especially if it turned out some of his clients wanted them delivered back to Tunbridge Wells. But short of looking for more funding, he didn't see what else he could do.

"Stop!" yelled Reggie. She put her hand onto his forearm and he stood on the brakes, stopping the Austin dead in the middle of the road. His heart pounded and his breath shallowed as he looked around for the emergency. Had he hit a child who had run out in front of him while he was busy with his thoughts? Had something terrible happened to the woman at his side? Did she need medical attention?

"What is it?"

"Sorry." She grinned, sheepishly. "I didn't mean you to stop quite that suddenly."

"Then what…?" He looked around. The road out of Tunbridge Wells was wide enough for two vehicles to pass, but it was also winding. They had driven past a large duck pond, then around a deep bend before climbing a steep hill with several smaller bends incorporated into it. To one side of the road were new houses, most of them only half built, their sturdy, square frames surrounded by scaffolding. To the other side were fields and woods, hedgerows and fences. Sheep grazed, totally ignoring the humans and the car just yards from them.

"What happened?" he asked. He checked his mirror, grateful no other vehicles had been on the road behind him.

Reggie cleared her throat. "It's just, I saw that." She pointed to a dirt track that led from the road, through the fields, and toward a cluster of farm buildings. A sign at the end of the track said, "Ramslye Farm." There was a farmhouse, a wisp of smoke rising from the chimney. To one side of it were low roofed buildings that Harry could only just see above the rise and fall of the landscape, and a couple of taller, longer barns.

Harry blinked and tried to figure out what was so noteworthy about the farm. This was, by and large, a rural area. Farms were scattered all over. Most of them were accessed by dirt tracks just like this one. Although, he would admit, the track leading to this farm looked to be in better shape than most. It was not rutted and potholed like so many would have been.

"Your building," she said, and she chewed her bottom lip, suddenly unsure of herself. "Does it have to be a custom-made warehouse? Or would an old barn suffice, for now?"

He stared at her for several seconds. She stared back. Slowly, her words—and their implications—filtered through his skull, which seemed thicker than normal today. As her meaning penetrated his brain, a slow smile spread across his face. "Let's go and take a look, shall we?" he said.

Her answering grin was wide and bright.

The farm's track was as smooth as it looked, with few jarring bounces. That boded well. Harry could not take fragile goods along a rickety road that might result in breakages, but this one was as easy as any public road. There were also a couple of passing places built in, which meant that vehicles going one way would not have to back up very far to let something coming the other way go past. That was an important consideration. While van drivers ought to be able to reverse as accurately and safely as they drove forward, it wasn't always the case. And although, in the short term, he would be the driver of the van, he hoped to expand the fleet eventually, and he didn't wish to have to find new premises simply because his future employees could not cope.

They drove past the first barn. It was set back from the track but still accessible. Made of red brick, it was two stories high, with a gabled roof made of tiles, many of which looked loose. Here and there was a gap where tiles had disappeared completely. Large corrugated iron doors took up much of one of the end walls. Grass grew around the barn, coarse and long, while nettles and brambles hugged the walls.

A few yards farther on, the second barn was in much the same state of disrepair, though it had noticeably more tiles missing from the roof. After that barn was a row of single-story buildings, which looked like they had once been stables. Then came a fence, flanked by bushes. Behind the fence was the farmyard, in which Harry could see chickens scratching and strutting about, while a goat grazed and a dog, chained to a kennel and looking decidedly bored, watched them.

At the end of the track was the farmhouse itself. A long building, two stories high, the lower story was made of the same red brick as the barns, the upper one of large stones that gave it a quaint, aged look. It had a tile roof and its woodwork was painted black and white. Three chimneys adorned the rooftop, though only one emitted smoke. Harry guessed that one was over the kitchen. A row of large plant pots lined the path that led from the track alongside the house. They held a variety of plants, some flowering, like lavender, others leafy and green. Harry recognized mint, parsley, and thyme, but he couldn't have named the others.

"Needs a little work," said Reggie, her wide smile coloring her voice. "Nothing insurmountable, though."

"Let's see if he'll rent it to me, shall we?" Harry climbed out of his car and hurried around to open her door. He knew he was slow, and she could have opened the door herself and got out a dozen times before he reached her, but she waited. She would likely never know how wonderfully capable that made him feel. Reggie Chilvers was a lady, through and through.

The farmer's wife came down the path from the house, wiping soapy hands on the bottom edge of her apron and frowning at her unexpected visitors.

"Can I help you?" she called, her Kentish burr clear in her soft vowels.

"Here goes nothing," murmured Reggie.

Harry took a deep breath, moved forward with his hand outstretched, and introduced himself.

An hour later, he thanked the woman for her tea, and for the delicious, freshly baked cake she had served with it, and walked with his new landlord to see the barn properly. He could see in Reggie's eyes that she wanted to come with them, but as keen as she was for women to be independent in business, she was also nobody's fool. She knew, as well as Harry did, this farmer was not a man to agree with her beliefs. As old as her father, if not older, the man's treatment of both his wife, whom he clearly saw as little more than a domestic servant, and of Reggie, who he treated as though she was fragile and easily shocked, left no doubt that he would not understand the modern woman.

Thankfully, Reggie was wise enough to know how to pick her battles. She smiled at the farmer's wife and asked her, sweetly, if the recipe for the cake was a family one, and would she mind sharing it? Harry threw her a glance that he hoped conveyed both his apology for her being sidelined and his gratitude that she took it so well, and then he left her with the woman in the kitchen while he went outside to the barn.

The corrugated iron door on the barn opened with a masculine groan, a pop, and a scrape of the bottom edge across the ground outside. Inside, the barn was dim, partly because there were few windows in the place and no electricity at all. In the center of the barn was a vast cavern of space, which stretched the whole length of the building. On both sides, and at the far end, there was an upper floor. It jutted out over the ground floor space by about ten feet all the way around. The place smelled of dry dust, old hay, and chickens, but it looked as sturdy and solid as any other building he had examined this week. Already, in his mind's eye, he was picturing the floor up there being cordoned off into smaller rooms, each containing shelving and cupboards to store goods. He imagined a walkway around the entire floor, allowing him to move from one space to another. At the far end of the ground floor he could see areas ideal for food storage, places where he could build cold pantries, install refrigeration units, and even somewhere to hang meat and birds where they might be safe from rats, mice, and other opportunity-taking vermin.

There was space to park his vans, and even a corner where he could put a hoist until he had the funds to install a lift, so that he could easily haul heavier goods up and down from the ground to the first story. He had negotiated to add one of the smaller buildings into the agreement, too, and now, on inspection, saw he had been right—that place would make the perfect workshop for a mechanic. The farmer had agreed Harry could paint the place and put in electricity and running water.

"You can put in electric, water, whatever you like," the farmer had said. "As long as the noise from your van and your business don't fret my chickens and stop them laying, that's all I ask."

"It's perfect," said Harry now, his grin wide. He shook hands with the farmer, and they agreed to draw up a contract.

Harry was in business.

Chapter Six

Over the next ten days, Reggie and Harry established a routine. He would pick her up at eight thirty every morning, at her parents' house. Three days a week, he took her to the tea shop in Fieldhurst, to fulfil her obligations there, while he went on and dealt with whatever needed to be done at his own workplace. There were lots of tasks to be completed there, and it pained Harry that he could not do them all on his own. Mundane acts such as sweeping the floor, moving debris from the buildings, and painting above shoulder height were not things he could easily do with legs as unsteady as his, and as Reggie had pointed out on that first day after he had leased the barn, it wasn't a good idea to risk falling while he was alone in the building and unable to summon help.

Reggie, of course, had couched her concerns in much more diplomatic terms than that. She never mentioned his limitations, saying instead that she wanted to be as much a part of this project as she could be, and if he did too much when she wasn't around to help, she would feel left out.

Harry was not fooled for a moment. He was, however, grateful that she didn't make a big fuss about her concerns, helping him and watching out for him while still allowing him to retain some dignity. Which was more than his own family had ever done for him.

He hadn't told his parents that he'd found this place. He didn't want to hear his father mocking him, nor did he wish to endure both of them making a song and dance about his injuries as they pointed out all the ways his shortcomings would prevent him doing things. Mother would wring her hands and fret about him hurting himself. Father would mutter and curse about wasting money—before he tried to either take over or force Harry to drop the whole project. It was, he knew, easier for him if they didn't know anything about it.

On the two days a week that she didn't work at the tea shop, Reggie spent her time at his workshop with him. On those days, she would still leave her home dressed in her usual fashionable outfits, not wishing to alert anybody to what she was doing. As soon as they arrived at the workshop, though, she made her way to a dark and private corner and changed into a pair of trousers, a shirt and a waistcoat, all filched from her brother's room. With her height, the clothes fitted her perfectly, and her slenderness meant there was no awkward tightness where she curved, either. Harry noticed, too, that she had been careful to choose clothes that had seen better days, with worn, frayed cuffs on the shirt, and trousers that were thin and shiny in places.

"James won't miss them," she'd said, the first day she brought them. "He doesn't even use these when he tinkers with his car anymore."

"If you say so," said Harry, doubtfully. The clothes looked comfortable and lived in, the sort of clothes a man would keep in his wardrobe forever, resisting all attempts to be rid of them. But then, he didn't know Reggie's brother, so he couldn't argue with her. Instead, he gave her mechanic's overalls to wear over the clothes, and some old gardening gloves to protect her hands.

She then set to, with impressive enthusiasm. She scrubbed walls, swept floors, and carried out years of debris, which she piled behind the barn. She washed the floors down, broke up cobwebs, and painted the newly cleaned walls in light colors, which made the space seem bigger and airier—and much easier to see.

Meanwhile, Harry prepared the mechanic's workshop and supervised alterations to the barn. The electricity and water supply were installed, and he had replaced the corrugated iron shutters with smart, well-fitted doors, as well as had the windows glazed.

He drew up plans for the various storage facilities and the walkway, then hired a team of builders to make those plans come to life. The only thing he hadn't started work on was the temporary hoist he planned to put into the corner.

On the tenth day, he stood in that corner, deep in thought.

"Penny for them?" Reggie said from behind him, and he jumped, then grinned that relieved, sheepish grin that said he had been startled but knew now there was no danger.

"I was thinking about the hoist," he told her. "And the lift that will replace it, once things get going and the money starts to come in."

Reggie frowned, puzzled, then studied the space herself, as if trying to see what he could see. "I thought you had it all drawn up," she said. "You only have to build it now."

He gave her a side-eyed glare and a sardonic grin. "I only have to build it," he agreed. "Which is, alas, very much easier said than done." He pointed out where the hoist would go, and all that was needed to make it work safely. "I can't do that myself. Not and guarantee it will be as sturdy as it needs to be. The last thing I want is for it to collapse while I'm transporting precious goods on it."

She stood beside him, hands stuffed into her pockets, which emphasized her slenderness, enveloped in the too-big overalls. Although she was taller than most women, and her legs were long, the trouser legs were longer. They bunched up around her ankles and dragged on the ground behind the heels of the brogues she'd invested in. The shoulder seams hung over her upper arms. She looked more like a little girl dressing in her parents' clothes than a worker who had pulled more than her weight in the race to get the barn ready for use.

Her face was clear of makeup, which allowed the smattering of freckles on her nose to show through and left her lips a dusky pink that was more alluring than all the dark red lip paints and glistening shimmers could ever be. Her hair was tousled, there was a smudge of dust on her cheek, and a string of gray cobweb stuck to the front of her overalls. She smelled of dust and paint, and turpentine. He'd never known anyone so beautiful, so alluring.

How could this woman think she was one of the nine out of ten? That she was plain and undesirable, and that men would prefer other women to woo? Did she have no mirrors? If Harry were whole and hearty, if he had anything to offer, he would be honored to court her, for real. He would have needed no deal with her father to sweeten the pot.

He closed his eyes and tried to tamp down the pain in his chest. The guilt and shame threatened to overwhelm him, rubbing the shine off this, the embodiment of his dream. He'd tried to assuage it by involving her, teaching her new skills, helping her discover what she was capable of, but it was no use. This was busy work. These were skills she was unlikely to use if—*when*—she did find a job.

She was enjoying herself. He could see it in the sparkle in her eye and the way she was constantly ready to smile. He savored those things now, while he could. Once she found out what he had done, she would never smile at him again.

"I see what you mean," she said, making him jump. Had he spoken his thoughts aloud? But Reggie wasn't looking at him. She still studied the corner where the hoist would go. "It must be strong enough to take whatever you throw at it, but you don't want it too heavy or it will pull the walls down."

"Yes," he agreed. He swallowed and pushed his thoughts aside.

"If the foundations are solid," she continued, "it'll take it." She knocked on the barn wall. "It seems well built, to me. I don't think there's anything to be concerned about."

At least where the barn was concerned, that was true. Everything had fallen into place so well, so quickly. Too well?

He didn't realize he had spoken aloud until she answered. "We've been lucky, I grant you. Why shouldn't we be? And it isn't all luck. We've worked quickly, yes, but we've also worked jolly hard. We deserve this. We deserve it to be successful. *You* deserve it to be successful."

She looked up at him with optimism and

encouragement. He held her gaze, hardly daring to blink lest the thread between them snap and take this moment from him, never to be returned. Her eyes were big and bold, the gray and violet flecks within them bringing the blue to life and filling it with a complexity that would take a lifetime to unravel. He could discern each individual lash around them, dark against the peaches-and-cream of her skin, the caramel freckles, even the gray dust smudge on her cheek.

Harry could not say if he moved closer to Reggie, or if she moved closer to him, but suddenly they were almost touching. He could feel the heat of her body, the soft caress of her breath on his cheek. The delicate scent of her seemed to underline the dry dust of concrete and the rubbery smell of new electric wiring, the sickly sweetness of oil, and the mustiness of old wood.

Outside, a bird called incessantly, while another sang melodically, its tone like a silver bell. A cockerel crowed and cattle lowed in the distance. The breeze made the barn doors rattle softly.

He reached out and caressed her cheek, very aware of the callouses on his fingertip as he brushed it over her silk-soft skin. He stroked her jawline, the lobe of her ear, touched the curl of her hair. She leaned into his hand, her head resting on his palm. Her lips parted, just the smallest fraction, and her eyes fluttered closed. He lowered his head. His heart sped up—he could hear it in his ear, feel it against his ribs. His thighs tightened, and his lower belly pulled as they came closer, closer…

The first kiss was gossamer soft, so light he barely believed it had truly happened. She sighed, and one hand touched his chest, as if she grounded herself, and him, through it. The heat of her fingers burned him through his clothes.

He brushed his mouth over hers once more, a little firmer this time. He felt the slight plumpness of her lips, the cool of her skin, the heat of her breath. She tasted of the cordial she had drunk with her lunch, the mint of her tooth powder, fresh air and musty interior, and that wonderful, indefinable something that was uniquely Reggie.

Her arm came around his shoulders and she leaned into him. Her soft breasts pressed against his hard chest, and her leg moved in between his, her belly against his center, so that she could not possibly be unaware of what she did to him. For a moment, he wondered if that part of him, growing ever larger, pressing against her, would frighten her, make her back away.

It didn't. He grinned against her skin, happier than he had ever been before in his life.

He ran his tongue across the seam of her lips and she opened them for him. His tongue pushed inside, dancing eagerly along the length of hers. She danced back, her tongue moving instinctively, picking up the rhythm. His body thrummed. A growl sounded deep in his throat and resonated through his chest, and she returned it with the softest mewl as she pulled him closer. He no longer knew where he ended and she began. Was that her heartbeat he could feel, pounding fast and loud, or his own? Her heat, or his?

*This.* He wanted to shout it to the world, let everybody know of the magic he'd found. He wanted to stay quiet, hold onto it, not let anyone else in to spoil it. He wanted it to go on forever. He wanted her, here, in his arms, in his heart, in his life…

The farmyard dog barked a warning. He wasn't

warning Harry, of course, but he might as well have been. It felt as if he had been doused in ice cold water, the madness of the moment thrust from him. He reared back, pulling away as if she had shocked him with a bolt of electricity. He moved so fast, he had to lean on his sticks and take two paces extra, to stop the stumble from turning into a full-blown fall.

"I…" He stammered while he tried to collect his breath, his thoughts, his equilibrium. His mind wouldn't tell him what to say. "I… I'm…"

"If you say you are sorry, Harry Pearson, I will knock you down."

"I'm not sorry. But I am… We… I have something I need to do. In the…" He pointed vaguely over his shoulder. "In the…mechanic's shed. I…erm, I…yes." He turned tail and left her. And even though his legs dragged and his sticks clicked on the floor, he felt as if he was running faster than an Olympic sprinter.

He didn't look back. He didn't dare. But he could feel her glare on him, all the way to the door. It was sharper than the point of any dagger, cutting through the flesh on his back and leaving him bleeding, in ribbons. And he didn't blame her. He had seduced her, drawn her in, kissed her…

He staggered into the former stable that he'd converted into a workshop for his vehicles. The door wobbled with a low complaint, and his footsteps and the taps of his sticks echoed on the empty air. "Harry Pearson," he muttered, "you are a bloody fool." *The biggest fool in England.*

He'd kissed her. She'd kissed him back! And then he had pulled away. He'd rejected her and run away.

"What kind of man are you?" he whispered.

That was easy to answer. He was, apparently, the kind of man who was terrified of a beautiful woman. Terrified of where a kiss could lead…

He slammed his fist into the door. The wood gave, but it still hurt, and he knew his knuckles would bruise. He called himself twenty kinds of idiot. He knew exactly where that kiss could lead. Exactly where it should have led, if he was half the ruthless businessman he ought to be.

He couldn't do this. Not to her. She was working so hard to give him his dream. He couldn't repay her by ending hers.

Not here. Not now.

There had to be a better way. A way to make them both happy. Though what that way was…

He still had four weeks to find it.

Four weeks? Ha! He'd be lucky to survive another four days of this.

He tidied the already tidy tools laid out on the workbench. They were shining and new. Untouched. His fingers ran over each one now, savoring the cold metal of the working edges, the warm rubber coating the handles. Outside, that cockerel crowed again.

This was not going to work. He could see that now. He was setting himself up to fail. Worse, he was opening himself to heartache and devastation. And there wasn't a darned thing he could do about it.

Every morning since they'd started, he had picked her up from her home, whether she was coming here with him or not. He had found himself looking forward to seeing her as she rushed out, tripped her way down the path, and almost jumped into his car, her smile wide and welcoming. He was sorry on the days when he left her at the tea shop, for then he knew he would count the hours until he could pick her up again. On those days, he threw himself into his work enthusiastically, more to stop himself counting the minutes than to prepare his company.

Then, when he took her home each evening, he stayed watching until she went inside and closed the door, giving him a little finger wave as she did so. Reluctantly, he drove away, imagining her taking off her coat and shoes, flopping into a chair and sipping at a drink until it was time to change for dinner. He thought of her shedding the clothes she had worked in all day, standing naked in her bathroom, watching the water splash into the bath, foaming into big, white bubbles that smelled of jasmine, lavender, and rose. She would step into it, those long, long legs, that perfect round bottom, the small curve from her hips to her narrow waist. He wondered if the hair in her most private of places matched the hair on her head. Were her nipples lightly pink, or were they darker? The color of her delectable freckles, perhaps? Did those freckles cover her body, or were they confined to her face?

When he slept, he dreamed of her. Awake, he thought of her. He heard her laughter on the playful breeze. Her out-of-tune singing as she painted seemed to echo in all the sounds that surrounded him.

It was not supposed to be like this. He was just supposed to spend time with her. Court her. Not fall in love with her. That was the last thing he should do. To himself. But, more importantly, to her. Reggie Chilvers deserved the best. And the best did not walk with sticks and haul his aching carcass gratefully into a chair at the end of each day.

Harry gave a heavy sigh and looked around the workshop. Like him, it was all set up with nothing to do. Yet. That would change, of course, once he had machinery in here. Then this space would have a better, more vibrant atmosphere. And Harry would be in a better, sounder frame of mind.

That was the solution, then. Keep busy. As busy as he could manage to be, in ways that kept him too occupied to think of her.

He looked around, as if the answer would jump out of the walls and announce itself to him.

Which, in a way, it did.

"I need to find a van," he decided. "Find a van, get it up and running, get the first deliveries underway."

If he did that, he could start to make money. His company would begin to be viable. And, in the process, he could exhaust himself to the point where he no longer thought of the delectable woman who took up far too much space in his life.

"Tomorrow," he promised himself. "Tomorrow, I look for a van."

****

Reggie stood in the center of the barn and watched Harry rush away. The urge to scream almost overwhelmed her as anger, frustration, and disbelief formed one big unholy mess within her. Her heart beat too fast and her breath was too shallow, as if it had stuck in her throat and couldn't move one way or the other.

Harry Pearson had kissed her.

It wasn't something she'd expected. Nor was it something she would have admitted to wanting. Far from it. Reggie had decided long ago that such trivialities were not for her. She would be too busy building a career and blazing a trail for other women to follow. Never would she crave kisses and caresses from a gentleman. Any gentleman. And yet, when it had happened, she couldn't say she hadn't enjoyed it.

Her first kiss. Not that she would ever tell him that. It mattered to her that she was seen as independent and ambitious, a woman of the world. The type of woman who would have been kissed before, and who set very little store by such things. As men did.

At least, she supposed they did. From what she could discern, they changed their lady friends as often as she changed her gloves. They thought no more of the women they escorted than Reggie thought of her gloves, either, barely remembering them by the next week.

That was how Reggie must be. Blasé. Indifferent. A kiss was a kiss was a kiss. If asked about the one she'd shared with Harry, she would say she didn't remember it.

She would be a liar.

Because his kiss had been memorable. Wonderful. More than wonderful. If that was what the fuss was all about, she could see why young women had chaperones and were never left alone with a gentleman. If that was what could happen, the duennas had their work cut out, and then some.

She had said she didn't want a man in her life. She didn't want kisses. But that was before. Before she'd been kissed. Before she'd known what it was like.

It had been delicious. Harry had tasted of coffee and chocolate, and the mint of his toothpowder. He was warm, his lips firm and sure, masculine and hard, yet light as a feather, drawing her in, making her want…

Reggie had wanted him. Wanted that kiss. She had

wanted it as much, if not more, than he did. For a moment, the world seemed brighter, clearer. More. *She* was more. Her skin had tightened around her, as if there was too much of her to be held within it. Every nerve was alive, every sense alert, aware.

His skin was warm against hers. He had shaved that morning, she knew, yet she could feel the rough rasp where new stubble already grew, even as she accepted the enticing fullness of his lips against hers. His hair was cool and soft and had flowed over her fingers like the best silk. Then she put her arms around him, around his shoulders, firm and strong, broad enough to carry the world. The thick cotton of his overalls was coarse and hard, the large buttons cold and unyielding as they pressed against her. Her breasts had grown heavy, tightening her clothes until her nipples rubbed against those buttons in a way that was at once luscious and terrifying.

That kiss changed everything. It made her question all she had ever wanted, drew her away to somewhere she hadn't even known existed before now.

And then…he had pulled away.

At first, she had clung on, clutching at him as if her life depended on him. She was all at sea, stranded, drowning, and he was all that held her up, kept her head above water. But he had clearly not wanted the same thing. He had not wanted her.

He'd pulled away so hard, so fast, that he'd stumbled. For an instant, she thought he would fall, and she braced herself to catch him, though she couldn't see what help she would be if he did go down. True, she was almost as tall as Harry, and she was strong, but not strong enough to bear his weight. Thankfully, he'd steadied himself, squaring his body and moving his center of gravity to where it should be, while his sticks pressed into the ground and gave him something to cling to.

Mortification showed plainly on his face and coated his voice in thick regret. For one terrible moment, she thought he would apologize. Apologize! For giving her the best, the most magical moment of her entire life! Her fists had clenched and her spine stretched, hard and straight as a ramrod, ready to defend herself from that, even while her heart still beat fit to burst, and every breath was hard won.

He hadn't apologized, thank God. If he had, she could never have looked him in the eye again. As it was, their next meeting was likely to be supremely awkward.

Her fault. It would be her fault. Had she not told him, in no uncertain terms, she did not want to be courted? She did not want a date. She did not want a beau.

She did not want the messy, disorienting, confusing emotions that now swirled within her.

No wonder Harry was confused. Appalled. Was it any wonder he had needed to escape her?

Reggie had always prided herself on her methodical approach to everything. She knew what she wanted from life and went after it with single-minded ferocity. She had mapped her path and dared anybody to try and change one step of her route. In doing so, she had exasperated her father, left her mother shaking her head in disbelief, and caused more than a little trouble for the sisters who followed her.

And now, she had made Harry run.

*He'll get over it.* The voice in her head sounded convincing. It was probably right. After all, it was just one—no, two kisses. A lifetime's commitment to the cause of freedom could not be blown out of the water by two kisses.

Could it?

She folded her arms tightly across her chest. What had happened here today could not happen again. It would not happen again. Reggie would make sure of it.

Although how she would do that... Decisively, she banished thoughts of the kiss and all it meant to the back of her mind. She wasn't here to think of such things. She was here to help Harry prepare for his company to begin trading.

With that in mind, she contemplated the space where he planned to put his hoist. It would be needed, if he was to make use of the upper floor, but he was unsure of his ability to build it. He could, of course, hire a firm to do it, but he would be reluctant to do that. He'd need money to pay the firm, and money was limited until the trading started. Yet, without the hoist, he couldn't trade to his fullest capacity, and couldn't make anywhere near the money he would need. A vicious circle.

He needed someone who would install it either at cost or with agreement to wait for payment. The thought had no sooner formed than she knew she had the answer. Her brother, James. He enjoyed doing this sort of thing, had wanted to learn to do it for a living, and would have done if Father hadn't bullied him into working for him. He'd probably jump at the chance to take a few days away from a job he loathed to do something he loved.

And if James was here, drawing up plans for a viable contraption, working on it, building it, well, he'd also be a buffer between Reggie and Harry, wouldn't he? There would be no more kisses. No more confusion, no more second guessing.

James would get to do what he loved. Harry would have his hoist, maybe even his lift. And Reggie would be safe in the knowledge that everything had gone back to where it should be. Where it was before *the kiss*.

She grabbed the broom and swept, a little more vigorously than was wise. Dust rose into the air, tainting it, settling on her skin, on her lips, on the taste buds on her tongue. She grimaced and scraped her top teeth over her tongue, trying to clear it, although she could still taste it everywhere. It masked the taste of disappointment. Disappointment in what, she couldn't say.

"Tomorrow, I will bring…" She shook her head, impatient with herself. "Not tomorrow," she whispered. Tomorrow, she was at the tea shop, working for Sally Ann. Which was a good thing. A very good thing. A day of respite. A whole twenty-four hours away from Harry and the way he made her feel. Twenty-four hours to pull herself together.

And then, the following day, she would bring James. Poor, unsuspecting James. She almost felt guilty at getting him here under false pretenses.

Well, partially false. He would be looking at the hoist, working on it. Protecting his sister was merely the icing on the cake.

But the most alarming thing of all, from Reggie's point of view, the thing that neither James, nor Harry, nor anyone else could ever know, was this. She did not need her brother to protect her from Harry.

She needed him to protect her from herself.

Chapter Seven

Two days later, Reggie came out of the house as she always did, a bright smile on her face. Today, she wore a skirt and jacket in a bold dogtooth check, with a wide apricot-colored ribbon at the neck, fashioned into a huge, loose bow. The ribbon matched the trim that edged the jacket, and the belt that sat on her hips. Her hat was an exaggerated chauffeur's cap, made in the same dogtooth fabric as her suit, with a peak on it which sheltered her face from the sun, and cocked a mischievous snook at officialdom. Behind her, moving at a more measured pace, was a young man who looked enough like her that he had to be her brother.

In contrast to his fashionably dressed sister, James Chilvers was staid. His suit was charcoal, with pinstripes in dark silver, the trousers baggy, the jacket long and loose. The matching waistcoat covered a crisp white shirt and a green tie that matched the band around his fedora. He held out his hand for Harry to shake, his smile diffident, but genuine.

"This is my brother, James," said Reggie. "Do you mind if he comes with us today? I'd like him to see where you want your lift. James is a bit of a whiz with that kind of thing."

James colored, uncomfortably. " 'Whiz' may be doing it a bit brown, Reg." His voice was soft and deep, and it made Harry think of the crooners he'd heard on radio shows. His eyes were the same gray-blue as his sister's, but his skin was darker, more tanned, as if he spent far more time outdoors than she did.

"It's not doing it brown at all, James. I know what you're capable of. You'll come up with a solution to Harry's problem in a trice. No, no, no." She held up her hand to stop his protest. "No false modesty. I won't allow it."

Harry had got out of the car and opened the front passenger door for Reggie to climb in. James sat in the back seat, immediately behind her.

"Reggie's been telling me about your workshop," said James, as they drove. "You've done a lot of work, according to her."

Harry nodded, his smile broad with pride. "I couldn't have done it without her."

"I must confess, that intrigued me." James turned to his sister. "How did you get the old man to let you do this? Even if you're not being paid, it's still 'work.' I can't see him allowing it." He curled his fingers to mime speech marks around the word "work."

Reggie laughed. "I decided it was better to ask for forgiveness than permission." James grinned and rolled his eyes, and she shrugged her shoulders, nonchalantly. "What the eye doesn't see, and all the rest."

Harry gave her a sidelong glance. Her eyes widened, far too innocently, before she brought the subject back to her brother and explained how she thought he could help Harry.

By the time they reached Ramslye, Harry had decided James was probably right. Reggie was doing it far too brown. He understood a sister's desire to sing her brother's praises and draw attention to his talents, but

Reggie's belief in James's abilities seemed too enthusiastic. It made him suspicious.

They'd almost reached the barn before he figured it out. She was using James as a chaperone! Harry was more than a little insulted that she thought she needed such a thing. Did she think he couldn't be trusted? Did she believe him the sort of man who would take advantage of her, even in a dusty, dirty, and primitive barn?

But then, he had thoroughly kissed her in that very place just two days ago. Perhaps she had a point. Perhaps she did need to bring her brother.

Harry had hardly thought of anything else but that kiss. He'd relived it in his dreams, replayed it when he should be listening to his family at the dinner table, conjured it instead of reading his book. He wanted, more than anything, to take her in his arms and do it again, but he knew he could not. He'd made a move far too soon, and frightened her. Why else would she feel she needed a chaperone?

Although, there was no denying there'd been two of them in that kiss. Her response, unpracticed and inexpert as it was, had been eager, too.

Which was neither here nor there. He needed to do better. He wanted her to trust him again. He wanted her to feel safe in his company. Without her brother.

James turned out to be a lousy chaperone. Once in the barn, he forgot all about Harry and Reggie after he had asked them the questions he needed answers for. Once he knew what Harry wanted, he tapped the barn's wooden walls, then checked the strength of the floor and the upper level. He clambered up into the roof space of the barn and swung on the rafters like a monkey on a tree before dropping to his feet to brush cobwebs from his jacket and clap them from his gloves.

"Do you want a hoist here," he asked, "or a lift?" He then launched into a long explanation on the pros and cons of both, before saying Harry should "leave it with me." He pulled a notebook from his breast pocket and scribbled for all he was worth.

Harry looked at Reggie, who grinned. "We can leave him to get on with it," she murmured. "What are we doing today?" She held her work clothes in her hand, although where she thought to change into them today was anyone's guess. Her brother was in the space she normally used.

Harry swallowed, the thought of her changing in a more visible space making his mouth dry and his breath short. It took him a moment to get himself under control enough to speak. "I need to look at vans," he said. To his ears, his voice sounded strained, as if someone had tried to choke him.

"Good idea." She stuffed the work clothes back into the bag. He pushed away his disappointment.

It was on the tip of his tongue to say he should go without her. If she'd felt the need to bring her brother as a buffer between them, it was hardly sensible to leave James here and go off alone together, was it? But then, it wasn't as if driving to various vehicle retailers was likely to get them into too much trouble. It wasn't the same as being here, in this barn, with nobody else around, no one to rein them in. Out on the roads, in the towns, in vehicle showrooms, they would be in public, surrounded by people. What could be safer?

Still, he had to ask, to make sure. She had brought James to protect her from Harry, after all.

"What about your brother?" He spared a glance at James, who was now pacing the space and murmuring to himself as he wrote down his findings.

"Oh, don't mind him," she said, dismissively. "You won't hear a peep out of him now, until either he's finished or we make him stop. Leave him to play." She threaded her hand into the crook of Harry's elbow. "We're squandering daylight," she pointed out, and hurried him to the car.

Over the next few hours, they drove all over Tunbridge Wells and Tonbridge, and even as far as Sevenoaks, looking at vans. Some were brand new, their paintwork gleaming, tires very black, and the leather upholstery filling the air with its woodsy, smoky scent. Others were slightly used, tires scuffed and the seats less rigid, molded to the shape of previous drivers. Some vehicles had wooden benches for drivers and passengers to sit upon.

They quickly discounted vehicles with longer, heavier crankshaft handles. Harry would, mostly, be working alone, and he didn't want a van that would take more time and effort to get going after each delivery than he felt he could spare. Other vehicles were cast aside because of the height of the cab, which would be difficult for him to climb into. Some vans were too small; they would carry next to nothing, forcing him to make several journeys instead of just one, defeating the object of having a local, efficient service.

A few of the vehicles were not really vans at all but small trucks, their flatbeds open to the elements. These would not be fit for his purpose unless Harry tied a tarpaulin cover over the goods. Not only was that time consuming, he didn't think he could manage it alone.

In Sevenoaks, they found a Thornycroft. It was the right size for the goods he hoped to haul, and it was easy for him to scramble in and out of. The driver's seat was comfortably placed, the pedals and gear stick within easy reach. It had a closed body, and sturdy springs.

"It's perfect in every way but one," said Reggie. She walked slowly around it, studying it from every angle, two vertical lines between her eyebrows showing him she was carefully pondering the question. His fingers itched to smooth those lines away.

"That subsidy," she continued. "I don't like it."

Neither did Harry. The van came with a £120 subsidy which, for some, meant the difference between owning a new van and not. It was an amount the government gave toward the purchase price, making the van significantly cheaper. However, there was, as there always would be, a catch. In order to get the subsidy, one must sign a legally binding agreement. In a time of national emergency, such as the outbreak of another war, the government would call up the subsidized vans. They would then pay the van owner a sell-on price, agreed at the time of purchase.

"If they took my van," he agreed with Reggie, "I would be out of business."

"How likely is another war?" she asked.

"How likely was the last one?"

"*Touché.*"

"The price they guarantee looks generous now," he continued, curling his top lip. "But a couple of years from now, it may not be."

"What they give you would need to cover the cost of a replacement van."

He nodded. "Which it won't do. Not when every

Jack and his Jill is shopping for the same thing at the same time."

It was a simple story of supply and demand. The government calling in all the subsidy vehicles would cause a spike in demand for replacements. Brand new vehicles would, of course, stay the same price as before, but few could afford them at a moment's notice. The difference between what the government gave for the van and the cost of a replacement would be far too much for most business owners. They'd all have no choice but to chase secondhand bargains. Bargains whose prices would rise significantly as demand suddenly outstripped supply.

"We'll keep it in mind as a last resort," he decided, and they walked away.

They nearly overlooked the Leyland van in Tonbridge. Like the Thornycroft, it was listed as a subsidy van. Because of that, Harry turned to walk away, but the salesman was not going to give up so easily.

"It isn't actually a subsidy van," he said. "Not like some of our competitors. You won't have to hand it over to the government on their say so. In fact, there isn't actually a subsidy on it at all."

Harry and Reggie exchanged skeptical looks. "Then why is it called a subsidy?" she asked.

"That is a good question, madam. The answer is simple. There used to be a subsidy."

"But now there isn't?"

He shook his head. "The moniker's historic. I wish they would change it, myself. You and your husband are not the first to think like that."

"Oh, we're not married," said Harry.

At the same moment Reggie said, "He's not my

husband."

"I do beg your pardon." The salesman grinned, making it clear he didn't believe them, and even if it was the truth, it wouldn't be too long before they were married.

Reggie threw the man a pained look. Harry cleared his throat and studied the showroom, comparing the gleaming, burgundy-red van they were being shown, to the navy-and-cream one in the far corner. His gaze rolled past the desks where other salesmen sat, ready to jump up and grab new customers and the generous commission if purchases were made. There were pictures on the walls, framed prints of advertising posters one might normally see on bus shelters. The place was a strange mix of elegant opulence and practical necessity. One would not come here if one were on or below the national average income. It reeked of success, ambition, and aspiration.

"She's steady and reliable," the salesman continued, determined to make the sale. "Four ton carrying weight. That's a guideline, not a set weight limit. In case you were wondering."

He led Harry around the vehicle, highlighting its benefits, extolling its virtues. Reggie moved to a chair between two sales desks and picked up the newspaper folded on the low table beside it. Harry mouthed an apology at her. She smiled, mouthed, "It's okay," and read the first article.

An hour and a test drive later, Harry had bought a van. He signed the papers, then took Reggie's hand and led her out of the hushed atmosphere of the showroom to the street where he had parked his Austin. Traffic drove past, tires swishing, engines chugging, the occasional graunching of gears betraying novice drivers. The air tasted of dust, oil, and damp.

"That's that, then," he said, opening her door for her and seeing her inside the car before starting the engine and climbing into the driver's seat. "The company is mobile."

"We should have a drink or something, to celebrate," she replied, her grin wide. "I have the feeling it is going to do very well."

"I certainly hope so," he replied, thinking for a moment of how much he had sunk into this venture. If it didn't work, he would be in dire straits. Not ruined, although if he were anybody else, that might have been a concern. It would be hard to claim ruination when one was the son of Walter Pearson, one of the twelve wealthiest men in Sussex. Walter might allow Harry's business to be closed down, he might leave his son feeling and looking a failure, but he would never allow him to live hand to mouth, and family honor would force him to pay his son's creditors, even as he complained about doing so.

Harry would work his fingers to the bone to avoid such an outcome. He did not think he could stand his father's never-ending carping if he failed. It was bad enough Walter still made mention, almost daily, of Harry's recklessness in joining up, and the results of that action. Eight years after the war had ended, and Walter still mentioned it at every chance.

"I know so," said Reggie. It took Harry a moment. She was talking about the company being a success. "This is exactly the right time to get into the transportation business," she continued. "The sky is the limit."

Harry chuckled. Her enthusiasm was pleasing, if a little premature. "Let's stick to one van at a time for now, shall we?" he cautioned.

She laughed. "I'm not advocating overstretching yourself. I'm stating a fact. The sky is, literally, the limit. I was reading about it in the paper in that showroom. It seems one can now fly directly from London to South Africa in one trip, using one aeroplane."

"All the way?" Harry's eyes widened. That had to be about twelve thousand miles.

Reggie pulled a face at him. "Don't be silly," she said. "They drop you off in Egypt and you have to walk the rest of the way." She rolled her eyes. "Of course all the way, you ninny. If it didn't go all the way to Cape Town, I would have said you can fly from here to Cairo, or Algiers, or wherever the flight's final destination was, wouldn't I?"

"I meant, does the plane do the whole journey in one fell swoop?" That was a heck of a journey. For a plane to make a nonstop trip halfway around the world, carrying the weight of passengers and cargo, the fuel needs would be horrendous.

Reggie frowned. "I don't think so." She thought for a moment. "It made refueling stops, of course. And it must have stopped at night to rest the crew and passengers. They wouldn't have just stayed in the sky all the time, would they?"

"It depends. How long did the epic journey take?"

"It set out last November, apparently."

"London to Cape Town in five months?" He nodded. "I'm impressed. I admit it."

"It's bound to get quicker. These things always do. It's not that long since it was quicker to walk than to drive a car, and now look." She sighed. "To fly all that way! How glamorous it sounds. The trip of a lifetime. Although you'd have to have a really good reason to go, wouldn't you? A trip so long, and presumably, so expensive."

"Perhaps it could be our honeymoon trip."

The moment the flippant words left his mouth, Harry knew it was the wrong thing to say. The smile fell from Reggie's face, happiness draining with the color in her cheeks. She stared at him for a long moment, then turned away and concentrated on the passing scenery, her arms folded tight across her chest and her ankles pulled back beneath her seat, her knees forced together in a way Harry could not imagine was comfortable.

He needed to move the conversation on. But how? If he apologized, it would give the comment more importance than it deserved, and reinforce the sudden barrier between them. If he tried to dismiss it, saying he'd spoken in jest, it might make things worse, making her feel awkward that she had taken his words so seriously.

And besides, he was not entirely sure he had spoken in jest. The way the thought had slid into his consciousness made him wonder if the idea hadn't been at the back of his mind all along. Ideas that came so quickly and seamlessly were rarely teasing remarks that shouldn't be taken seriously.

But he couldn't say *that* to Reggie, could he?

"We should get back to Ramslye," she said, her voice stiff and strained by the rigidity of her body. "Poor James will think we have forgotten him."

From what Harry had seen of 'poor James' and his enthusiasm for his work, he didn't think her brother would have given them a second thought since they'd left, unless he had wanted to show someone a breakthrough he'd had in designing the lift. Even then, Harry suspected James wouldn't have cared who that 'someone' was. If the farmer's wife had shown her face at the wrong moment, she would have done equally as well, for James struck him as a man single-minded in his approach to machinery and all but indifferent to his fellow human beings when automation was nearby.

Not that Harry would ever point that out to Reggie. James was, after all, her brother. So all he said to her now was, "Right."

"Right," she repeated. There was a finality about the word that Harry didn't like.

Without saying anything more, they U-turned at the next junction and headed back the way they had come.

## Chapter Eight

Over the next week, Harry saw nothing of Reggie. The morning after his honeymoon *faux pas*, she had sent a note telling him not to pick her up, citing family reasons. The following day she begged off a lift to the tea shop, saying Sally Ann had asked her to come in early and would pick her up. The tea shop was busy, she had said in the second missive, and that meant she would need to go in every day for the foreseeable future. She would, she said, let Harry know when she was free to help him again.

He phoned the Chilvers' house several times but was unable to speak to her. They said she had gone out with her friends, or she was busy with her sisters, or some other, even flimsier, excuse.

Harry had no choice but to accept the fact that she was avoiding him. He didn't like it, but there seemed little he could do about it, except mutter under his breath as he continued to ready his van, his warehouse, and himself for the Grand Opening of his company. Although it was what he had always planned to do, he found working alone incredibly lonely, and he caught himself yet again banging his tools louder than was strictly necessary, just to fill the silence. He longed to hear Reggie's pithy observations about what he was doing, her melodic laugh when something unexpected happened. He wanted to see her wander through the warehouse, the baggy ankles of her too-big overalls threatening to catch her feet and tumble her to the floor but never quite managing to do so. In his thoughts, she always had a smudge of dust on her cheek, and a twinkle of mischief in her eye.

He banished the image of her and bashed at the workbench as hard as he could with his hammer. The work he did wasn't even necessary now. It was just busy work, work for the sake of it, designed to stop him thinking of her.

It didn't.

Over the last few days, he had driven into Tunbridge Wells as well as to some of the other towns and villages nearby, handing out the cards and flyers he had had printed, advertising his services. He'd had several inquiries, and three firm offers of contracts, which was a better beginning than he had hoped for. Thrilled, buoyed with confidence for the future, Harry wanted to share that news with her, for she would be almost as happy as he was about it. At least he thought she would be. The Reggie who had helped him find and ready everything most certainly would be. She would be ecstatic. But the Reggie who didn't take his calls? He couldn't say.

The thought that she might not even care started a dull ache in the middle of his chest. He rubbed at it, massaging the area around his breastbone, trying to make the pain go away, but it didn't. Instead, it seemed to spread, radiating outwards, filling him with its misery, until it was almost more than he could bear. He firmed his jaw defiantly and did his best to ignore it. It just grew stronger.

It wasn't the only agony he lived with at the moment. The long hours of walking along the hard, unforgiving streets to deliver his flyers to every shop and business that might be interested had almost finished him. He had walked farther on each day of this week than he had walked in the last six months combined, and his body objected strongly. His legs and back were sore, his hips and knees stung, and his ankles felt as if they had been set on fire. Even a long soak in a warm bath didn't fully take away the pain, and his evenings were spent lying on his bed, a pillow under his knees to take the pressure from his lower back. If Reggie had been with him when he delivered the flyers, he thought bitterly, she would have delivered half the leaflets. More than half, probably. Then it might not hurt so much afterward. Not only that, but her cheer and happiness would have made the work lighter in many other ways, and would probably have garnered more customers, to boot.

And really, what was it all for? Here he was, working himself to the bone to get things up and running, but with the best will in the world, he knew he could not make enough, quickly enough, to repay the loan in full by Reggie's birthday, which was now just three weeks away.

Yet, it seemed, that was exactly what he was going to have to do.

He hammered the workbench again. One little remark. A careless, throwaway sentence, and his dream had become a nightmare, his life drained of all color and joy and promise. And it wasn't just because her father was about to demand his money back, either. It was because of Reggie herself, and the way he missed her.

That truth hit him, as heavily as the hammer had hit the workbench. He missed her. That had nothing to do with the deal he had made with her father, and everything to do with Reggie herself. William Chilvers could go to the devil, for all Harry cared. The deal he had concocted was Machiavellian, bordering on sadistic. It had no place in the modern world. Women were no longer commodities, chattels for men to barter with. Harry should have told the odious man that when he first offered him the deal. He was heartily ashamed that he had not done so.

His temporary lapse in judgment and integrity had cost Harry dearly, he knew. Not only was his company on the line, threatened with extinction before it could even come fully into being, but, worse, he had come to know a wonderful woman. A woman who was going to hate him once she knew what he had done.

He hammered the workbench once again. At this rate, the surface would be splintered and pitted before ever an engine part needed fixing here. Harry didn't care. It was unlikely ever to be used for business anyway. Not by him. Unless he could, in the next three weeks, figure out some way to persuade Chilvers to change his mind about calling in the loan, or find an alternative source of funding, he was ruined.

It might be possible. It might not. Either way, he had nobody to blame but himself.

Just as he had no one but himself to blame for the way things were with Reggie. That was the bigger regret. Whatever else happened, whether the company survived or not, he didn't want to be estranged from Reggie. He wanted their easy friendship back, the camaraderie they had built. He wanted to go back to what they had been before he'd been so stupid.

Honeymoon, indeed! Could he have uttered a more damning and inappropriate word? If only he could fix it, somehow…apologize to her, beg her forgiveness…

Could she forgive him? Give him a second chance?

There was only one way to find out. He threw the hammer down onto the bench and all but ripped off his overalls. Then he hobbled to his car and drove as quickly as he could to the Fieldhurst tea shop.

Chapter Nine

The tea shop was busy when Harry got there, most of the tables taken by middle-aged couples or small groups of ladies sharing tea and scones. The queue at the counter was long, made up of men and boys in cheap suits waiting to buy their lunches, and women wearing the unmistakable uniform of domestic servants, picking up orders for the households in which they worked. Elsie was one of three women behind the counter today, all of them wearing mid-calf-length black dresses covered by crisp white aprons, their hair tucked under lacy white mobcaps. They worked methodically and smoothly, clearly used to coping with this volume of customers every day.

Joining the queue would mean standing for longer than his legs would allow, so Harry sat down at an empty table and waited for the rush to pass. Most of the customers took their purchases and left the shop, so he didn't feel guilty about taking up the space. Besides, he intended to order when the traffic allowed.

He'd been there for a couple of minutes when a shadow fell across him. He looked up, hoping to see Reggie, but his spirits plummeted when he realized it was Sally Ann. She was not smiling, and she did not seem particularly welcoming.

"I'm sorry, sir," she said, in a flat monotone that said she wasn't in the least bit sorry. "The tables are reserved for customers."

"I am a customer," he answered. "I'm waiting for the queue to go down." He indicated his sticks.

Sally Ann nodded. "I can take your order, sir. What would you like to drink?" The way she spoke made him think she would happily bring him arsenic or prussic acid.

He ordered a pot of tea and a piece of cake for himself, then added, "And whatever Reggie would like." Sally Ann's eyes narrowed, suspiciously, and he continued, quickly, "I'm sure she has a break. You're not the kind of employer who wouldn't give her staff a break."

Sally Ann's voice was quiet but full of steel. "As I have told you before, sir, Miss Chilvers is not on my payroll."

"But she *is* in your office."

"I fail to see how that is any concern of yours."

Harry clenched his jaw and bit the tip of his tongue against what he wanted to say. It would serve no good purpose to be disrespectful to Reggie's friend and it might hurt his cause. So instead, he said, "I was hoping to speak with her."

"She may not wish to speak with you."

*I know.* "Surely that should be her choice." He sighed. "Please. Tell her I'm here. I don't want to upset her. I just…" He waved his hand, as if grasping for the words he needed.

"Just wanted to talk to her," Sally Ann finished his sentence for him. "I will tell her you are here, but I don't promise she'll come to you. And if you upset her…" She let her words trail off, leaving the implied threat hovering in the air.

"I don't intend to."

Sally Ann turned on her heel and disappeared into the back of the shop.

\*\*\*\*

Reggie sat in her office staring at the figures in the ledger. These were numbers she had written herself. She knew them as well as the lines on her own hands. Today, for the sixth day in a row, they might as well be Chinese symbols for all the sense they made to her.

It had been this way ever since Harry had taken her and James home a week ago, then driven off with a polite but distant goodbye. Not that Reggie could blame him for that. She'd been curt to the point of unfriendliness all the way home, and she had clearly left him in no doubt she didn't wish for his company.

Even James had noted the tension and frigidity in the car. "Did you and Harry have an argument?" he asked as they trudged up the path toward the front door.

"No." It wasn't exactly a lie. There had been no fight. "Why?"

"Seemed like you had. You didn't even come into the barn when you got back."

"I was tired."

"I wanted to show you what I'd been doing." He sounded hurt. "It was very good, considering I had no blueprints, nor could I just run out and buy all the materials I'd have liked. But I had a good rummage, and, it turned out, most of what I needed was already there. I did have to cannibalize a couple of pieces of machinery to get..." He talked enthusiastically at her, explaining every step of the process he'd employed to make whatever he'd devised.

Reggie didn't hear a word he said. His voice,

together with all his mechanical jargon, disappeared into the ether, pushed away by the volume of her own thoughts.

*Perhaps it could be our honeymoon trip.*

It had been the last thing she had expected Harry to say. Honeymoon? He *knew* how much she dreaded the idea of marriage. It wasn't just that she wanted a career, or her independence. It ran deeper than that. She had vowed she would be no one's wife, her life in his hands, every activity she took part in monitored and approved, every friendship inspected by his gimlet stare. She had seen that happen to her mother, and it was not happening to her.

Elizabeth Chilvers had, judging by the photographs Reggie had seen, been a beautiful, vivacious young woman. Even in the stiffly posed photographs of the late Victorian age, Elizabeth had been full of joy and spirit that the formal settings and long exposure times of those days were unable to quench. Anybody else in the photographs seemed stern and wooden in contrast to her. Nobody more so than the dour and serious man she had married.

By the time the photographs included James, then Reggie, a complete change had occurred. Elizabeth the mother was flat and lifeless, her face solemn, back stiff, all trace of a warm human being gone. The woman Reggie knew now was even more stilted than her photographs, with nothing left of the joyous girl at all. These days, Mother sat languidly on her sofa, knitting baby bootees for the local children's home, or she served tea and made polite conversation with her husband's colleagues whenever he deigned to bring them home. She admonished her own children for showing any sign of exuberance, and voiced such gems as, "Young ladies do not run down corridors, dear. They glide." And, "Do refrain from humming to yourself over there, darling. It is so common."

In 1916, when conscription depleted the civilian workforce and women did their patriotic duty by taking up the jobs, Elizabeth Chilvers had played her part, with her husband's permission, leaving the house daily to take her place in the great machine that was Britain at war. For a time, she'd flourished. Her eyes had sparkled and her back had straightened, and her confidence had been restored. She had laughed then. More than Reggie had ever heard her laugh before.

Six months later, William said he needed her to be at home. She had left her job and, within weeks, the lively woman had been put away in a cupboard somewhere, and the dutiful, quiet, and somehow sad Mrs. Chilvers had taken her place.

Reggie had learned two things from that. Firstly, working outside the home, doing something independent, had been very good for Mother. It made her someone in her own right, not simply an accessory for Father to put on and off whenever he wished. She'd had her own money, and spent it as she wished, made her own friends, and chosen her topics of conversation. Reggie had desperately wanted Mother to keep those things and had been upset to see that Elizabeth Chilvers fade into memory.

Which led to the second lesson: a married woman obeyed her husband. Even if it made her unhappy and robbed her of things that gave her satisfaction.

Reggie would never forget that lesson. She would not repeat her mother's mistakes. So she would not marry. She would work, and have her own money. Nobody would control her.

In many ways, the freer, more easygoing society that had developed after the war had helped her in her resolve. Many women now worked and had their own income, although, to be fair, there were so many women and so few men that being single and independent was not necessarily a path chosen by all who followed it.

But still, there were so many things a woman could do, these days. Some went to university. Others trained for professional careers that would have been unthinkable just ten years ago. Some women had the vote, although, if Mother's experience was anything to go by, many of them consulted their husbands and, presumably, voted as he said they should. On the whole, though, women had much greater freedoms now, and Reggie was damned if she would sit back and meekly let her opportunity pass by.

When she learned the new Property Act would allow a grown woman to hold property in her own right, without needing permission from her father, or anybody else, and that it would come into force the year she reached her majority, Reggie took it as a sign. Freedom would be hers. She had planned for it and prepared for it, and she was not going to give it up just because a handsome man with an easy charm mentioned honeymoons.

"What do you say to that?" James' words had cut through Reggie's thoughts like a hot knife through butter, and she realized they had reached the front door of their home, which he now held open for her. He had clearly told her something which required a reaction, but she had no way of knowing what he had said, or what reaction was called for.

"Have you heard a word I've said?" James frowned at her, though if he meant it to be intimidating, he needed to work on it. Then he'd shrugged, his good nature overriding his irritation. "Never mind. You'll see it when you go to the workshop tomorrow."

She pulled a face. "I'm not going there tomorrow."

"Oh, right." He grinned, conspiratorially. "Tomorrow, you'll be…" He looked over his shoulders, furtively, and Reggie rolled her eyes at the theatrics. "…with your 'friends.' " He gave her an exaggerated wink. "In that case, you will see it the next day."

"Actually, I won't," she said. "I have…no plans to go there again."

James stared at her, his face inscrutable. It was impossible to know what he was thinking, or how he'd interpreted her words, until finally he said, "You've had a row, then? I thought you had, when you didn't come into the workshop." He gave her a squeezing hug. "Don't worry, old girl. Lips sealed and all that. Shan't tell anyone any of the details."

Reggie refrained from pointing out he didn't *know* any of the details.

"Are you at home to him?" She shook her head. "Right you are."

Then, clearly deciding enough had been said, he strode away toward the billiards room, where, presumably, he would knock seven bells out of a set of billiard balls until it was time to change for dinner.

It had been disappointingly easy to avoid Harry. She'd sent him a note, telling him not to pick her up, saying she was going into the tea shop early with Sally Ann. That lie had been rewarded with a trip on the overcrowded omnibus, where she was squashed between a rotund businessman who had covered his need for a bath with copious amounts of cologne, and a buxom young woman in the livery of a popular bakery, who smelled of flour and yeast. Reggie sat between them, pulling her shoulders round, trying to shrink herself, while her arms felt pinned to her sides and her thighs were bruised by the way the man's briefcase and the woman's basket collided with her on every corner, stop, and bump in the road.

She'd thought about Harry's spacious car with its comfortable seats, and the way he transported her door to door, and sighed her regrets. If only... *If onlys,* she scolded herself, *are dangerous things.* She had made up her mind not to see him again, and she would not go back on that. Doing so would only leave her open to the risk of...

Risk of what? Encouraging him? Making him think there was hope of that Cape Town honeymoon in their future after all?

She swallowed, hard. It was not that at all. The risk she faced in seeing Harry again wasn't that he might misinterpret things and build false hope. The risk came in the fact that the ideas his throwaway comment had planted weren't repellent to Reggie, not in the least.

After that first day, Reggie volunteered James to take her to the tea shop. He moaned about the early start, but he did what she asked, in the same way he complained about doing her dirty work, yet still made her excuses each time Harry phoned the house.

"Thanks, James," she had said when he complained after last night's phone call. She reached up and kissed his cheek, catching him even as he tried to pull away from her. "You are a pal. You'll never see what I buy you for this."

"I don't doubt that," he'd answered, unimpressed.

And now, here she was, at her desk, ledger open, and no work done because she was too busy lollygagging. She shook her head, annoyed at herself for wasting so much time, and resolved to stay as late as she could tonight, to make sure the day's work was finished. It wasn't as if she had anything else planned, was it?

"Well," said Sally Ann, as she came to stand beside Reggie's desk, hands on her hips and a wry smile on her face.

"Well, what?" Reggie's return smile was intrigued. In one of her hands, Sally Ann held a bunch of till receipts, which looked quite crumpled beneath her dough-coated fingers. Her blonde hair was tucked under her white hat, though a strand had escaped and now curled over her cheek. Her complexion held the rosiness of working in the hot kitchen, but the sparkle in her eyes was pure amusement. Reggie laid down her fountain pen and sat back in her chair, prepared to laugh at whatever Sally Ann had just witnessed out in the shop.

"Well, you were right," Sally Ann said.

"Good to know. What was I right about?"

Sally Ann laid the receipts on the desk. "You said he'd come here."

The curious smile fled Reggie's face and she felt the blood drain. If she looked into a mirror now, she was willing to bet her cheeks would be the same shade as the dough Sally Ann had been kneading.

"Here? Now?" There was no reason to ask who they were talking about.

Sally Ann nodded. "Large as life and twice as... I

wouldn't call him ugly, personally."

Neither would Reggie, but she didn't say so. Sally Ann already looked amused enough. Besides, just because Harry was here, it didn't mean...

"Lots of people come to this shop every day," said Reggie, trying for nonchalance.

"Yes. But not all of them ask to see you."

The breath caught in Reggie's throat and there was a strange fluttering inside her, around where her heart might be. She willed it to stop. "Did he now? I may not want to see him." *Drat!* There was a distinct quaver in her voice that she did not want.

"I know that," agreed Sally. "And, more importantly, *he* knows." She shrugged her shoulders and moved toward the office door. "But he still asked to see you."

"I'm busy." Reggie bit her bottom lip and wondered what she should do now. Part of her wanted to rush out there and have tea with him, and carry on where they had left off, chatting and laughing and building his business. Then again, the other part of her...

*Perhaps it could be our honeymoon trip.*

What did he want from her? Had he been hinting that he felt more for her than the friendship they had agreed upon? Or had his comment been a joke, which she had taken more seriously than he had intended?

He hadn't said it was a joke. He'd seen her take umbrage and he hadn't argued. Which did not mean his intentions had been as she suspected. He may not have realized...

*Don't be an idiot, Reggie! You left him in no doubt how you interpreted his words. And the effect they had on you.* A blind man could have seen. Yet Harry had not taken them back, nor had he corrected her misconceptions. So what was she supposed to think?

Then again, perhaps she was refining upon it too much. Perhaps he'd been so astounded at the way she'd misconstrued his meaning he had been speechless. Or maybe he thought that correcting her would make things worse, protesting too much. Or...

Reggie couldn't say what he thought. She'd thought she knew, but she could have been wrong. She'd thought he meant that he hoped to deepen their relationship, despite whatever she had told him. But if that was what he wanted, would he really have stayed away from her for a whole week? Would he have accepted the way she'd avoided him, without demur? Surely, if he harbored deeper feelings for her, wouldn't he have made some effort to put things right between them before now?

She felt her cheeks heat at the idea that she may have been so wrong. That she may have been so full of herself that she thought... She took a deep breath and put her head down, ready to add the new receipts into the ledger.

"So, do you want me to tell him you are not coming out? " asked Sally Ann.

Reggie looked up, sharply.

"I told him I would tell you he's out there. I didn't say you would join him. I'm quite happy to go back and tell him—"

"No!" The word came out forcefully. Sally Ann's eyebrow rose. Reggie gave a half smile and an embarrassed chuckle. "I can...spare a few minutes. I need to stretch my legs anyway, so I might as well see what he wants."

Sally Ann nodded. "I'll be in the kitchen if you need me," she said, and she left the office. Reggie stood up and smoothed her dress.

****

The queue had shortened now, most of the customers having been served. The tea shop buzzed with the sound of several quiet conversations, each building on the volume of the others, to increase the level of noise in the place. The door to the shop opened and closed regularly, making a bell tinkle each time.

Minutes passed. He began to wonder if Reggie had refused to see him. If so, he didn't know what he could do to change her mind. But surely, if she'd said no, Sally Ann would come out and tell him so. His stomach roiled at the thought that she was just going to leave him here, to get the message, eventually.

Then she appeared at the door to the back of the shop, and he forgot to breathe.

She was every bit as beautiful as she had been the last time he saw her, and then some. It was as if his memory of her had been a poor copy that did her no justice, like the newsprint copy of a photograph that blurred and hazed the image which was so clear in the original.

Today, she wore a dress in lavender blue, with box pleats below a dropped waist that was emphasized by a wide, satin ribbon. A bolero jacket matched the dress, and she wore a long string of pearls around her neck.

She looked around the room, though he did not believe she had been searching for him so much as for anyone else who might know her and tell her father they had seen her here. Satisfied there was no one, her shoulders lowered and her face relaxed a little as she strode across to him, the heels of her shoes clicking in a brisk, no-nonsense fashion.

"You asked to see me?" Her voice was low, almost a whisper, and the glare she levelled at him was less than friendly.

"Take tea with me?" He smiled, hopefully.

"I am busy."

"You should have a break from your work, whether you are being paid for it or not. You know what they say. All work and no play makes Jack a dull boy."

Reggie stared at him for a moment or two longer, then nodded once. "Fine." The word was cut by the clench of her jaw. She looked over to the counter and nodded at Elsie, then sat down across the table from him, her hands clasped and resting on the tabletop.

Having got her to sit here with him, Harry was desperate to make sure she stayed. He racked his brains for something to talk to her about. Eventually, he blurted, "My van is being delivered tomorrow. I can start making pickups and deliveries after that."

*Scintillating conversation starter, Pearson.*

"That's good," she replied. "I am pleased for you."

"The salesman threw in a set of pneumatic tires."
*What are you doing? She doesn't want to know about pneumatic tires!*

She frowned. "Pneumatic? Are they better?"

"Better than solid tires? Much better. Plus, the government are changing the law, or so I've heard. It will not be legal to go as fast on solids as you'll be allowed to drive on pneumatics."

"I see."

Elsie brought over a tray laden with a pot of tea, two cups and saucers, milk and sugar, and two pieces of sponge cake. Harry pulled out his wallet and paid the waitress, including a decent tip. She grinned at him, appreciatively, and dipped a curtsey before she went back to the counter.

"Is it wise?" asked Reggie, then she clarified, "Being able to go faster? This is, as I recall, the van where the weight limit was a guideline? Will it be safe at speed, should you happen to have it overloaded?"

Harry grinned. "I won't overload it." Reggie looked skeptically at him. "Oh, ye of little faith," he continued. "I will be fine. I'll use my common sense."

Reggie raised her eyebrows and stared at him as if to ask, *What common sense?* Then she looked away to pour the tea.

"I missed you," said Harry.

She did not respond.

"It's not the same without you. In the workshop and whatnot, I mean. Getting everything ready. It's not the same."

Reggie poured a splash of milk into both cups, then handed him his. He picked up the sugar tongs and added a couple of lumps of sugar into his cup.

"Your brother made a really good job of putting in the lift. You should see it, Reggie. It takes all the heavy work out of getting things up to the top level. Even I can do the job now. By myself, if I have to."

She stirred her tea. "I am busy, *Mr. Pearson.*" There was a slight emphasis on the formality of his name.

"Harry," he corrected her, anyway.

"I have work to do."

"Listen, what I said the other day…that nonsense about honeymoons…" She bristled and he winced. "I didn't mean to upset you."

"You didn't." The cut-glass edges of her words highlighted their untruth.

"It was…a flippant comment. A joke. I was trying to say Cape Town is a long way to go, and you would need a lot of time to…" He sighed in defeat. "I suppose I laid an egg."

Reggie stirred her tea once again, though it didn't need doing. Then she brought the cup up to her face, her right hand holding the handle, the fingertips of her left pressed against the cup's far side as if to balance it. She blew daintily, making the brown liquid ripple. "I am not getting married," she said. Her voice was soft, quiet, but determined.

"I know." He looked down at his own cup, more to avoid her gaze than to see his drink. In that moment, he was terrified of what she would see in him, the secrets she would discern.

The silence between them stretched. Ten seconds. Fifteen. Not long in the grand scheme of things. Hardly enough to blink twice. Just enough to take in three breaths. To Harry, it seemed an eternity. Finally, when he could stand no more, he looked up and met her steady gaze, taking in everything about her.

Today, her eyes were the silver gray of pewter, cold and unrelenting, yet their effect on Harry was the same as sitting by the hearth when the fire roared. His cheeks felt warm in her glow. His throat was dry and scratchy, and he reached, with a shaky hand, to pick up his cup. He was amazed it reached his lips without a major spillage.

Electricity arced from her to him. It quickened his pulse and filled him with a tingling buzz from his hair down through his body, his arms and fingers, his stomach, his thighs, even his useless numb toes. He tensed and prayed he didn't look like the fool he felt himself to be.

The temperature in the room rose. Perspiration beaded on his brow and at the nape of his neck, soaking the tips of his hair. The backs of his eyes burned. There was a lump in his throat. It tasted like regret.

She turned her head away, swiftly, looking as uncomfortable as he was. "I really do have work to do."

He swallowed and studied his tea again. "I'll…leave you to it, then. I just—I just wanted to clear up that misunderstanding."

Reggie nodded and sipped her tea.

"And…" Harry wondered if he was about to make the biggest blunder of his life, or his best-ever decision. There was only one way to find out. "And I would like to take you out to dinner."

Her eyes narrowed.

"Nothing fancy, not a date," he said, quickly. So quickly, the words seemed to join up into one long word. He cleared his throat and tried again. "Not a date." He was relieved that he now sounded normal. "Just two friends out together, sharing a meal and having a good time."

She shook her head. "I don't know…"

"I mean, I would have said let's go dancing, but my skills are a little, er, rusty in that department." He grinned. "I've got two left feet. Or, at least, I might as well have, these days."

He was rewarded by one of her low chuckles. "What am I going to do with you, Harry Pearson?"

"I really don't know," he said, rejoicing inside because she had called him Harry. "Although I suspect keeping me off street corners and out of pokey may require your presence at dinner."

"Dinner." She glared a warning at him. "But not a date."

"Not in the least." Mentally, he crossed his fingers.

Reggie sighed, drank more of her tea, and dabbed at her lips with her napkin. The movement was so delicate and fussy, so unlike the Reggie he had come to know. Yet, at the same time, somehow it suited her completely.

"All right," she told him, finally. "Pick me up at seven."

When she had returned to her office, he hobbled toward the exit and, although his knees were creaking and complaining with every step, he felt lighter and more flexible than he had been for years. In his heart, he danced.

## Chapter Ten

Harry maneuvered himself out of his bathtub, using the specially designed hoist his father had paid a fortune to install for him, then sat wrapped in a towel in the tubular steel chair by the custom-made low sink with the vanity mirror above it. Here, he brushed his teeth and shaved his cheeks and jaw, ridding himself of the day's stubble before rubbing brilliantine onto his palms and dragging them through his damp hair, softening it while making it glossy. His aftershave stung slightly, but it also refreshed him as the menthol in it released against his skin.

He had booked a table at a hotel in Lewes. His brother had been there and given it a glowing review, and Harry looked forward to trying it out for himself. He looked forward to entering the place with Reggie, already felt his chest swell with pride at the thought of her on his arm, and the envious glances he would get from other men, just because she was his and not theirs.

That thought made him stutter to a halt and he almost dropped the bottle of aftershave into the heavy porcelain sink. He caught it before either bottle or sink could be damaged, though some of the lotion spilled, scenting the room with its strong, fresh scent. Carefully, he replaced the stopper and rested it on the shelf, then stood to dry himself properly.

"You can get those thoughts out of your head right

now, Harry, my boy," he muttered to himself as he dragged the towel back and forth across his back. "She is not yours any more than she is theirs. She is hers, and hers alone. You forget that at your own peril."

That was true. If Reggie Chilvers had the smallest inkling he had ever thought of her as "his," she would have a conniption. He suspected she had a temper to reckon with and, if she knew his thoughts, he would see it, up close and in its full glory. It was safer if he remembered that, even in his private thoughts. It was bad enough that he'd made that stupid deal with her father. He didn't need to make things worse by parading her like the prize filly in the owner's enclosure at Ascot.

"For God's sake!" he hissed, rubbing the towel over his skin so harshly it hurt. "What were you thinking?"

It wasn't the first time he'd asked himself that question since he'd shaken William Chilvers' hand. It most likely, almost certainly, wouldn't be the last. The answer was easy: he hadn't been thinking at all. Or, if he had been, his thoughts had been selfish, concerned only with what he wanted and never once wondering how a woman, any woman, might feel about two men striking a deal over her entire future, as if she was a chattel to be owned and bartered by them. The days when women were the property of their menfolk were long gone, as Reggie would, no doubt, remind him, even as she slapped his face and marched away, flinging over her shoulder words to make a sailor blush, as she cast aspersions on Harry's person and his character.

Yet what could he do about it now? He pulled on his trousers and tucked in the long tails of his shirt before ringing the bell. He had worked hard to recover as much as he could, but there were still some things he would never do for himself again, one of them being putting on his own socks and shoes, and tying his own laces.

"What am I to do about it all now?" he whispered.

"Beg pardon, sir?" asked Jefferson, his father's valet, who had, uncomplainingly, taken on the extra duties of being Mr. Harry's man whenever he was needed. Harry's father had decreed that, since Harry never went anywhere worthwhile, and didn't have to look either promotable for a job nor marriageable for a decent woman, he didn't need a man of his own. Since Harry had done everything for himself in the army and hadn't been the worse for it, and since he'd always thought there was something less than ideal about a grown man being dressed by somebody else like a child in the nursery, he had not argued.

"I'm sorry, Jeff," he said, calling the valet by the nickname he and his brothers had called him when they were still in short trousers. "I was thinking aloud."

"Perhaps it is something I could help you with, sir?" Jeff looked very eager to go and fix whatever problem Mr. Harry was having. But Harry was not about to scandalize the man with the tale of what he had done, and how low he had sunk. He cared too much for the valet's good opinion of him to confess that.

"Would that you could, Jeff," he said, with a rueful smile. "But unless you can find a way of me being able to put on my boots unaided," he lied, "there is nothing to be done. By you or anyone else." Briefly, he crossed his fingers, then reached for his cufflinks while Jeff laced his shoes.

"Ah. I see, sir."

"Not that I don't think you do sterling work," Harry added, quickly.

"Of course not, sir. But I do understand. It must be galling. To be a man so young and so active as yourself, sir, and be unable to do all the things you wish to do."

"Yes." The backs of Harry's eyes burned, and there was a bitter taste on his tongue.

"You mustn't feel badly about it, though. I mean, it's only your footwear that you need me for."

"Yes." Harry grimaced. Jeff was right. It might have been much, much worse.

"And who's to say, given time, that won't change, sir?"

*For the worse, or the better?* "Yes," said Harry. "There is that."

Jeff knew as well as Harry did that his legs and hips had healed as well as they ever would. After eight years, hoping for any more improvement was wishful thinking. Although, perhaps now, with the benefit of modern medicine, with all the improvements that had come because doctors had had to treat war injuries far worse than his...

But no. There were improvements in treatment, but even now, they would only make a difference if the injured men reached the hospital quickly enough to access them. If a man was knocked down by a motor car in the middle of the High Street, and could get to help within thirty minutes, perhaps. But if he lay in a blown-up trench for hour after hour, trapped from the waist down beneath sucking mud and fractured timber, dead horses, and God knew what else, waiting and praying for a rescue that might not come, while all around him the air was filled with the moans of the dying and the pounding of the guns, and the bombs... Nobody fully recovered from that. It was good enough to have survived.

Harry straightened his tie and shrugged into his evening jacket, grabbed his sticks, and made his way out of the house, to pick up the other sacrificial lamb.

He snarled, angry at himself, then began trying to justify his actions, although, he knew, there was no justification. The truth was simple, if unpalatable. He had wanted his own dream so much he had put it before all decency. He had decided it mattered more than a young woman's future, and now there was no getting out of it. He had spent the money Chilvers had loaned him, and he couldn't afford to replace it. No one else would lend it to him. If they had been willing to do that, he would never have gone to Chilvers in the first place. It would be months—years, even—before his company made enough profit to keep him, let alone pay off lump sums on demand.

Faced with the thought of his son going bankrupt and bringing shame upon the family, his father would probably pay off Chilvers for him, but that wouldn't help Harry. Not really. Walter wouldn't pay for everything and then just hand it back to Harry and let him pick up where he had left off. No, Walter would either run the enterprise for himself, taking it into his empire, or, more likely, he would sell everything and try to minimize the losses. Then he would use the whole sorry incident to point out, yet again, what a useless waste of flesh and bone Harry was.

"It's not just your legs that don't work anymore, is it, lad?" he would sneer. "I think you hit your head, too." Then he would purse his lips in disappointment, write the check, and throw Harry back onto the garbage heap.

That was not happening. Harry stiffened his

shoulders and straightened his spine, defiantly. He would succeed. Somehow. He would succeed, and he would not bury Reggie's dreams as he did it. He would... He didn't know what he would do right now, but there was no cause for panic. He still had three weeks to figure it out.

The lady who came down the stairs in the Chilvers home sent all thoughts of business loans and dodgy deals skittering from Harry's head. He watched her descend and he forgot to breathe, until his heartbeat pattered hard against his ribs to remind him. He thought his jaw sagged. He knew his eyes were big and round, because they hurt from staring at her, while other parts of him stood up strong, reminding him that, whatever the state of his legs, there were ways in which his body worked perfectly.

She wore a calf-length black silk dress with a cream lace insert at the neckline, which took the outfit from scandalous to modest but didn't make it any less seductive. A matching width of lace hugged the hem of the skirt, while a long, loose, cream lace scarf looped down her back covering the length of her spine, then was draped over her shoulders and fastened between her breasts by a silver brooch studded with rhinestones and pearls. A pearl choker emphasized the length of her slender neck, and she wore a pair of shiny, black, almond-toed shoes with Louis heels. Her hair was hidden under a black cloche hat, and when she reached the bottom of the stairs, she handed Harry a black-and-cream coat. He helped her into it, admiring the shape of it: wide and roomy across the shoulders, it tapered to a narrow hem which made her seem taller and more slender than she already was.

He swallowed, but still his voice sounded gruff to

him. "You look beautiful."

Reggie gave him a skeptical look.

"No. Really," he insisted. "You do."

She didn't answer. She simply allowed him to open the door, and then she glided elegantly toward his car.

At the hotel, he had booked a table in the rear corner of the dining room, away from the other patrons. They followed the maître d' across the lushly carpeted room to a mahogany table set for two. A candle sat in the center of the table, inside a ring of flowers, and its subdued light gave the corner an ambiance of romantic coziness. Harry held out Reggie's chair for her, then sat himself.

"So," she said, when the maître d' left them with their menus. "Here we are."

"Here we are," Harry repeated, for want of something better to say.

The waiter came for their drinks order. Harry ordered a whisky on the rocks, while Reggie asked for a Campari.

"How have you been?" he asked, once they were alone again.

She shrugged her shoulders. "Much the same as ever. What about you? I imagine you've been busy?"

He spent the next few minutes telling her all he'd done over the last week, and of the first orders that had come in, following his campaign with the flyers. "I can make a start on the deliveries, now that the van is arriving."

Reggie nodded. "It's coming tomorrow, isn't it?"

"It is." His grin was so wide it hurt his cheeks. He must look like a child given the run of a sweet shop, but he couldn't help it. He couldn't be blasé about something that mattered so much.

"Perhaps I could come and see it?" she asked.

Harry's heart soared. "How about a ride in it?"

Her smile lit her face, and melted the last of the ice between them.

They talked amicably, about nothing in particular, over a leisurely dinner which began with a small glass of tomato juice and Worcestershire sauce, followed by perfectly cooked roast lamb with tomatoes, cauliflower, beans, carrots, and new potatoes, before it ended with a platter of water biscuits and French cheeses. Rich, red wine flowed, just enough to make the evening relaxed and fill it with laughter.

Harry held his glass up in the candlelight and peered into the liquid as if he expected to find the knowledge of the ages in its depths. Perhaps he did. "Do you know," he said, "if we were in America and drinking this, we'd be breaking the law?"

"Hmm. So I've heard."

"Prohibition. Gives me palpitations just thinking about it," he joked, putting his free hand to his chest and shuddering, exaggeratedly.

Reggie laughed. "Careful. You'll spill it."

"God forbid." He put the glass down carefully, looked over both shoulders as if checking for eavesdroppers, then spoke in his best imitation of an American accent. "Okay, sweetheart, I don't think the Feds are watching us tonight, so what's your poison?"

"Aw, gee, Harry," she answered, in an even more atrocious accent than his had been. "I thought you'd never ask."

Harry hooted with laughter. "Who told you Americans speak like that?"

"I don't know," she said, her expression one of

mock offense. "How would I know what they sound like? I've only ever heard one American speak in my entire life." He raised an enquiring eyebrow and she explained. "He came to dinner once. I think he was contemplating investing in something with my father. Charming man, if a little garrulous. My sister, Florence, flirted shamelessly with him all evening, although poor James was somewhat overwhelmed."

Harry could imagine. All the Americans he'd ever met were confident and outgoing, with a can-do outlook that took them a long way. James Chilvers struck Harry as a diffident man who would find that hard to deal with.

"How about you?" Reggie asked, pulling his thoughts back to the here and now. "Where did you learn how Americans speak?"

"There were Americans in the military hospital when I was there."

"Oh? What were they like?"

He thought for a moment. "Vibrant. You wouldn't think so, would you? Confined to a hospital ward, and all that. But they were…full of life, and…" He waved his hand through the air in front of him, as if that could magically produce the words he was looking for. "They made one…hopeful, I suppose."

"That's a good thing, isn't it? In a time and place where everything is bleak?"

She was right. It had been a good thing. In a narrow world where everyone was in pain and dealing with injuries that changed the future for all of them, and shortened it for far too many, the optimism, and sheer bloody-mindedness of the more memorable Americans among them had been a tonic. Many patients, including Harry, had been spurred to greater healing than might otherwise have been the case, because of their American comrades' "never-holler-uncle" attitude.

He shook himself, as if to dislodge those memories, then grinned broadly at Reggie. "Very much so. More wine?"

Thankfully, she took the hint and said no more about that time.

They had been in the restaurant for three hours by the time Harry paid the bill and helped her out of her seat. He'd had his fill of good food, which had made him mellow, while the two glasses of burgundy he'd drunk were enough to relax him without impairing his senses. The waiter brought Reggie's hat and coat, and he helped her to put them on. His hands rested on her shoulders for a moment longer than was necessary, and he pondered the wisdom of what he wanted to do next. It was, he decided, risky, but then, nothing ventured…

He kept his voice light and tried to make himself sound as if it didn't matter to him which way things went, as he said, "I do believe this is the part of the evening when a gentleman would usually ask a lady if she would like to go dancing. But I'm not especially fond of cutting a rug these days, so would you rather do something else instead?"

Reggie frowned. "Such as? The kinema will be closed by now. What else would there be to do? We're too far from London, and nowhere else is going to have the all-night entertainments they've got. I'm not really the sort who likes just sitting in a bar all night."

"Neither am I." Harry smiled sadly, and gestured that she should move to the exit ahead of him. It was all well and good wanting to keep the evening going, but she was right. There was nowhere to go. They passed the other diners and nodded their thanks to the maître d', who hoped they would return soon, then stepped out onto the road.

The wide street was almost deserted, the shop fronts dark, though one or two windows in the shiplapped walls above the shops were still lit. The street lamps were well spaced and not particularly bright, so they did little to diminish the darkness, although comforting yellow squares of light shone through the windows of the hotel and painted the footpath. Farther along the road, tinny piano music escaped a pub.

It was a clear evening, not exactly cold, but chill enough that Reggie pulled her coat more tightly about her. Not wanting her to be cold and uncomfortable, he walked her briskly to his car, which he had parked against the double-stepped curb just a few yards from the hotel door. He helped her inside, where she would be a little warmer while he cranked the engine.

"It's a lovely evening," she mused, as he climbed into the driver's seat. She looked out of the window and tilted her head to see the sky. "The stars are lovely."

Harry glanced up. There were a few dim pinpricks of light against the rich blackness of the night. One or two of them stood out more brightly than the rest. "You can see them much better outside of town. On the Ashdown Forest, for instance, they look as if they go on forever."

"Truly?" She smiled at him as he pulled away from the curb. "We have to go near the Forest on the way home, don't we?"

"We can do, yes. Why? Do you want to see for yourself?"

She nodded, her face a picture of eager delight.

\*\*\*\*

Reggie looked out of the window as Harry drove them through the streets of Lewes and onto the road to Fieldhurst. The High Street was adequately lit, not only with streetlamps, but also a couple of illuminated shop windows. They crossed the bridge over the River Ouse, where the Harvey's brewery sat on the riverbank, with its distinctive square towers and the yard between them, and the water well lit to allow the night-shift workers to see. The tall, thin chimney behind the building was silhouetted against the night sky.

Within a few minutes, they left Lewes and drove up the hill through Malling and Clay Hill. As the buildings grew fewer and farther between, and the countryside disappeared under a veil of darkness, the stars became clearer. Harry's car headlamp beams pointed along the road, painting the air before them a lemon yellow.

Over the next twenty minutes, they drove through small towns and hamlets and along narrow, winding lanes. Gorse bushes and sparse clumps of trees stood, dark shadows on the darker background.

"I come up here by myself sometimes," Harry said as they drove through a hamlet and then across the heathland that made up the forest. "When it's dark, like tonight. No moon. No cloud. Just the stars."

He pulled off the road and bounced over an uneven area of stones, rutted mud and deep puddles, then stopped the car beside grass, gorse, and bramble. A few yards ahead of them was a wide mound of earth, higher than the rest of the land around it. A clump of trees grew from the mound.

"Where are we?" she asked. Her voice was hushed, respectful of the quiet night.

"King's Standing," he announced, as he turned off the headlamps and cut the car's engine, plunging them into complete darkness and silence. "So named because, they say, the king waited on that mound when he hunted deer here. You could see animals moving across the land for miles from there, and you didn't have to stalk them and possibly miss them. Apparently."

"Which king?"

Harry pulled a face, as if he tried to think about his answer. Then he shrugged. "Allegedly, Henry the Eighth, I believe, but I don't know that for sure."

Reggie raised her chin and eyed him with mock haughtiness. "You don't know for sure?"

"I wasn't there."

She sighed. "What kind of an excuse is that?"

He chuckled and she grinned. A moment passed. Then she cleared her throat, and reminded him of the reason they were there. "Stars."

Without more ado, Harry opened his door and stepped out of the car and into the night. Reggie waited as he made his way around the vehicle, opened her door, and gave her his hand. She stepped daintily onto the running board and then down onto the hard, uneven ground. Her foot slipped slightly and she stumbled. Harry caught her, preventing her fall and she clung to him. They stayed like that for a few seconds longer than was necessary, neither making any attempt to let go. She could feel the warmth of him through his shirt, his breaths, short and shallow, felt his heart beating beneath the palm of her hand. The night air carried the coconut scent of the gorse, the clean smell of the pine, the dampness of the earth. They mingled with the scent of Harry, his sharp, clean cologne, the soap he'd used, the wine and whisky on his breath, and that something she couldn't define, the something that was uniquely, wonderfully, him. He looked down at her as she looked up at him, and their eyes met. Time stood still. The world around them faded away. The crickets stopped their chirruping, the breeze stilled.

Reggie didn't know if she moved closer to him, or he moved closer to her. Maybe they both moved together, but suddenly his lips were on hers, kissing her, claiming her, making her feel… She hardly knew what she felt. His skin against hers was warm with life yet cold from the night air, soft yet with the rasp of new beard growth. Her heart did a strange flippity-flop, making her breath catch in her throat, and there was a peculiar heaviness in her lower belly that spread out, through her thighs.

Without any conscious effort from her, her arms wrapped around him, her fingers playing with the ends of his hair, cold and smooth like wind-washed silk above the coarse wool of his coat collar. She moved closer, until the front of her coat touched the front of his, and the softness of her body pressed against the hard muscle of Harry. His arms held her, making her feel warm, protected, loved.

*Loved?* The word, echoing through her, was like a splash of icy water. She didn't love Harry. She didn't love anybody. Not in that way. She was free and independent. One of the nine. This was wrong. This was…

She pulled away. He let her go, and she took a step back, her thin-soled shoe no protection from the unevenness of the rutted ground. She hardly knew what to say, what to think, or do.

Harry cleared his throat and half turned away. He said nothing. What was there for him to say? They both knew it should not have happened, could not happen again. But oh! It had felt so right!

Which was where the danger lay.

Reggie knew she should cut short this evening, demand they get back into the car and drive home. She couldn't bring herself to say it, couldn't even bring herself to want it. So she just stood there, uncertain what to do, what to feel, what to be.

The breeze was chilling. Reggie hunched her shoulders inside her coat and curled her hands into fists in her pockets, yet still, she shivered. Harry must have felt it, because he opened the car door again for a few seconds, then settled a heavy warm blanket over her shoulders. Immediately, she was warmer. He held the blanket in place, adding extra heat that flowed from his body through the layers of clothes and into hers. She felt his arms encase her once more, warm and strong and enticing. Too enticing.

She stiffened and took a step away. He let her go. She missed his touch at once. She wanted to go to him, lean into him, feel him surrounding her, taste his kiss... Instead, she stood back and tilted her head to look up, pretending fascination with the night sky.

It was so dark it seemed a pillow, close enough to touch, soft enough to sink into. Hundreds of thousands of stars were woven into it, some bright, standing alone, others in dimmer clusters, as if a whole star had shattered and only the dust remained.

"Wondrous, isn't it?" he whispered, and for a moment, she was at a loss how to answer him.

*The stars! He was talking about the stars.* Reggie

swallowed, hard. "They're so clear." Did her voice sound strained, or was that her imagination?

"The whole of the universe on display," he said, "just for us."

The breeze dropped. The air stilled. There was no sound. No movement. Nothing but Harry and herself, alone in this universe, made just for them. Her heart sped up and her mouth dried. Her breath caught. Her lips parted the slightest amount.

Suddenly, nothing else mattered. All her plans for her future were dross, nothing to what was happening here, under a million stars. She turned and faced him, moving ever closer…

The first kiss was soft, gentle, the slightest brush of her lips against his, for—she had no doubt, this time— *she* kissed *him*. Harry had held back, allowed her to take the lead, and she had done so. Then he kissed her back, and his lips cushioned hers, pulling her in, closer and closer, until she could not have said where she ended and he began. He was a strange combination of bitter and sweet, warmth and chill. He was everything she had thought he would be, and yet, nothing she had expected. He was…Harry.

He groaned softly and triumph soared within her as his arms circled her once more, strong and warm, making her safe, although safe was the last thing she wanted to feel.

Reggie arched her back, slightly, the movement subtle. He kissed her jaw, her cheek, her chin, tormenting her with the softness of his kisses, the barely-there touch of his lips to her skin, his night-cooled kiss scorching her, making her long for…something.

She pulled him deeper into her embrace and touched

her mouth to his once more. This new kiss was stronger, deeper, undeniable, full of promise, and full of danger. His tongue caressed the seam of her lips and, instinctively, she parted them, then gasped when his tongue entered her mouth, scraped gently over the top of her teeth, and danced sinuously alongside hers. The ache between her legs grew, almost unbearable now, her most private places hot and damp, her nipples heavy and sensitive, puckering against the silk of her shift. A soft mewl sounded, and it was a moment before she realized it came from her.

Somehow, her coat was unbuttoned and his hands were inside, stroking her waist, her hips, the side of her ribs, setting her on fire. He brushed against the underside of her swollen, sensitive breast and she almost exploded with desire.

His lips left hers and she groaned her displeasure. It changed into a moan of delight as he feathered kisses along her jawline, then her neck, nipping at her, then licking softly at her skin. He cupped her breast, and ran his thumb over the sensitive nipple, which grew to a taut point, painfully seeking his fingers. She moaned again and felt his lips curve, smiling against her skin.

On the nearby road, a car growled and jerked as the driver changed gears. Like a disapproving uncle clearing his throat, the gears graunched, and the engine roared its disapprobation, the yellow beams of its headlamps searching as it drove past. Reggie pulled back, sharply, jerking into wakefulness, and awareness. She all but jumped back, startling away from the drugging kiss, away from his hypnotic caress.

She pulled back so quickly, Harry stumbled. He grabbed the frame of his car, holding onto it to steady himself, and Reggie felt guilt wash over her. She should have been more careful, not pulled back like a frightened rabbit, making him overbalance, losing his center of gravity. Lord! If he had fallen, out here, miles from anywhere… She started to reach out to him, then froze, uncertain what she should do. Should she steady him, hold his arm until he was in no more danger? Should she let him find his equilibrium alone? What would he want?

In deference to his pride, she pulled farther back.

Harry's breathing was as heavy and labored as her own. She fancied she could hear his heart beating, so loud and fast she feared it would burst, his shoulders rising and falling as if he had just run the race of his life. But was that because of the kiss they had just shared? Had it affected him as much as it had her? Or was his reaction more for the fear of the tumble he had very nearly taken? He clutched the car for a few seconds more, then straightened. Now that he was steadier, he smiled and moved away from her, though she noticed he still rested his hand on the car's sleek bodywork.

The car on the road moved on past them, its headlamps growing smaller, fading into nothingness as it rounded a bend.

"I…" Reggie swallowed the gruffness in her voice and tried again. "I should be getting home." Her words were as stiff as she was, and she was stiff enough to break if she tried to bend. She made a conscious effort to drop her shoulders. It didn't help.

"Yes." Harry agreed with her, but it sounded as if it was the last thing he wanted to do.

"Yes," she repeated. She rebuttoned her coat, her actions stilted. "My father will wonder where I am."

At those words, he pulled himself to his full height.

His hand still rested on his car, the way they might rest on a banister when going down stairs. Then, quickly, eagerly even, he pulled open the passenger door.

Reggie had no choice but to climb into the car. She sat primly on her seat, feet flat on the floor, ankles pressed together, her hands folded into her lap, and her eyes fixed on the windscreen, though she could see little beyond it.

Harry shut her door with a decided thunk and teetered round to the driver's side.

"Let's get you home," he muttered.

Then he peeled out of the car park and onto the road as if he couldn't do it fast enough.

Chapter Eleven

Reggie let herself into her home as quietly as she could, aware that it was well past midnight and half, if not all, the household would be asleep. She hung her coat in the closet and took off her shoes, savoring the feel of the cold tile floor on her tired feet before padding toward the stairs, all the time berating herself for what she had done.

How could she have been so stupid? They had had such a wonderful evening, renewing their friendship and building bridges, and she had ruined it all by kissing him again. And after she had made such a fuss about not wanting more than friendship, too!

He'd told her he had missed her. Well, she'd missed him, too. There was no denying that, although she hadn't admitted it out loud. Instead, she'd tried to tamp down the feelings within her, refusing to acknowledge them, refusing to admit how frightened of them she was. Because here, in the cold, lonely, middle of the night, she knew that to be true. She was frightened—terrified—of the way Harry made her feel, and by how quickly and thoroughly the man had become so important to her.

It was that fear which had caused her reaction to his silly quip about honeymoons in the first place. The reaction which had caused such a rift between them, and then had led them to tonight: to dinner, to friendship, to all that had followed on.

"He made a joke," she muttered as she padded into her room and shut the door with a quiet snick. If anyone else had said it, she would have laughed it off, given a comeback retort and forgotten it. But when it was said by Harry…it hadn't sounded so funny, then.

"He meant nothing by it," she whispered. "A joke." Certainly, there had been no call for her to play the Outraged Miss the way she had.

She had been ridiculous and oversensitive about it, she decided. She sat at her dressing table and used the vanishing cream to remove her makeup, peering at her reflection to make sure she'd got every last piece of it.

"It's not as if he was pestering you with unwanted proposals." Her reflection glared at her, agreeing that she had read too much into it. "For goodness' sake, Reggie Chilvers! The man has never even asked you out on a date." Dinner with a friend did not count. Especially when that dinner, which was most definitely *not* a date, was to make up after a senseless quarrel she'd caused by her unreasonable behavior.

But then, would it have been so bad if they had been on a date?

She unrolled her stockings and draped them carefully over the chair back, so they wouldn't snag or tear, then stared into the mirror, pondering the question.

"Suppose it had been a date," she murmured, resting her elbow on the dressing table and her chin on her upturned fist. "What would have been so bad about it?"

She had fervently declared herself uninterested in love, basing her decision on what she knew of men. Now, she realized, all her assumptions were based on a very limited sample study. When she thought about it, the men she knew well enough to judge boiled down to just two: James, and Father. Most other men of her acquaintance were people she'd met through Father. Most of them worked for him, and did his bidding, so they really didn't count.

A man like James would drive her to distraction. He was too shy, too easygoing. He let Father ride roughshod over his dreams and desires, suppressing his passion for making things work to sit in his office, day after day, letting life slowly ebb from him. Reggie could never fall for somebody like James. She needed someone stronger, someone willing to stand up for what he wanted. Someone with a strong personality.

Although not someone strong in the way Father liked to be strong: bombastic and bullying, supremely confident—or at least, at pains to appear so. Those things may be an asset in his business matters, but they were not at all attractive qualities in a husband. Or a father.

But Harry was not like that. He respected Reggie. Took her wishes into account. Had he not done so tonight? They'd been caught up in the moment, the two of them. Those kisses had been hot enough to burn them both to a crisp. Reggie knew, from talking with her mother, that it was difficult for a man to hold back. A woman, Mother had said, should be careful never to flirt too much, because men could not control themselves the way women could, and they couldn't stop once things were started.

Harry had proved Mother wrong tonight. He had wanted her, she knew. She had felt it in every kiss, every caress, in the way she'd felt his body behave. Yet he had stopped when she had. He'd made no effort to override her wishes, or to take what she hadn't freely given. That's what she loved about him. He…

Loved? That was the second time tonight she'd used that word. Did she love Harry Pearson?

Panic rose within her, making her heart flutter and tightening her chest. She had to work to calm herself. Honestly! She was being foolish. Of course she didn't love Harry.

At least, she didn't think she did. The feeling she had whenever she thought about him, that warm glow that made her want to hug herself and hold him within her heart, that wasn't love. Was it?

She liked him. Liked being with him. Seeing him always brightened her day. That didn't mean she loved him. Neither did the fact that she thought about him constantly when they were apart, counting the minutes until she saw him again.

"He's delightful company," she whispered. She hung her dress in her wardrobe and pulled on a nightgown, then sat, hairbrush in hand. She began to count the strokes, then stopped, cross with herself. A hundred brush strokes each night made sense when a woman's hair was the length of her spine, but Reggie's hair was shorter, more manageable, and a hundred strokes was just silly. She put down the brush and made her way to her bed.

"He's delightful company," she repeated, as she settled herself between her sheets and reached up to the light switch that hung like a pendant above her bed. "He's interested in me."

That was why she liked being with him. He liked her. He was interested in her life. He liked to see what she'd bought when she went shopping. He liked to hear news of her day. It would never occur to him that events in his life were more important than events in hers.

Those things did not mean that he loved her. And though they made her like him, very much, they didn't make her love him. Nor did it mean anything that she enjoyed the feel of his arm under hers when they walked, or the way his fingers encased hers whenever they held hands. He was being a gentleman. And she…

She had been the one who had orchestrated tonight's kiss. Or had she been? Certainly, she had leaned in to him, put her lips to his, and started something she could neither control nor stop.

Though he had kissed her first. Hadn't he? Or had the first kiss been her, too? She'd wanted it. Wanted him. He made her feel…things she had no business feeling. Things that did not sit well with her future. With all she wanted. She could not, would not give up her dreams because a man made her feel as if she'd only just come to life. As if…

"No!" Reggie took a deep breath and blew it out. It was wrong. It wasn't supposed to be. "And it can never happen again," she whispered into the darkness. "Never."

She turned on her side, bashed her pillow into shape and shut her eyes, then opened them again to dispel the images of the two of them, entwined, kissing, more.

"Never," she reiterated.

It was going to be a long night.

**\*\*\*\***

Harry couldn't sleep. For hours, he lay in bed, tossing and turning, sitting up and drinking water from the glass on the bedside table, lying down again, then starting his fidgeting from the beginning.

He had kissed Reggie.

He had kissed her before, of course, that day in the

barn. Those kisses had been wonderful, but they paled beside the kisses they had shared tonight. Tonight, when their lips had met, it had been one of the most wonderful moment of his life. Tonight's kiss had been as perfect as a kiss could be.

To be fair, he wasn't exactly an expert on kissing. Which was hardly a surprise, when one thought about it. He'd had very little experience of girls and kissing before he'd run off to join up at the age of fifteen—unless he counted the time with Daisy Mae Benton behind the cowshed, and that, if he was honest, had been more confusing than pleasurable. Then, after he'd joined the army, there was precious little chance of kissing and romancing. There had been the intensive training grounds and, all too soon, the stinking, swamping trenches, until he had been wounded. After that, he'd needed to concentrate all his attention on his convalescence, which had been long and arduous. He'd had to learn to walk again, to strengthen his legs as much as he could, to build hope and possibility back into his future. There had been very little time for anything else, and very few chances for encounters with females of the kissing variety.

Not that most of those females would have been interested in him. Like everyone else, they wanted to push away the memories of the war and the grim struggles of the first years of peace. Injured men like Harry reminded them of too much. Not to mention that those who had survived intact were intent on frivolity in a world where there were no problems, and all they had to do was have fun and throw themselves energetically around the dance floors.

Theoretically, there were women enough for every

man who had come home from the war. But these women were learning to be independent, accepting there was no guarantee a husband would be available to take care of them as their fathers had their mothers. The very shortage of men that should have given Harry a good chance of finding a mate had, in fact, worked against him, for once the stigma of spinsterhood had been lifted, many women chose to remain single rather than tie themselves to somebody who was broken.

Reggie was like them in that she preferred singleness and independence to the idea of marriage and family. But, unlike all the other women he had met since the war, Reggie didn't think of Harry as a figure of pity. He didn't see charity in her eyes when she looked at him, or hear discomfort in her voice as she took care with every word, frightened of saying something insensitive. When Reggie looked at him, she did not see a broken cripple. She saw a whole man, a man whose legs might have been mangled but whose brain functioned fully. A man with prospects, whom she could respect and admire and…love?

It was a lot to hang onto a few kisses. Although, what kisses they had been! The passion and heat of them had taken Harry completely by surprise, and almost knocked him off his feet.

He had wanted to kiss her all evening. When he'd picked her up, when they'd parked outside the hotel, all through the meal, his only thoughts were of how beautiful she looked, how desirable. He had imagined her in his arms, her eyes staring into his, her lips meeting his. It was almost more than he could manage, to sit and talk with her, pretending she wasn't drawing him in with the way her sensuous lips wrapped themselves around her words, spoken in that deep, husky voice. He was glad that his trousers were loose-fitting and his coat was long or she would have been under no illusion about the effect she had on this "mere friend." His quip about other men taking their ladies dancing had been a kind of lament—his disabilities meant he had no way of prolonging their evening, and making light of that prevented him from howling in anguish. Anguish which turned to joy when he discovered she wasn't ready to go home either.

Stargazing on Ashdown Forest wasn't necessarily his first choice of activity on a cold night in late March, but it was the first thing that had come into his head when she'd looked at the stars, such as they were, in town. He'd been telling the truth when he said he often drove up to King's Standing, and watched the heavens, which meant he'd be able to talk to her about the constellations without seeming too much of an idiot.

And then one thing led to another, and…

It was the best night of his life. *She* was the best thing that had ever happened, in his entire life. She was everything he'd waited for, all he had hoped for, and now that he had found her, he couldn't contemplate the idea of losing her.

But…if she learned of his deal with her father… He closed his eyes against the pain that shot through him at the very thought. The look of hatred and betrayal he would see on her face, the way she would turn away from him in disgust, their friendship in tatters, shot down before it even had time to grow and develop into something more.

Lord, what a mess!

He scrubbed his hand across his face, trying to wipe away the despair threatening to engulf him, wanting to replace it with hope and forgiveness.

Perhaps if he explained it to her…

He scoffed at that. She would be furious. There was no way Reggie Chilvers would sit and listen quietly to him while he confessed, then benignly pat his hand and tell him it didn't matter, and that she was perfectly all right with the knowledge that he had gone behind her back, arranged a deal to not only thwart her ambitions but force her to be something she detested instead, then romanced her in a sly, underhanded way to ensure his success…

She wouldn't be all right with that. Not for an instant. She would… Well, at the very least, Harry would get his face slapped.

But what if he confessed to her in such a way that she could get past her anger? If he explained why he'd done what he had done, worked with her to see she got what she needed, what she deserved to have…

Reggie was an intelligent and practical woman. She was pragmatic enough to know that, sometimes, one had to roll with the punches and make the best of what one had. She wasn't missish about things, and she wasn't unreasonable. If he made his confession now, before she could find out from some other source, show her he was being honest with her now, that he truly did regret his part in it, maybe he could head off the worst of her anger.

He would have to repay her father sooner than he wished, of course. But he would have to do that anyway. There was no way Reggie would change her mind between now and her birthday, and that would be clear to her father.

But, if Harry was honest, that part didn't matter anymore. Much as it would hurt to lose his own dream, he would survive. Perhaps he could find a way to rebuild it later.

But if he lost Reggie…that was something he would never survive.

Guilty secrets had a way of being exposed, usually at the worst possible moment. This one would be no exception. He felt the truth of that to his core. Which meant he had no choice.

He must tell her the next time he saw her. He must explain everything to her, beg her forgiveness, then promise to spend the rest of his life making it up to her.

Would that be enough? He could but hope. There was always hope.

On that thought, he finally slept.

\*\*\*\*

It was four days before Harry saw Reggie again. In truth, he knew he could have made more effort to meet her sooner, and his tales of appointments, meetings with potential clients, and sundry family matters were little more than excuses. He knew why, too.

Much as he wanted to see her and spend time with her, he also dreaded it. Now he had decided to come clean and tell her about the deal he'd made, he didn't want to do it. He knew, in his heart, no matter how he explained it, whatever justifications he gave and however much he said he was sorry, Reggie was unlikely to forgive him. From the moment she learned of it, she would hate him, and he wanted to put that off as long as he could.

It wasn't a decision he was proud of; it smacked of cowardice, to say nothing of conduct unbecoming. They were charges he would plead guilty to when the time came, but for now, he wanted—needed—to put everything off.

On the fourth day, she telephoned him at his new warehouse. He'd had a couple of calls here already, from prospective clients, but the jangle of the bell still sent a thrill through him. He cleared his throat, picked up the candlestick phone, and held the earpiece to his head.

"H. Pearson, transportation," he announced, crisply and clearly into the mouthpiece.

"Harry?" Her voice was tinny along the line.

"Reggie," he said, and wondered if she could hear the beaming smile he suddenly sported.

They exchanged good wishes, and a little small talk, and then she asked him out to the kinema that evening. "It's nothing special," she said. "Not a new film or anything. It's *The Thief of Baghdad*. I know it's a couple of years old, but I haven't seen it, and I thought, if you hadn't either…"

Harry had seen it when it first came out, but he had enjoyed it and wasn't averse to seeing it again. "I'd love to come," he said, and he arranged to pick her up that evening.

As he put the phone down, he felt a twinge of guilt because he knew he would not keep his promise to himself and tell her everything. Not tonight.

"It's an evening out," he murmured. He rearranged the things on top of his desk, only to put them back in their original places. "Why spoil an evening out with something that can wait?" It wasn't urgent. Nobody was going to die if he put off the evil moment. It would give him more time to come up with a way of confessing all without making her hate him.

He had to think of something. He simply had to, because he could not bear the thought of losing her regard, her friendship. Her. For one simple truth now shone through, clear as the beam from a lighthouse. He would never feel about any other woman the way he felt about Reggie Chilvers. He loved her, and he wanted her to love him. He wanted to spend his life with her. If, when she discovered his secret, she didn't want him, could not forgive him, he would be shattered. And he would spend the rest of his life alone. No other woman would ever do for him now.

Guilt jabbed him like a stiletto to the ribs and he sighed. "I will tell her," he promised himself. Again. "Just not tonight."

If that made him a coward and a cad, so be it.

He finished work early and went home to clean up, wearing his best suit and his most expensive cologne, although he told himself several times that this was not a date. But then, he argued, it could be.

"Slow and steady wins the race, Harry, my lad," he whispered as he walked along the corridor to the front door.

"Beg pardon?" asked his brother, Frank, startling Harry.

"What are you doing here?" he asked, far more belligerently than he should have.

Frank did not take it amiss. His eyes twinkled with humor as he answered, "I live here. You might remember me turning up at dinner every so often."

"Not so often everyone would notice," Harry answered. "But I meant, what are you doing here, now? At this time of the evening. Aren't you usually out and about, chasing some flapper or other?"

Frank's smile dimmed, momentarily, then brightened again, and he chuckled. "I'm having a night off. Those girls wear a man out."

"You're getting old."

Frank called Harry something that would once have had their housekeeper washing his mouth out with kitchen soap. Then he carried on to the stairs and ran up them two at a time. Harry felt a pang of regret that he could no longer do that, before he raised his chin, defiantly. "At least I've got a lady to take out this evening," he told himself.

"I heard that," called Frank from halfway up the stairs. "Just watch it, or I'll have to steal her away from you."

"Where would you like to be buried?"

Harry left home with Frank's easy laughter ringing in his ears. He couldn't remember the last time he and his brother had teased each other in such a way. It felt good to be doing it now, as if some barrier, erected after Harry's time in the hospital, had finally been breached, and things were getting back to normal.

"I certainly hope so," he said as he cranked the car's handle, then drove toward Reggie's home.

She was waiting at the door for him, swathed in a big, broad shouldered coat with a velvet collar and a narrow hem, her hands encased in leather gloves with velvet wrist trim. She blew on her fingers as he pulled back onto the road and headed for Tunbridge Wells. "There is a definite nip in the air," she said. "Winter isn't done with us yet."

"Good job we haven't planned a picnic on the beach, then," he replied. She laughed.

They reached the Great Hall at the bottom of Mount Pleasant Road in plenty of time for the evening showing. Which was just as well, because the road was lined with parked cars on both sides, as far as they could see. The only spaces were opposite the Hall, outside the Central Train Station, and those spaces were jealously guarded by taxicab drivers. If he parked there, Harry would likely return to find his tires removed, or some other inconvenience. He could try parking farther up Mount Pleasant Road, but the hill was steep, and it would be hard to climb back to the car after the show. In fact, it would be equally difficult for Harry to walk down the hill from the car to the kinema.

"I'll drop you off here and then park on Grove Hill Road," he decided. That street was just around the corner and, although it wasn't completely flat ground, it was nowhere near as steep as Mount Pleasant Road was.

"Or," she argued, "you could wait here at the Hall, and I will park the car."

Harry opened his mouth to object. It went against everything he was to leave a lady to walk the evening streets unattended.

Reggie raised her hand to stop his protest. "It's a well-lit street, and I should be able to park just a few yards in. I'll be back before you know it." She frowned at him then, clearly sensing his disquiet. "How do you think we women got about when all you men were off fighting the Hun? We didn't sit at home, twiddling our fingers and not daring to move for the lack of an escort." He gave her an old-fashioned look and she grinned. "I can do this, Harry."

He realized, then, he wouldn't win this argument. "When did you learn to drive?"

"Years ago. James taught me." She chuckled, naughtily. "I blackmailed him into it when he had Father's car. Can't remember what I threatened him with now, but whatever he'd done, it was bad enough that he kept me quiet with a few weeks' driving lessons on the roads around Fieldhurst."

"I take it your father didn't know? About the driving, I mean. Not the blackmail." Harry knew the answer before she gave it. William Chilvers was not the kind of man who would let his daughter drive his car.

Reggie laughed louder at that. "Can you imagine? He'd have a conniption at the very thought." The smile faded and she looked at him more solemnly. "But whatever my father may think of women drivers, I can do it. Your car will be safe with me."

That decided Harry. He would not be yet another man who restricted her activities and doubted her abilities, simply because she was a woman. He would have every faith in her, and he would make sure she knew it.

"If you're certain," he said, and he climbed out of the car. She slid along the bench seat and took the wheel. She did graunch the gears the first time she engaged them, and he winced, wondering if he had done the right thing. But then, watching her drive off up the hill, he could see she had quickly got the hang of it.

He watched her turn right and settled in to wait for her to drive around in a big circle to where she would park. At least they'd be facing in the right direction when it came time to go home, he mused.

Minutes later, she sashayed around the corner and met him at the doors to the Great Hall. "Your pride and joy is safely parked across from the Renault and Rover garage," she said. "It's perfectly all right."

"I never doubted it." He crooked his elbow for her, and they went inside.

The Great Hall had once been a concert hall and theater, and it was furnished much as it had been then. The screen was hidden behind thick red velvet curtains, embossed with sturdy gold thread. It was mounted on a stage, behind a proscenium arch. The orchestra pit separated the stage from the rows of plush seats. Along each side were the boxes that privileged theatregoers had once paid a fortune to reserve, now mostly curtained off, used only for a sellout performance. There were boxes either side of the stage, too. One of these now held the piano, which would be played to accompany the film. The other box held two rows of seats, as if it awaited the guests of honor, though why anyone would want to sit there during the show was beyond Harry's comprehension. The carpet throughout the kinema was thick and luxurious, while the lighting was subdued.

An usherette led them to their seats and asked if they would like drinks brought over. They ordered those drinks for the entr'acte, then made themselves comfortable. Two men in the seats behind them lit up cigarettes, blowing the thin blue smoke out to join the haze caused by other smoking patrons. Reggie batted it away from her with her hand, grimacing her distaste.

"Would you like me to see if we can find better seats?" asked Harry.

"No point," she said. "there'll be people smoking everywhere." She sighed. "I do wish they wouldn't. It makes everything smell so. My coat will need a clean after tonight."

"Just one of those things, I suppose," he answered, with a shrug. Most men of his generation smoked. It had been actively encouraged in the army, where it was said tobacco calmed nerves before a battle. Harry had tried it, but he had hated the taste and had been violently sick afterward. Some of the other soldiers had laughed at him over that, but they'd been happy enough to swap some of their other ration items for his cigarettes.

"My father smokes," said Reggie, bringing him out of his memories. "But only in his study. Mother doesn't like it in the rest of the house, thank goodness. I hate going into his study. It stinks in there. I honestly think he cannot smell it for himself, for he sits in there quite happily every day." She grinned, sheepishly. "You must think me pernickety in the extreme."

"Not at all. I don't like the smell of it either. Though I fear we won't stop people doing it. I've even heard that some women have taken it up."

She shook her head. "And Father calls me an unfeminine hoyden."

The lights dimmed and the first film began. It was an old film, apparently from France, about a cannon-propelled flight to the moon which, as far as Harry could make out, owed a great deal to the works of Jules Verne. The moon landing, when the spacecraft hit the Man in the Moon right in his eye, got a round of applause.

That film ended and the lights came up for a short interval, after which they laughed at the deadpan comedy of Buster Keaton as a man who must marry by midnight or lose a fortune. After that film, the usherette brought their drinks, a whisky for Harry, wine for Reggie. He sipped, savoring the taste of his drink, then held his glass in salute.

"Here's to you, Reggie Chilvers. May your life be filled with happiness and health."

"And to you, Harry Pearson," she replied, clinking her glass against his. "And to a very successful business venture."

At last, they reached the main event of the evening, when Douglas Fairbanks fought his way through myriad adventures and past numerous villains, to triumph in the final reel.

Afterward, while most patrons left for the nearest pubs or nearby restaurants, Harry and Reggie sat quietly in the Great Hall's lounge, enjoying a second drink and discussing the films they'd seen that evening.

"How did you like *The Thief of Baghdad*?" Harry asked.

Reggie scrunched her face as she thought about it. "It was…action-packed," she said, at last. "And Mr. Fairbanks is an undeniably handsome man."

Harry cocked his head to one side. "Better than me?" He preened, playfully.

"We-ell," she joked, and he grasped at his chest over his heart.

"Cruel, cruel maiden," he cried, dramatically.

"Is everything all right, sir?" asked the waitress. He fought his laughter long enough to assure her that everything was fine.

"It was an enjoyable evening," said Reggie when she stopped laughing. "But I have to say, that film was exactly like a dozen others. To say nothing of its similarity to books, and theater shows. In all of them, the men get to go out and have adventures and do the exciting stuff. They fight the villains and swash their buckles, and all the rest of it. And the women? The women stay at home and wait to be claimed. They are the first prize, given to the victor. Most times, like in that film, they don't even get a say in what happens to them."

Harry could see her point, though it had never

occurred to him before. "I suppose that's how it is in fairy tales," he said.

Reggie guffawed. "That's how it is in real life," she corrected him. "When you think about it, you might almost say we were living in the twelfth century, not the twentieth. Women are still mere chattels. Pieces on a chessboard for men to move into whatever positions they choose."

The fun of the evening drained away, as he heard the truth behind her words. She was going to be very upset when she learned the truth. Shame washed over him, threatening to drown him, and guilt lodged in his throat like a large rock in a narrow stream. If he took another swig of his whisky, he would choke on it.

"It's time to go home," he said, quietly. And, he vowed silently, when he got to her home, he would tell her. He could not put it off any longer. When she hated him and refused to have anything more to do with him, and all he faced were the lonely years ahead, he would take comfort in the memory of this evening.

"Want me to fetch the car?" she asked, cutting into his thoughts.

No, he didn't. It was late now, and all the shops on Grove Hill Road would be closed. The street would be in darkness. Most of the kinema goers had left, as well. The pubs were starting to kick out the die-hard drinkers, those who had stayed to the very end. The last thing Harry wanted Reggie to do now was to walk through the streets unescorted.

"We'll walk together," he said. She nodded, but he saw the disappointment in her eyes. He could guess the reason.

This was something he could do for her, one small

thing to make her happy, before he crushed her with the truth. "Would you like to drive us home?"

Her eyes widened and a huge smile spread across her face. "Would I?" She stood and let him help her into her coat before picking up her clutch bag.

The night was cold, a white coat of frost already forming on cars and street furniture. Their breaths formed small clouds before them. Reggie shivered and Harry pulled her closer, telling himself it was to keep her warm, nothing more. She didn't object to his embrace, and he took that as a win.

A man stepped out of a shop doorway and blocked the pavement. They were less than a dozen feet from the safety of Harry's car, but he had a sudden feeling it might as well be a dozen miles.

The man's hat hid his features, the shadow of its brim obscuring his face. He drew on a cigarette, the end of it lighting orange red, but even that wasn't enough to show him properly.

There was the slightest chance this wasn't as threatening as it appeared. The man might be a shopkeeper, heading home after working late, stopping for a moment to light his fag, and not thinking of how his actions might be interpreted by others.

Nevertheless, Harry tightened the muscles in his arm, drawing Reggie in closer, more securely. Thank God he hadn't let her retrieve the car on her own.

Then a second man came out of the shadows of the Renault and Rover garage, crossed the road, and stood beside the first man, and Harry's faint hopes died.

## Chapter Twelve

The second man was smaller than his companion, although he was stockier, and he looked as if he might be used to brawling in the street. Even with the shadows thrown by his wide-brimmed hat, Harry saw the misshapen nose that spoke of past fights. Like his friend, he wore a loose-fitting suit and an unbuttoned coat, perfect for moving easily and quickly.

Footsteps sounded on the pavement behind Harry. He prayed they belonged to other filmgoers, but when they stopped dead and nobody said anything, he knew they did not. His escape, Reggie's escape, had just been cut off. He was outnumbered and outmatched. He knew it, and the cold grin on the first man's face said they knew it, too.

All Harry could do now was keep their attention on him and hope Reggie could get away. As long as she was unhurt, he would be happy.

"We don't want to hurt you, old man," said the first man. His voice was soft, not much more than a whisper, and all the more menacing for that. His friend, standing beside him, smirked and pushed his hands nonchalantly into the pockets of his coat.

Harry answered him. Partly, it was to draw their attention and keep it away from Reggie, but there was also a piece of him that was incensed. *Old man?* He wasn't yet twenty-five years old. He'd be damned if he'd let anyone call him an old man! No matter how many mates they'd brought to the fight.

"Old man?" he said, injecting every bit of outrage he could muster into the words. "I bet I'm younger than you are." It was a bet he would probably win. The two men in front of him were either well into their thirties or life had treated them very harshly.

And who knew? Maybe a friendly bet could defuse this situation. Harry had seen unexpected challenges soothe ruffled feathers in the army barracks. It might work here.

Reggie squeezed his bicep, sending him a silent message that he should not antagonize these men. He flexed his muscles in return, willing her to trust him and praying her trust would be rewarded. He didn't dare to look at her to see if she understood.

"Old, young, I don't really care," said the man.

So much for a friendly bet. Adrenaline began to pump through Harry, making his blood sing, tensing muscles and readying nerves.

The man took one last drag on his cigarette, threw it to the ground, then squashed it with his foot.

"What do you want?" asked Reggie. Her voice held the slightest quiver. She had to be terrified, thought Harry, and he admitted, at least to himself, that she wasn't alone in that. *He* was frightened, too.

Being threatened here, in the middle of civilization, with a young lady on his arm, was like a knife to the heart. Anything could happen. Reggie could well be hurt, and that made what was happening here more terrifying than any of the times he'd gone over the top of the trenches, advancing into no-man's-land and the sights of the German guns. When he had done those things, there had been a sort of rightness about them. A reasonableness to the unreasonable actions, a defense for the indefensible order to go.

But this? What was happening here, now? This was pointless and wasteful. There was no reason for it. No defense. This simply did not belong.

Besides which, when he had been sent on those suicidal runs from foxhole to foxhole, Harry had only really had his own safety to concentrate on. Oh, he looked out for the men either side of him, and they looked out for him. But all those men were trained. They were primed and ready to do their duty. They didn't truly need his protection. Not like Reggie did.

"We want what you've got," the man in front of them answered Reggie's question. Harry pushed aside his memories and concentrated all his attention on what was happening here. The man's companions laughed, low. At him, Harry realized. At the utter hopelessness of his situation. The first man held out his hand in supplication.

It stung, but Harry couldn't really blame them for their confidence. His situation was every bit as bad as they surmised. There were at least four of them to his one, and they were all hale and hearty, physically whole. The man had every right to expect easy pickings. That was what he would get. Harry had no other choice.

Harry pulled out his wallet and held it at arm's length. The man with the misshapen nose took it, rifled through it, took out the money within, then tossed the leather wallet to the ground. Reggie handed over her clutch bag and he treated that with equal disdain.

"Your watch," demanded Man Number One. Harry glanced over his shoulder at the two men behind him, then unbuckled the watch his father had given him for his birthday. Nose Man pocketed it.

Man Number One turned to Reggie. "Jewelry."

"You can take it," she said. "It's all paste. Costume stuff." She took off her ear bobs and handed them over to Nose Man. Harry bristled. He felt useless, worthless.

Nose Man examined the ear bobs, then swore.

"Gash!" he spat, using an old slang word for cheap jewelry. Harry made a mental note of it. Perhaps it would help identify the thief later.

Nose Man threw the ear bobs to the pavement.

Man Number One was not happy. Harry supposed he'd expected rich pickings. To an extent he'd found them—Harry's wallet held at least ten pounds, and his watch would raise a pretty penny, too. But it wasn't enough for that man.

The thief stepped forward, glaring at Reggie as if she was to blame for his disappointment. Harry tensed, ready to punch him as hard as he could before yelling at her to run while he lay about the others with one of his sticks and prayed for a rescuer to be nearby.

Man Number One eyed Reggie, thoughtfully.

Reggie eyed him right back, her gaze steady.

The man chuckled, then raised his hand slowly, and caressed her cheek.

Harry's blood boiled, but before he could do anything, Reggie slapped the man's hand away and took a step back. Quick as lightning, the man grabbed her arm. His other hand gripped the nape of her neck and he pulled her nearer, licking his lips and leering at her.

She squirmed to keep him from kissing her. Harry dove into the fray, jabbing at him with his stick. He caught the man in the stomach and the breath whooshed out of him. He doubled over and Harry brought the stick up, hard and fast, connecting with the man's nose with a sickening crunch. The man yelled in pain and Harry had the hysterical thought that he would match his mate, Nose Man, now. Harry swung again, and this time his stick connected to the man's most tender parts. He clutched at them, fell to his knees, and vomited.

"Run!" Harry shouted at Reggie, swinging his stick in a wide arc to keep the other thieves at bay, though he knew he could not hold them off forever. He only got a few swings in before the inevitable happened. One of the men behind him kicked at his second stick, the one still helping him to stand steady. The stick flew from his hand and clattered to the pavement, Harry's legs gave way, and he went down.

He rolled himself into the smallest ball he could manage, arms over his head, protecting it. Boots kicked and stomped on him. Men grunted and swore, their breathing growing heavier with the effort of each blow. Reggie screamed, yelling blue murder.

A boot got past his defenses and connected with Harry's cheek. Another kicked his jaw, snapping his head back sharply. He pulled his arms even closer to his skull. All he knew was that he had to stay awake. He could not lose consciousness. It was the only way to keep Reggie safe.

The copper tang of blood filled his mouth and pooled in the back of his throat, threatening to choke him. His stomach was on fire and his chest stung. His breaths came, short and shallow as the light began to fade.

No! He had to stay awake. Both their lives might depend upon it.

\*\*\*\*

They were killing him! And for what? A watch. A wallet. A cheap clutch bag that held no more than five pounds.

The man had been angry to find Reggie's ear bobs were made of glass and pasteboard. But then, ear bobs generally were. Real gemstones were usually far too heavy to wear comfortably on one's earlobes, and besides, it was too easy to lose one and not notice until hours later, when there would be no hope of finding it. If the jewels were real, that loss would hurt, whereas losing this pair would hardly register.

That they'd been surprised by the paste ear bobs told Reggie these were not experienced thieves. Experienced men would have ignored them and gone for her necklace instead, and that was most definitely not paste.

For a moment, when the first man had put his hand to her cheek, she'd thought that was his intent. She'd expected him to grab the necklace and pull it from her neck. Instead, he had caressed her, sneering as he did so. Instinctively, she'd pulled back, batting away his unwelcome advances. The way he'd run his tongue along his lips as he stared at her was frightening, and she had fought back. Now, of course, she knew it had been designed to provoke her into acting like that. He had wanted her to do so, knowing Harry would be bound to rush to her rescue.

But why did the man want to fight with someone like Harry? What possible benefit was there to be had in attacking a man who walked with sticks? Did he feel big for putting down his man so quickly? Was it a way to ease his frustration at his failure to net a bigger haul?

Or was it something else? Did the man know Harry?

Was there bad blood between the two of them?

Not that the why mattered right now. All that mattered now was that they were killing Harry. There were four of them, kicking and stomping on him, over and over and over, and she didn't know how much more he could take.

She had to stop them. So she yelled and screamed at the top of her voice, hoping someone would come and chase the men off. Had no other filmgoer parked along this road? Was there no one living above the shops who could yell at the men? That might be all it took to frighten them off and stop this brutal assault.

The kinema ushers were only just around the corner. Trained to deal with drunk and unruly patrons, they were handy with their fists and knew how to take care of themselves. Surely, they could hear her cries? Why did they not come?

Nobody came. Nobody seemed interested in discovering what the noise was about. The street remained completely deserted, apart from Harry and Reggie and the thugs attacking them.

The men didn't stop. They didn't slow down, though their shoes and trousers were spattered with Harry's blood now. By the time rescue came, it could well be too late. He might be dead, and these men... Reggie refused to think about what they would do next.

It was up to her to save them both.

Reggie darted around the gang. They paid her no attention, so intent were they on hurting Harry. She grabbed one of his sticks, surprised and pleased by how solid and heavy it was. It could do a lot of damage, she thought. Holding it in a two-handed grip, like she would hold a golf club, she gritted her teeth and swung with all her might, almost over balancing as she whacked the man nearest to her. Her hands tingled and her arms hurt from the jarring blow, which caught him across his shoulder blades. He roared with pain but it didn't knock him down.

He turned and glared at her, swore, and called her a name she wasn't supposed to know. A part of her was triumphant. While he concentrated on her, there was one less man beating on Harry. Another, bigger, part of her knew she was now in real trouble. She stepped back. He moved toward her. She brandished the stick like a sword. He grinned.

Clearly, he expected her to swing at him as she had done before. He was ready for that. As the stick came round, he would grab it, snatch it from her grasp and use it himself. She would be unable to stop him, his strength too much for her.

So she changed tack. Instead of swinging at his head or torso, the way he expected, Reggie bent her knees and swung it low, near to the ground.

The speed of the swing turned her in a full circle, so she didn't see the full impact of her move, but it must have worked, because with a cry of surprised pain the man was upended, his legs taken from under him, his feet shooting up as his torso went down.

Surprised and dazed, he sat on the pavement, his face a study in bewilderment that would have been funny if the situation hadn't been so serious. Before he could recover, she swung again, this time catching the side of his head and leaving a red mark that rose immediately on his cheek. One more swing and he lay unconscious.

Reggie's breaths were shallow and jagged, as if they were cut by the blade of a jigsaw. She felt sick but at the same time elated. Her wrists ached and her pulse pounded in her ears. Hot tears stung her eyes.

A second man glanced over his shoulder. He did a double take at his downed friend. "Hey!" he shouted, his voice filled with outrage that she had dared to attack his mate. He charged at her, but he was big, and that made him slow. Reggie stood her ground until the last second, then she sidestepped him. He flew past her, and she hit him across the back of his shoulders. He stumbled.

The man righted himself and turned to face her. Fury glittered in his eyes, but she was not about to give up. Not only did her own life depend on this, but Harry's too. And if it was too late for him, if they had already killed him with their vicious kicks, well, then she would make sure he got justice. She would see every one of these men hang, if she had to.

From further down the street, a man shouted. Footsteps rang on the pavement, coming nearer. Reggie chanced a look and saw two men, dressed in the kinema's livery, rushing toward her.

Seeing the writing on the wall, her attacker turned tail and fled. The kinema employees dove at the last two, pulling them off Harry. Reggie dropped the stick and fell to her knees at his side.

Within seconds, the fight was over. The last two thugs ran as if the devil himself were stepping on their heels. The fourth man, the one Reggie had hit first, was dazed, though he was no longer unconscious. He moved and tried to get up, but the kinema ushers were having none of that. One of them sat heavily on the thug, who collapsed back onto the pavement.

"You're not going anywhere, mate," he told the thug, in a polite and deferential voice that was totally incongruous in the situation. "So just lie still and be a good villain, eh?"

Reggie fought the urge to laugh at his words, knowing if she let it out, it would quickly turn to hysteria.

"Are you all right, miss?" The second usher leaned over, his face full of concern. She stared up at him, taking a moment to process what he said. "The manager called the police," he added. Then he glanced at Harry. "And an ambulance, I think."

"Thank you," she whispered. She cradled Harry's head in her lap and gently stroked his blood-soaked hair. She could feel the holes in her stockings, the edges of the silk pressing into her legs and the grit of the pavement embedding itself in her exposed knees. Her gloves were in shreds. She pulled them off and threw them aside. Her heart lay on the ground beside her bag and Harry's emptied wallet.

Harry seemed to be less than conscious, but he wasn't fully unconscious, either. He groaned and tried to say something, but she couldn't make out his words. His face was a mess of bruises, cuts and grazes, his nose broken and one eye socket swelling nastily. Blood trickled from his nose and one side of his mouth, his cheek was lumpy and out of shape, his clothes torn, and there was a clear footprint on his coat.

"Ssh," she said, as he groaned again.

"Reggie," he managed to get out, but it cost him. It sounded as if he spoke around a mouthful of plum stones wrapped in thick layers of cotton wool.

"It's all right, I'm here."

"Re-Reggie," he said again. Speaking was clearly an Herculean task.

"Ssh. Don't speak. Ambulance is coming."

"Sorry. So sorry."

"You have nothing to be sorry for."

"Could…couldn't protect. Couldn't f-fight."

"It's all right, my love," she whispered. "Just rest. Don't talk."

It seemed an eternity before the ambulance arrived, although it was likely no more than ten minutes. They put Harry's neck in a restricting brace, loaded him onto a stretcher, and sped away toward the hospital in Pembury, a tiny village on the outskirts of Tunbridge Wells. Two police officers led the captured thief away in handcuffs, while other officers interviewed Reggie and the two ushers. The officers were very thorough in taking their statements. Too thorough, Reggie decided, growing more and more anxious about not being with Harry. She didn't know how badly he was hurt, or what he would need. She didn't even know if she would be of any use, or if he would want her there.

None of that mattered. She *had* to be by his side.

"Can you ask me the other questions later?" she asked the policeman. "I need to get to the hospital."

He looked her up and down. "Are you hurt?"

"No, but my friend is. Please?"

The policeman frowned, then nodded. "We'll be in touch."

She smiled her thanks, got into Harry's car, and drove out of town to Pembury.

The hospital was built on the site of a Victorian workhouse, and some of the wards were housed in the original building. It gave the place a grim, stark atmosphere. Nurses in long dresses and crisp, white pinafore aprons walked briskly between the buildings, or dealt efficiently with newly arriving patients, directing porters in dark uniforms similar in style to the ones worn by footmen. At this time of night, there were few people wandering about, and the only arrivees were would-be patients and their families.

It didn't take long for Reggie to discover Harry had been admitted to the men's ward. She raced across the hospital grounds toward it, taking off her shoes to allow her to move faster and with more freedom. A nurse in a dark blue dress which seemed to denote her as someone with status held up her arm, forcing Reggie to stop.

"We don't run in hospital corridors, young lady."

*We do if we're in a hurry.* Aloud, Reggie asked, "Can you tell me where the men's ward is?"

"Yes, I can," said the nurse, "provided you walk. Running in a hospital is dangerous." She looked at Reggie, who was willing to bet that glare made junior nurses quake in their walking-only shoes.

"Sorry," said Reggie. She thanked the woman for the directions and moved off in a strange way, not quite running, but too fast to be termed walking.

When she got to the men's ward, however, the ward sister was not helpful at all.

"You cannot come in here whenever you feel like it," she told Reggie, quietly, but firmly. "These men need their rest. Visiting hours are seven to seven thirty every evening. Are you his wife?"

Reggie should have said yes, she realized as soon as she said, "No. I'm a friend."

"Then I suggest you ask a member of his family for news of his condition."

Reggie wanted to scream. The ward sister seemed determined not to be helpful.

"Are you saying I can't visit him if I am not family?"

"I'm not saying any such thing. But patients are restricted to two visitors at a time and, naturally, his family will come first. Now, though, nobody is coming in. The ward is closed to visitors. If you would leave quietly and not disturb my patients, it would be appreciated."

She wasn't going to get anywhere arguing with the sister, so Reggie thanked her with an insincere smile and made her way back to the hospital entrance. She was almost at the door when she heard a woman pleading with the receptionist.

"He's my son," she said, tearfully. "Please."

"I'm sorry, Mrs. Pearson," said the receptionist. "You can't see him tonight."

Reggie turned, wondering whether she should talk to Mrs. Pearson. They didn't know each other, and she wasn't entirely sure the woman would want to speak to her. Or if she did, what she should say.

The entrance door was pushed open brusquely. It slammed against the door stoppers, whose scuffed condition told Reggie it wasn't the first time they had been so abused. The receptionist looked up, then looked away again, her expression carefully neutral, but somehow leaving no one in any doubt as to what she thought.

The man who strode into the hospital was someone Reggie would know anywhere. Tall and lean, he was the graven image of his son except his hair was iron gray where Harry's was dark.

"Well?" he demanded of his wife, who seemed to shrink before him.

"They said visiting hours are…"

"Never mind that! I want to know what he's done to

land himself in here."

Reggie glared at him. She longed to say Harry had been a hero, fighting off four thugs, and his father should be proud, but somehow, she knew her opinion would not be appreciated. So she stood in the shadows and hoped someone would come and give them a report on their son's progress, so she could eavesdrop and learn his condition for herself.

"He was attacked by thieves," said the receptionist. "I can get the police officer to come and see you..."

"Thieves? Did they get much from him?"

*What did that matter?*

"I couldn't say, sir." The receptionist was curt. Mrs. Pearson looked uncomfortable.

"I knew something like this would happen," said Mr. Pearson, angrily. "Boy can't take care of himself. He's no business going out on his own, so that decent, law-abiding people need waking in the middle of the night to come and see to him. Where is he?"

"I just explained to your wife..."

"She can tell me later. I need to take him home now."

"I'm sorry, sir. That will not be possible. You see..."

"I don't want your excuses! I want the boy. I will take him home where he can be looked after, and I can see to it that he doesn't get himself into any more trouble. Now!"

That was the final straw. After everything she and Harry had been through tonight, this pompous idiot thought he could come here and belittle everyone, Harry included?

Reggie stepped forward from the shadows. "He

can't go home tonight," she said. Her tone was quiet, but anyone who knew her would realize it was the one she used when she would not brook any argument. "His injuries require a stay on the ward."

Mrs. Pearson put her hand flat against her throat and the color drained from her.

"And," Reggie went on, "he's not a boy. He's a man."

"What's it to you?" Mr. Pearson's tone was sneering and contemptuous. He looked Reggie up and down. She knew she looked a fright but, frankly, she didn't care. If it hadn't been for Harry, she would look much worse, she was certain.

"He's my friend, and he's a hero, and I won't have you, or anyone else, denigrating him."

Mr. Pearson glared at Reggie as if he had never heard anything so audacious in his life. "You won't have? You. Won't. Have?" He stalked over to her, clearly thinking he would intimidate her. Having grown up with her father, Reggie was not easily intimidated.

"Your son gave a good account of himself tonight, against four vicious opponents. He saved me."

Mr. Pearson curled his lip at her. "I take it he hasn't settled your bill yet."

The implication of his words shocked Reggie, but she didn't allow it to show on her face. "I am going to ignore your rude manners, and your indifference to your lady wife." She turned from him and gave a small bow to Mrs. Pearson, then addressed herself to the woman. "Your son gave a very good account of himself tonight. He was a credit to you, ma'am."

"Thank you." The woman swallowed, hard.

"This is intolerable," muttered Mr. Pearson. He

turned to face the receptionist again and opened his mouth but, before he could say anything else, Reggie spoke again.

"What is intolerable, *sir,* is you, coming in here, throwing your weight around like a crass bully, and treating your son as a child. He deserves better, as do the staff at this hospital."

Out of the corner of her eye, she thought she saw both Mrs. Pearson and the receptionist smile briefly, but since they both adopted straight, emotionless expressions again immediately, Reggie couldn't be sure.

Mr. Pearson glared at Reggie for long moments. Reggie stared back, evenly.

At last, he turned his head and spoke to the receptionist. "I want my son discharged. There's nothing a hospital can do for him that cannot be done at home. And a damn sight cheaper, too."

Mrs. Pearson closed her eyes, clearly embarrassed. The receptionist sighed and repeated her earlier statement that Harry could not go home until the doctor said so.

Reggie pasted a smile on her face and said, in the sweetest voice she could manage, "If you're worried about the cost, Mr. Pearson, I believe there's a poor fund one can apply to."

Mr. Pearson looked as if he would explode. His color went from pink through red to purple. His mouth puckered and his cheeks quivered. Then he turned on his heel and stalked out of the building, almost taking the door off its hinges. Mrs. Pearson followed him. When she reached the door, she turned and gave Reggie an apologetic smile.

"Sarah!" Her husband barked from outside the

building, and Mrs. Pearson hurried through the door.

When they had gone, Reggie asked the receptionist if she might use the phone. Wearily, suddenly aching all over, and worried that she would burst into tears if she wasn't very careful, Reggie phoned her brother and asked him to come and pick her up.

Chapter Thirteen

The visitors' bell clanged and people poured into the ward. Harry was unsure whether he would get any visitors on this, the second evening of his enforced stay in the hospital. He was even less certain that he wanted them. That was, he hoped Reggie would come to see him, although expecting her to give up two evenings in a row to him seemed a little presumptuous. But when it came to his parents, it was a different story. He loved his mother and would be happy to see her, but she would, undoubtedly, fuss over him and leave him feeling exhausted and depressed. She had done just that when he recuperated after the war and, to be honest, he could do without it.

As for his father—he hoped he wouldn't come here tonight. A little piece of Walter Pearson went a very long way.

However, the man who approached his bed at exactly seven o'clock was a surprise. Just as Walter had done last night, William Chilvers pulled the curtain around them, giving them a little privacy in this very public space.

Chilvers sat down and stared hard at Harry. "This was not the smartest thing you could have done."

*I didn't do it on purpose.* Harry said nothing aloud. It didn't seem worth it.

"Still, I daresay we can overcome it if we put our

minds to it," continued Chilvers.

"I don't see how." Harry felt at a distinct disadvantage, lying on this bed, wearing his pajamas. His face was unshaven and stubbly, and this was, most definitely, not the time or place to conduct a business interview. But, it seemed, that was exactly what Chilvers planned to do.

In which case, Harry needed to state his case, see if he could make the man see reason, in light of all that had happened. This attack might turn out to have been the silver lining in the cloud over him, if he played his cards right.

"Clearly," he said, "the deal we made cannot be completed. Under the circumstances, I would ask…"

"Why can't it be completed?" Chilvers' brow pleated, his puzzlement genuine.

"Because I'm in here," Harry answered, in a way that said that should be obvious.

"You'll be out in a couple of days."

"Then I'll be recuperating. There is simply no way I can—"

"If you are ready to give up so easily, young man, it doesn't bode well for your business and its future."

"That's different."

"I don't see why." Chilvers said. "I compromised when I said you didn't actually have to marry her. I can see how that wouldn't work in this modern world. But the rest of it…we agreed."

"Mr. Chilvers—"

"It's not something we can reschedule until you decide you're feeling better. Regina's birthday is a little under two weeks away. That is not a date that can be changed."

"I know. But—"

"Believe me, if it could be, I would. I have tried to delay things. I cannot."

"I beg your pardon?" The man made no sense. "You can't just change her birthday."

"Not her birthday," said Chilvers. He waved a hand in the air, dismissively. "That's set in stone. But I hoped other things might not be. I went to the solicitor handling the inheritance to see if there was any way to tweak it. I pointed out to them that she is a very young twenty-one and needs protecting." He grimaced. "Apparently, it takes a court order, and I wouldn't get one on the evidence I have."

*Thank goodness for that!* "Reggie is perfectly capable of managing her own affairs." Harry heard the indignation he felt on her behalf. It sounded loud and clear in his words. Chilvers clearly heard it, too.

"Don't get on your high horse with me, young man. I was trying to protect my daughter. That's not something a man should be condemned for."

"If you ask me, we should both be—"

"Cold feet, eh?" Chilvers chuckled. "Thought so. You need a thicker skin than that, lad, if you're ever going to succeed."

"Mr. Chilvers…"

"A deal is a deal, Pearson, and you signed up to this one. You should be proud of what you're doing. It's not every man who can say he's making sure my daughter doesn't go off the rails." He sneered. "Moving out." He gave a mocking laugh. "Getting a job, and all that other guff she comes out with."

"Sir…"

"She is perfectly serious, too. At the moment, I can

prevent her making all these monumental mistakes myself. But on her birthday, I lose that."

"I think—" They had no right to do this. It was Reggie's life, and she had to be able to live it how she wanted, regardless of what they thought. Before he could say so, Chilvers cut him off.

"This, you being…" He gestured at Harry's battered body. "It plays to our favor. Or it could do. How long can you eke it out?"

"Eke it out?" Harry frowned, pulling on the bruises to his face.

"Your recovery. I've been watching the two of you. She likes you. She's worried about you, and feeling sympathetic. Not to mention guilty."

"Why should she feel guilty?" Harry grew angrier by the second.

"She just does. And that is useful."

"I don't—"

"It means she will want to take care of you. And while she's doing that, she'll delay what she's threatening to do to me. Which gives you more time to change her mind for good. The longer you can keep this going, the longer you will have."

Harry gritted his teeth so tightly, he was surprised he didn't break them. "I am not a malingerer."

"Needs must, lad. Look, all I am saying is, you should play on her sympathies."

"I can't do that."

"Hooey! Of course you can. And it would be all to the good. Women love a wounded hero. And if that hero was wounded protecting them? You've hit the jackpot, Pearson."

There was so much Harry wanted to say to that. But

what was the point? It was clear Chilvers wouldn't allow him to disagree with his point of view.

"You've less than a fortnight to go, Pearson. You've been making good progress. I know you can do this." Chilvers stood and walked around his chair as if to leave. Then he gripped the chair back with his hands and stared at Harry. "She's yours for the taking. You have her eating out of the palm of your hand. Hold your nerve and all will be well."

Harry was glad to see Chilvers leave. He felt used, soiled by his presence. How could he have contemplated, even for a moment, the deal between them? He was thoroughly ashamed of himself.

He would not do what Chilvers wanted. Not anymore. He'd decided that, even as the man had reinforced his orders. Harry had hoped to talk sense to him, to renegotiate, but he could see that would never happen. Chilvers was too used to getting what he wanted, and now he would accept nothing less.

So be it. If Chilvers wouldn't compromise, the man would have to get used to disappointment. And if that cost Harry his dream, then that was no more than he deserved.

Next time he saw Reggie, he would tell her everything and…

The rail holding the curtain rattled quietly. Harry looked over at it and knew he had run out of chances to put things right. For there was Reggie, standing stiffly, a large box of chocolates clutched in her hand. She did not look pleased to see Harry. Nor did she look as if she worried for his well-being. Instead, her lips were pursed, and her eyes were hard and icy.

"Reggie," he said. He cleared his throat. "Reggie,"

he repeated, more clearly.

"Eating out of your hand, am I?"

*Oh, hell.*

"Yours for the taking?"

"That's not how it—"

"Hold your nerve and all will be well." She raised her chin, magnificent in her defiance, both of him and of the pain that showed in her eyes. "You must think me a dolt."

"Reggie—"

"Miss. Chilvers."

"I can explain—"

"I'm sure you can. Unfortunately for you, I'm not interested."

"I was going to tell you—"

She thrust his chocolates at him. They hit his chest in the most tender spots, causing him to wince. He grabbed at them instinctively, stopping them falling from the bed, and that hurt him again. He grunted and fell back.

"I hope you choke on them." She turned her back to him and moved to the curtain.

"I didn't know you when I agreed—I tried to tell you—I was—"

She whirled back to him. Her eyes blazed blue fire. He could feel the scorch go through him, searing his soul. Her voice was a little above a whisper, but filled with venom. "Don't say another word," she said. "And don't you dare come near me again. Ever."

She took a deep breath, transformed herself into a model of ladylike calm, and left him. It seemed to Harry that she took all the air with her.

****

Reggie was halfway along the corridor when she had to stop. The tears, which had been stinging the backs of her eyes since she left his bedside, now escaped. They rolled down her cheeks, making her skin itch. She half turned to the wall, lowered her head, and pretended to rummage in her bag so that passersby wouldn't realize she was crying. Reggie did not show her emotions to all and sundry. She did not cry in a public place, and she was not about to start now. Not over him.

When she was sure the worst had passed and no more tears were likely to fall, she made her way to the nearest powder room and did what she could to repair her face. It didn't take too much, thank God. Unlike her sister, Florence, Reggie wore only as much makeup as she felt she needed.

How could Harry have done that to her? How could he be so duplicitous? She had thought they were friends, and all along he'd...

Frankly, she should have known better. She had nobody to blame but herself, for had she not met him because he'd come to make a deal with her father? She knew, more than anyone, that William Chilvers only struck deals that benefited him, and he would make sure he had got everything he wanted from any associate. And somebody like Harry, desperate to get his business up and running, with nowhere else to turn... If her father wanted somebody to seduce Reggie into behaving as he thought she should, Harry was the perfect candidate.

She had let her guard down. Harry had been extraordinarily good at the job he'd been given. He'd certainly taken her in. Completely, and absolutely. All his talk about there being nothing more than friendship between them had been a stroke of genius, putting her at ease, reeling her in. And now, she would pay the price. More tears burned her eyes. She blinked them away. She would not give him—either of them—the satisfaction of making her cry.

James had parked his car at the far side of the hospital car park, which suited Reggie, for she used the extra moments in the fresh evening air to compose herself fully. When she finally reached him, she pulled open the passenger door and smiled so broadly, it hurt her cheeks. "Ready?" she asked.

He looked up, nodded, folded the newspaper he had been reading into a neat square and tossed it onto the back seat. "That was quick."

"Yes."

"Where to now then, miss?" He saluted, his fingers touching the peak of an imaginary cap.

Reggie was not in the mood. "Take me home."

He gave her a sidelong look that lasted for less than a second. Then, without saying anything, he got out and cranked the handle to make the engine roar into life. Jumping back into his seat, he asked in a casual voice, "Fancy a snifter on the way?"

"Not really."

"My treat." He gave her a cajoling grin.

"Just take me home, James." *Where I can rant and rail to the walls in my room until this sick, searing pain subsides.*

James kept his eyes on the road. "You've been crying."

"I got a bit of dust in my eye. The wind blew it up in the car park."

He sniffed. "No, it didn't."

She didn't answer. She didn't want to go over it all.

Not now.

"What happened?" he asked, then frowned, concerned. "Oh, Lord! Harry's not...? I didn't think his injuries were that bad..."

"Harry is fine."

"Well, something's not."

"James. I just want to go home."

James pulled over to the side of the road. It was still early enough that the roads were busy, and several cars passed them, their headlights lighting them for a few seconds before they moved on, tumbling James and Reggie back into the darkness of the evening. Trees on the side of the road swayed in a stiff wind, giving the scene an eerie, alive feeling.

"I know I'm not always the quickest on the uptake," said James, quietly. "I don't always see what's going on right under my nose. Tend to get myself bogged down in what I'm doing, and let the rest of the world pass me by. Quite honestly, it's usually easier that way. But, sometimes, even I can't ignore things."

"James..."

"This is one of those sometimes, Reggie. No ifs. No buts. Something's not right with you, and I *will* know why."

*Of all the times for James to notice something is wrong.* Reggie sighed. That was unfair. She made James sound self-absorbed and uncaring, and he was neither of those things. He just didn't feel the need to pry, to winkle out every detail, giving his ha'p'orth of opinion and getting involved. So why did he have to involve himself tonight?

"It's been a long day, James," she said. "I'm tired. So if you don't mind..."

"Well, here's the thing, Reg. I do mind. I want to know what's happened. Because you're my sister, and you are upset, and I don't like it. If I can, I want to help."

She smiled. "Thank you, but—"

"Does it have anything to do with our father?"

Startled, she snapped her head around and stared at him.

"Only, I thought I saw him coming out of the hospital about ten or fifteen minutes before you came back. I wasn't absolutely sure it was him at the time. I mean, it looked like Father, but he was quite a ways away, and it might not have been, and I thought, why would he be at the hospital?" He sniffed. "But you're upset, and he does have that effect on people. So, the more I think about it, the more convinced I am that it probably was him."

"It probably was," she conceded. "He was there."

James nodded, knowingly. "What's he done now?"

"What makes you think he's done anything?" Reggie tried to sound light, but instead it sounded strange.

James laughed. "Because I know him." He turned in his seat to fully face her and took her hands in his. "Look, Reggie. The man is a—a—"

"A bully?"

"That's one way of describing him. It's a tactic he uses in business, and it works for him. Keeps people in check. It certainly works on me, I admit. But then I work for him, I'm an employee, and that makes me fair game, whereas—"

"No, James. It does not make you fair game. Nobody should be treated the way he treats people. He shouldn't be allowed to do the things he does. The way he rides roughshod over other people's wants and desires, belittles them and their dreams…" She took a deep, ragged breath, pushing down the emotion that threatened to explode from her.

James gave a half smile. "Thought so." He patted her arm, then faced the road again. "We'll stop at the Duke of York and have a drink, and you can tell me everything that's happened." He winked at her. "I'll even let you cry on my shoulder, if you like."

That was a huge concession for James. Reggie knew her brother hated tears. It was almost a phobia with him. That he was prepared for her to shed some now was a testament to how much he truly cared for her. And an indication of how terrible she must look.

Not that she would cry, she promised herself. She owed it to both James and herself not to do so. She did not want to make her brother uncomfortable when he was being so kind to her, and, for herself, she was determined she would rise above it.

She blinked a few times until the sting in her eyes dissipated. "I'm not going to cry," she promised.

"I'll buy the drinks," he said. "You tell the tale."

And with that, he rejoined the traffic headed toward the Pantiles on the south side of Tunbridge Wells.

****

The following day, Harry was discharged from the hospital. He asked Frank to drive him home, so he wouldn't have to listen to his father lecture him on the journey. Once he got there, his mother did her best to make him comfortable, as he had known she would. Every twenty minutes or so throughout the day, she came into his room, to make sure he wanted for nothing. Was he too hot? Too cold? Did he need tea, coffee, something to eat?

When she knocked on the door for what seemed the thousandth time that day, Harry closed his eyes and bit the end of his tongue to stop himself saying, in that super calm tone one can only achieve when one has reached tether's end, *No, Mother, I do not need food, drink, cushions plumping, blankets, or anything else, except to be left alone.*

*She means well*, he told himself silently.

A moment later, he was glad he had said nothing aloud. "Harry dear, you have a visitor. Shall I send them in to you?"

*Reggie.* He hoped, prayed it was her. It must be her. It couldn't be anybody else. He didn't have friends who were close enough to call on him, and his siblings wouldn't have asked permission. William Chilvers wouldn't come here, and besides, he'd already made his position clear. He wouldn't think a further visit was necessary.

It had to be Reggie.

He sat with a welcoming, and very relieved, smile on his face as he utilized the few seconds between Mother announcing the visitor and showing her in to rehearse all that he would say to her.

First and foremost, there would be his groveling apology. He would make no excuses for his behavior because when it came down to it, there were no excuses. None that held water, anyway. Excuses were for children. As a man, Harry must accept full responsibility for his actions.

Which didn't mean he wouldn't promise to make it up to her. Whatever she wanted him to do, however he must earn her forgiveness, he would do it. And he would do it willingly.

He would not tell her he loved her. Not yet. Considering her aversion to courtship, and the fact she was angry precisely because he had made a deal to court her, declaring his love for her would probably not be his smartest move. He would bide his time on that. And if biding his time cost him his business, well, he only had himself to blame for that, too.

The door swished open. Mother showed his visitor in. It wasn't Reggie.

Harry's grin stayed in place, but all the warmth and happiness leached from it as James Chilvers walked in.

"Harry, old chap. How are you feeling?" James asked, but there was something about it that was…off. His smile, like Harry's own, was too practiced, and it did not reach his eyes. There was an awkwardness about him that said he was trying too hard to show his pleasure at seeing Harry, and the glitter in his eyes was dangerous. His voice was too bright, full of too much bonhomie.

"Would you gentlemen like tea?" asked Mother. "Or is coffee more to your liking?"

"Neither, thank you, Mrs. Pearson," James told her, pleasantly. There was a difference in his tone when he spoke to Mother. He was less menacing, more polite, but the change was subtle, and so well done, Harry doubted it could have been heard by anyone who wasn't looking for it. He tensed. This did not bode well.

"Don't go to any trouble for me." James bowed to Mother in a sweetly old-fashioned way she would love. "I cannot stay long. I just wanted to come by and let Harry know I've been thinking of him."

Judging by the anger Harry could see behind James' eyes, he could guess exactly what Reggie's brother had been thinking about him.

"Oh, that is a shame." Mother smiled. "Enjoy your time together, and if you change your mind, just ring the bell."

"Thank you," said James, and he bowed once again. Mother had a grin like a Cheshire cat as she left the room.

The door clicked shut behind her, and James' smile disappeared. "You blackguard," said James.

It wasn't what Harry had expected him to say. It was an old-fashioned word, rarely used anymore, and certainly not by anyone of their generation. Although, Harry had to admit, it served the purpose and summed up the way Harry felt about himself perfectly.

"Be thankful I'm trying not to use words that are any stronger than that," James went on, in a strange half whisper. "I wouldn't wish to shock your mother, or any of your sisters if they are about."

"Thank you." It was all Harry could think to say. Although, he added in silent irony, his sisters could probably teach James a word or two he had never heard before.

"Some of us are gentlemen," retorted James.

*Ouch.* "And some of us are not." Best to acknowledge the hit. After all, James had implied nothing that wasn't true.

"No," said James. "And one does not need to be a genius to know which side of the divide you sit. You really are the outside of... There is no common decency in you, at all."

"Steady on. I admit I've behaved badly, but that doesn't mean—"

"Behaved badly? Is that what you call it? I'd say that is putting it mildly, wouldn't you? Although it's good to hear you admit you're in the wrong. I'm sure many a rake would think he's perfectly justified in treating a lady the way you have treated Reggie. I have to say, my first inclination was to call you out, but even for me, it wouldn't be a fair fight." He looked pointedly at Harry's battered body. James himself did not have the physique of a bodybuilder, which made the insult even more pointed. Harry felt the warmth in his cheeks as shame burned them.

"Plus," James continued, "Reggie wouldn't like it if I did that. Besides, I can't really call you out unless I also call out your co-conspirator, and no matter that he deserves it, what son wants to do pistols at dawn with his father?"

There was a moment of silence, broken only by the loud, deep tick, tick, tick of the mantel clock. James paced back and forth over the carpet, agitation marking every step. He ran his hand through his hair, pushing it back from his face and leaving it sticking up.

"How is she?" asked Harry, at last. His voice was quiet, barely there, as if he didn't dare to ask any louder, didn't want to be heard, because he didn't deserve a reply.

"She's angry," James told him. "Very. Angry."

"She has every right to be."

"She most certainly does, and I can testify, she is busy exercising that right. In fact, I'm surprised she hasn't come and called you out herself."

Harry huffed. "Give her time." He wasn't sure he was joking.

James sighed. "She'd probably call me out too, if she got wind I was here."

"She didn't send you?" Although she must have told

her brother the whole sorry saga.

"That shows you how little you know her. My sister doesn't need or want other people to fight her battles for her. But that doesn't mean that I won't."

Harry nodded. At least Reggie had somebody in her family who cared for her. Her father most certainly did not.

"You stay away from her, do you hear?" James faced him fully now, and he pointed his finger at Harry, accusingly.

Harry began to reply. "I need to apologize…"

"You need to stay away from her. Or the next time we meet, it will be so I can plant you a facer."

"But I can't make it right with her if I…"

James moved swiftly across the floor. He leaned over, his hands on the arms of Harry's chair, his face inches from Harry's. "You can't make it right! Full. Stop. All you will do, if you try, is upset her even more, and I will not allow that."

The two men glowered at each other for several long seconds. Then Harry nodded, admitting defeat. James was right. He'd had his chance, and he'd muffed it. Trying to make things right between them now might make him feel better, but it would not be of benefit to her, in any way. He should do the right thing and leave her alone, as her brother demanded.

"Yes. You are right."

James watched him for a minute longer, clearly trying to discern whether Harry was serious or not. Eventually, he must have decided that he was, because he stood up straight.

"I'll see myself out," he said, and he left.

Harry stared into the flames in the hearth for a long

time. There was an ache in his chest that had nothing to do with his broken ribs, and a pain in his head that dwarfed the pain from the kicks he'd received. He had a feeling that these particular hurts would last much longer than the ones the thugs had inflicted, too.

A lifetime, probably.

Chapter Fourteen

A week after he was released from the hospital, Harry went back to work. His bruises had faded to a sickly yellow-green color and the swelling around his eyes and on his jaw had gone down until they were barely noticeable. His ribs were still tender, but the pain was, for the most part, bearable. He could drive without difficulty, and his brother, Frank, had made himself available for the next few weeks, should Harry need any heavy lifting done.

"I'm really grateful for this," Harry told Frank when they picked up a vanload of groceries that Harry's ribs were just not ready to handle yet.

"So you should be." Frank pushed the groceries toward the front of the van to make room for other things. He grinned. "What are big brothers for?" His eyes sparkled, mischievously. "Besides, it ticks our dear old papa off, something rotten. I'd do it for that reason alone."

"Is he still at you to find a job?" Frank had quit his job at the family business after a huge row with their father. He was currently filling his time with pleasurable pursuits. Harry suspected that was also to upset Walter, who could do nothing to force his son to return to the business. Frank had more than enough money to live on for some time to come, and so was immune to all of Walter's threats. Harry suspected their father's recent bouts of temper were further fueled by the fact that Frank not only refused to return to the business or, failing that, to find some other paying job, but he then chose to use some of his free time helping Harry grow the business which Walter had predicted would fail.

Apart from the necessity of help while his short term disabilities healed, Harry had another reason to be grateful Frank was here. His brother's presence forced Harry to actually turn up and do something himself, when he didn't have any inclination for it.

His motivation was lacking, partly because he knew the business was doomed. There was less than a week to go until Reggie's birthday and, barring a miracle, there was no way William Chilvers would relent on his insistence that Harry pay off the loan in full at that time. Since he also knew the chances of meeting Chilvers' demands were zero, next Wednesday, Harry would be on the hook for more money than he could afford, and he would have no choice but to forfeit everything.

Not that he had told Frank this. Frank would want to help him, and Harry was determined that would not happen. The amount he owed to Chilvers was enough to leave Frank vulnerable to their father's demands—if, indeed, his brother had enough to cover the entire amount, which was doubtful. Harry would not see his brother left penniless for his sake.

So Harry told him nothing about the complex finances of his company, and pretended all was well. He told nobody. It wasn't necessary for anyone else to know. He'd made the mess, and he would live with it. And while he waited for the axe to fall, he saved every penny he could, optimistically wishing on stars each night that, in the cold light of a business day, Chilvers would see the company as a viable concern and have second thoughts about destroying it.

His hopes were buoyed by the fact that the company was doing much better than he'd predicted it would. The money had started coming in, faster than Harry had hoped for, and he had high hopes that, if he squirrelled enough away to make a sizeable repayment, it might go in his favor.

He didn't need much to live on. He was a bachelor, living in his parents' house. He had no dependents, and no plans for any. All hopes he might have harbored in that regard had flown when Reggie discovered what an idiot he had been.

Although he kicked himself daily for what he had destroyed, and grieved for what might have been, there was a silver lining to the cloud, in that he was able to put more money into his savings than might have been the case if he was squiring Reggie about. Which, in turn, built his hopes up even more that his company might actually survive, even if it was touch and go for a while.

His occupation of the barn was safe. He'd paid the rent for a year, so he'd have somewhere to store goods and to work from, at least. The telephone company was also paid. Those were things Chilvers couldn't take in lieu of payment. Plus, it would do him no good to strip the barns of the fixtures and fittings Harry had installed, so presumably those were safe.

The biggest loss would be the van. Seeing it as a tangible asset, Chilvers was sure to seize it, along with the money Harry still hadn't spent from the loan. He had been judicious in his spending, largely thanks to Reggie. She had looked at everything he needed and worked out the most cost-effective way to get it. Thanks to her, there was quite a bit of money left. Along with the value of the van, it should be enough to cover the bulk of the debt. His personal savings would cover most of what was left. If he was lucky, it would be enough for all of it.

He smiled now. It was ironic, he thought, that Reggie's budgeting might thwart her father's attempts to destroy the man who had failed him and hurt her.

Once he'd paid Chilvers, all Harry would need was enough cash to buy an old jalopy, so he would at least be able to do his deliveries. It wouldn't project the same image as the brand new Leyland, but needs must.

An idea had occurred to him in the middle of one of his sleepless nights. Chilvers was a man of business, and a good one at that. If Harry could persuade him it would benefit him to allow Harry to keep trading rather than seizing everything, he might be persuaded to lease the Leyland to Harry. Then Harry could stay in business properly, showing off his brand in a way he was happy with, while Chilvers got a good return on his investment.

The idea, while it had merit, didn't make Harry feel better. Not inside, where it truly mattered. Only one thing could do that, and it was far beyond his reach. The loss of his friendship with Reggie was like a never-healing bruise, a bittersweet ache that tempted him to press on it addictively, just to remind himself of its pain.

Now and again, something would cause it to flare. Then, it became a sharp burning sensation that penetrated deep inside him, as if someone had cut him with a knife. It would stop him in his tracks, steal his breath, and make him want to double over, groaning in agony.

That was when he knew this—the business, his independence, everything—all meant nothing. Not without her. She had been with him from the start, helped him with every aspect, part of what it took to build the company from the ground up. She had made suggestions, given him ideas, helped him form his plans. Together, they'd chosen the van. Designed and built the warehouse. She had listened while he practiced his telephone voice, worked out the timings of his routes, decided on his prices. She was in every moment, every brick and nail, every nut and bolt. Without her, he was sorely tempted to walk away and never look back.

Except, Reggie wouldn't want him to. She wouldn't want her hard work, and his, to have been for nothing. She would want something she could point at and proudly say she had helped build it. She would want this company to be a success.

For her sake, he would make it one. He would fight tooth and nail to keep it afloat, to see it survive and prosper. He would do it all, for her.

Harry took a deep breath, pushing down the sting of the jagged-edged knife sawing at his heart, checked he had everything on board the van, and closed the back doors. "For you, Reggie," he whispered.

Frank got into the van on the passenger side while Harry pulled himself up into the driver's seat, and they set out to make the delivery.

****

Wednesday the fourteenth of April was cold and gray, with a drizzle of rain that suited Reggie's mood perfectly. She had been in a state of funk for days, and the mood wasn't going to lift simply because today was her birthday.

She told herself she was feeling nervous of the future, and that was all there was to it. Today was a big day for her. She had now reached her majority and could do whatever she wished with her life. Nobody had the power to gainsay her anymore. Her inheritance was in her hands. She could leave this house, be what she wished to be, do what she wished to do.

On the other hand, she was now responsible for herself, her actions, her money. Nobody would be there to catch her if she made a mess of things. Nobody would save her from herself.

Father had tried. At least, that's what he said when she discovered he'd talked to the solicitor handling her inheritance. He had wanted to break the terms of the inheritance and force a delay in her receiving it.

"For your sake, Regina," he had said when she confronted him. "You're very young. I don't want to see you hurt, or taken advantage of."

"The only person trying to take advantage of me is you," she'd retorted, before adding that she would live as she saw fit and not as he dictated, although in her heart she wanted to believe him, wanted to think that, as her father, he would want only what was best for her. That they just differed on what that might be.

She could, she realized, forgive him for trying to delay the inheritance. It had been arrogant and high-handed of him, but that was his way. He'd grown up in the last years of Victoria's reign, and his attitudes and beliefs reflected that. When his opinions were forming, women were little more than chattels. They went from being under the control of their fathers to being controlled by their husbands, and when they married, they gave up all rights to everything they owned. Father had been a young man before the Married Women's Property Act allowed women to keep and control their own property.

In those days, no woman from a well-to-do family sought employment, either. Women worked because they had to, because they were of the classes that provided servants or shop workers and such, or because they'd fallen on hard times and needed to make their own living. They did not take jobs simply because they wished to do so.

The war had changed that, of course, when so many men marched off to fight and women were needed to take their places. But even then, men like William Chilvers expected it to be temporary. Once the war was over and the men returned, they thought women should step back into their drawing rooms and resume their tea parties and charitable support.

They had certainly not expected their daughters to take up where their mothers left off and demand careers for the sake of them.

With all that in mind, Reggie knew she would forgive her father his heavy-handed attempt at managing her fortune and her future. But she would never trust him again. And she was determined to move out from under his roof as soon as she could.

Harry was a different kettle of fish. Not only had he grown up in the modern era, when women had more freedom, he'd been as much a victim of patriarchal control as she had. He'd had to fight to establish himself as his own person and to do what his heart decreed. He should have understood and empathized with her. Yet he'd happily fallen in with her father's plans and machinations. He had manipulated her, preyed on her emotions, drawn her in. In his way, he was no better than the fortune-hunting would-be bridegrooms of the last century, whose long shadows frightened her father and powered many of his protestations.

"If I hadn't overheard that conversation in the hospital…" she murmured, then she shook her head. "I'm well shot of him. And I won't let him spoil my birthday."

With that resolution cemented by having said it aloud, she left her bedroom to join the family for the small tea party they were holding in her honor downstairs.

James stood at the foot of the stairs, waiting to escort her into the parlor. He grinned, broadly, at her as she descended toward him.

"Look at you," he said, "all grown up. It's not five minutes since you were all legs and freckles, your hair in pigtails, and your dress torn."

"Probably torn on some adventure you led me into!" She laughed. "I haven't been that hellion for years, James, and you know it. So stop pretending otherwise."

"Who's pretending? I know you've been a beautiful, elegant woman for quite some time now, but it happened so gradually, I didn't notice at first. But today, with it being your birthday, and the big birthday at that, it sort of makes one stop and take stock. I'm looking at everything with fresh eyes. And you, I have to say, clean up very well."

"There he is," she answered. "That's the brother I remember. A backhanded compliment, and a suspiciously naughty grin. You had me worried there, calling me beautiful and what-have-you. I thought someone had paid you to say it."

"Maybe they did. After all, a man does have to keep himself in the manner to which he's become accustomed somehow, does he not?"

Reggie stared at James, surprised. It was rare for him to 'get' jokes made by other people. It was almost unheard of for him to come back with a witty riposte. He was one of those people who blinked and looked blankly at you, leaving your humor to fall flat.

All of which meant his lighthearted banter made today even more special.

He pulled Reggie to him, squeezing her in a tight hug. "Happy birthday, sis," he whispered. He kissed her cheek, then patted her head, in a teasing remembrance of the days when he would ruffle her hair and run off with her ribbon.

Reggie smiled and hugged him back.

"But I do have to remind you of one thing," he said, shaking a finger at her as if he was about to lecture her. "Twenty-one today or not, you are still my baby sister. You have always been my baby sister, and you always will be. Perhaps you're not quite so red and scrunched up as you were when I first met you…"

"Oh, you!" Reggie swatted his arm and he grabbed at where she'd hit him, pretending she had hurt him.

Then his smile dropped. "Seriously, how are things?"

Her grin faded, too. "Fine."

"You're sure? Because if they aren't…"

"They are. All is well, James. I promise."

He sighed. "If you say so. But I want you to know, if you need anything, I am here. I mean it. Whatever you need me to do, I'm here to do it." He frowned, thoughtfully. "Except lifting heavy furniture. I'm not particularly good at lifting heavy furniture."

Reggie rolled her eyes at his absurdity. "You're an

idiot—what's he doing here?" Her smile disappeared as she peered out through the window beside the front door. Through it, she saw Harry park his car in the drive and pull himself out of the driver's seat. As she watched, he grabbed his sticks, and a large bouquet of flowers before he closed the car door.

Reggie groaned. She hadn't expected anything from Harry, and she wasn't sure she wanted it, yet at the same time, she felt a frisson of pleasure go through her at the thought that he had made the effort. And there was a part of her—a very small, very silly part of her—that was pleased to see him here, that wanted to invite him in, forgive him, take things back to where they had been…

Which was ridiculous. It was just because it was her birthday. She was caught up in the emotions of the day, that was all. The last thing she wanted was to see the man who had so badly betrayed her, who had conspired to destroy her future for his own gain.

James turned to see who she had seen. He swore, then apologized for his language.

She waved his apology away. "He's enough to make a saint swear."

"I'll go and deal with him."

It was tempting to let her brother do just that, to avoid Harry altogether. But that wasn't fair on James, and Reggie had the feeling it wouldn't do any good anyway. She needed to talk to Harry herself, and nip in the bud any delusions he might have of them making up and going back to what they had been.

She needed to talk to him. She didn't *want* to talk to him. She needed solely to make sure he got the message and knew he was *persona non grata* in this place. Or anywhere she might be. There was no other reason to meet him. She definitely did not want to listen to what he had to say, to listen to his deep, dark voice. She wasn't expecting an apology, and she didn't want to hear it from him, even if he brought one.

Not that his apology would be of any value. Fine words made of smoke, wrapped around paper flowers. Nothing more. Harry had lied to her. He had used her, betrayed her, conspired against her with her own father. The last thing she wanted was to talk to him.

But if she didn't go out to Harry, James would, and one of them would be bound to hit the other. She did not want that.

"I'll wait here for you," said James, as she opened the front door.

"You don't need to. Go on into the parlor. Join the fun. I'll be in, in a minute."

James raised his eyebrows in mock horror. "You would send me in there, alone and unaccompanied? You want me to venture into the Tea Party of Doom?"

Reggie laughed. "It is not that bad."

"Not that bad? Not. That. Bad? Mother and Father are in the same room. Together. Plus, the whole gaggle of our sisters are in there, none of them behaving as they ought to. There are…" He clutched his throat like an elderly lady clutching at her pearls, and adopted a look of sheer horror. "Cucumber sandwiches! And a sponge cake, for goodness' sake! With butter icing! And you want me to go in there, brave all of that, without any protection?"

Reggie patted his arm in grateful thanks. She knew what he was doing, and she loved him all the more for it. "All right. Stay here. Do not come to the rescue unless it's a matter of life and death."

James saluted. Reggie went out to meet Harry, who was now hobbling up the drive.

She met him halfway along the path. The air was damp, although the drizzle had stopped. The grass had a fresh green sheen, as though someone had painted it with gloss, while the soil was dark and plump. The scent of spring flowers and fresh earth swirled through the afternoon, and a bird chirruped repetitively in a tree. Reggie was aware of the goosebumps on her bare arms, and the cool breeze caressing her hot cheeks.

Henry smiled, tentatively, at her. "Happy birthday," he said.

This time two weeks ago, he would have hugged her and bussed her cheek. She would have welcomed it, wished it could have been more, a proper kiss that left nobody in doubt as to how she felt about him, and hopefully, how he felt about her. She would have taken his arm and let him lean more on her than on his sticks. They would have walked into the house, where she would have introduced him to her family. Some of whom, she reminded herself now, already knew him as well as, if not better than, she did.

On that thought, her back straightened and she pushed her shoulders down, her chin rising to an almost haughty level as her heart hardened. "Thank you," she said. She was glad to hear her voice was devoid of all emotion. "You didn't need to come."

"I wanted to wish you well."

"You have." *Now, please leave me alone before I beg you not to.*

"And to give you these." He held out the bouquet. "Along with my heartfelt apologies for what I did."

There was the magic elixir. The potion she needed

to bolster her resistance to him. For a moment there, she had been in danger of overlooking his crimes, deciding they didn't matter. His apology reminded her that they did.

"I'm not interested, Harry. Please, just go away."

"Reggie…" He reached out the hand holding the flowers. It may have been an entreaty for her to take them, but it looked more. Reggie stepped back.

"I mean it, Harry," she said. She hoped the flat tone she used made him think she was indifferent to him, that he hadn't hurt her too badly, that she had quickly recovered. Inside, where nobody could see, her heart hurt. A lump formed in her chest, hard and rocky and tear-inducing. She knew she could not stand here and talk to him for much longer, not without bursting into tears in front of him. And that, she promised herself, she would never do.

So she took the flowers and lowered her gaze to them, as if she found the folded red petals fascinating. There were a dozen of them, all a deep, dark burgundy, ready to unfurl and fill the world with their perfume and their beauty. There was no blemish on any of them.

"Thank you," she said. She glanced up at him, then looked down at the flowers again. "I mean it, though, Harry. I do wish you all the best. I hope everything works out well for you, I truly do. But I want no part of it. I want no part of you. Please, leave me alone."

She turned from him and returned to the house. It took a gargantuan effort to keep her steps steady, her pace unhurried, when what she truly wished to do was run as fast as she could.

At the door, she risked a glance back over her shoulder. Harry stood where she had left him, his head bowed, shoulders slumped. Another two steps and she was inside the house.

James closed the door softly. He didn't say anything—and somehow, that made it worse. A sob escaped her.

James took the roses from her and laid them on the hall table. The ends of their stems had soaked the paper wrapping them.

*That'll ruin the French polishing on that table.*

The mundane thought was the last straw. She let her brother gather her into his arms, and she cried into his chest, the heartbreak of the ages pouring from her.

## Chapter Fifteen

The next four weeks were a nightmare for Harry. He missed Reggie dreadfully. Barely a moment went by when she wasn't in his head, occupying every thought, driving all else away. If he saw something interesting, his first thought was, *Reggie would like that*. When a large contract came his way, he wanted to tell her about it before he told anybody else. Without her, the celebration of it was muted and wouldn't have happened at all if Frank hadn't been with him. Frank expected Harry to toast his first big success, and Harry did not want to give Frank a reason to speculate about why he didn't do so.

When he should be at his desk, doing his paperwork, Harry found himself thinking of her. He dreamed up impossible ways of meeting with her, so that he might beg her to listen to him. He would give everything he had for a few moments with her, for the opportunity of a second chance. And if she ever granted him that chance, he would spend the rest of his life proving to her that he was worthy of it.

He had been so stupid! Whatever had possessed him to agree to her father's deal in the first place? He'd known it was wrong. People were not assets to be bartered, nor were they pieces on a chessboard, to be maneuvered into place to secure a victory. He'd known that, and he'd said yes anyway.

Thank God he'd refused the original deal, to marry her. She would never even consider forgiving him if he had agreed to that. The thought of an arranged marriage was intolerable to him, and he had known, instinctively, it would be more so to her. If he was ever to marry the woman he loved, it would be because of their mutual feelings, and not because…

His head jerked as if he came to from a doze. He looked around his office, relieved to find himself alone. Frank was out on a delivery, so wasn't there to notice Harry's strange behavior. Frank had been a godsend, stepping in to help when Harry's newest injuries hampered his abilities, but he was too quick and too perceptive by half. Harry did not want him—or anyone else—delving into his feelings for Reggie, or into the mess he had made of them.

His feelings for Reggie. That was the second time in as many minutes he had acknowledged them. Oh, he'd known they were there. He wouldn't feel so bad now if there were no feelings for her. His conscience might still trouble him if there were no feelings for her, but not by anywhere near as much as it did now. Misery would not sour his mood and take away his pleasure in all he had achieved so far, if it wasn't for how he felt about Reggie.

Harry had known all these things before, but this was the first time he had put them into coherent thought.

Not only did he have feelings for her, he'd just thought of her as the woman he loved. *The woman he loved!* Was that true? Did he love Reggie?

Part of him wanted to say no, it wasn't true, he didn't love her. He *cared* for her, but love? He couldn't love her. He hadn't known her long. Surely one could not love someone in such a short time. Although, he had heard of people who fell in love at first sight, so maybe…

How would he know? He'd never been in love before, so how could he possibly tell whether what he felt now was love?

"What is love, anyway?" he muttered.

"Why are you asking that?" asked Frank, making Harry jump.

"Where did you come from?"

"Just now? Tunbridge Wells. Originally? I'd say it's Father's place to tell you that."

"Very funny."

Frank grinned. "Why are you asking about love?"

"I wasn't."

Frank raised an eyebrow.

"I was… It was… Someone said something that made me think." Harry shuffled the papers on his desk unnecessarily. "I've got a delivery in Fieldhurst to do. Do you fancy getting onto it so I can finish up this paperwork?"

"Paperwork to do, love to ponder." Frank elongated the word "love" so that it took three syllables. Harry gave him a sidelong look, and he continued, "It's got nothing to do with that doll you went to the kinema with, has it?"

"What do you know about that?" Harry frowned. That night was not amongst his fondest memories. Not only had he been attacked and hospitalized, but it had been the reason William Chilvers had sought him out, and why Reggie had discovered his betrayal of her before he could confess to it.

"Only what I heard when Father was ranting about her being at the hospital."

Harry bristled. "What did he have to say about her?"

Frank swatted away the question as he would swat a

fly. "Sounds like she put him in his place." He chuckled. "I would have paid good money to see that."

"You're just angry with him because he fired you." And Harry was picking a fight to avoid talking about Reggie.

"He did not fire me. I quit. And stop changing the subject. Is she the reason you are contemplating love?"

"No." Harry knew he answered too quickly. "I'm not even seeing her anymore," he added, hoping he sounded unbothered, although it probably didn't help that he spoke the words to his accounts book.

"That's a shame. I liked the sound of her."

Harry didn't answer. Instead, he concentrated on the paperwork. It took all his willpower to do so, especially with Frank trying to wheedle answers from him.

Eventually, though, his brother saw he was getting nowhere, gave up, and prepared to take the goods to Fieldhurst. "Anywhere else after that?" Frank asked.

Harry handed him two more job sheets.

Frank looked them over and nodded. "You're going from strength to strength. You'll need a second van soon." He took the job sheets and left the office.

A second van. Harry grimaced. Things were going well, Frank was right there. But what his brother didn't know was that, barring a miracle, it didn't matter how much work he did, or how much demand there was for it, H. Pearson Transportation was unlikely to be buying a second van.

In fact, Harry was surprised he still had use of the first one.

Ever since Reggie's birthday, Harry had been on tenterhooks. With every day that passed, he expected a communication from Chilvers, demanding immediate repayment of the loan. After their conversation in the hospital, Harry knew Reggie's father was unwilling to compromise. Renegotiation of the loan was out of the question, and since Harry had missed the deadline for fulfilling the criteria, there was only one possible outcome.

He'd heard on the grapevine that Reggie had started the job her father hadn't wanted her to take, although he didn't know where it was. He'd gone back to the tea shop, hoping to find out, but he had been unwelcome. Oh, they'd served him, but they hadn't been pleased to do so, and they made sure he knew it. Elsie had thrust his cake at him and plunked his tea down so belligerently he half expected to wear it. She made it clear she wouldn't talk to him. When he'd asked one of the other waitresses about Reggie, he got a shrug of her shoulders, a mumbled, "Don't know, sir," and a studious avoidance of his table for the rest of his visit.

Whatever and wherever her job was, he wished her well with it and hoped it lived up to her expectations. He wished he could have shared it, celebrated its good points with her, commiserated over the bad. Alas, those moments were no more going to happen than his purchase of a second van.

He had racked his brains for ways to pay Chilvers without destroying the business. It was impossible to raise another loan to do that. The banks were no more likely to lend him money now than they had been before, and there was nowhere else he could, or would, turn to. Father had the money, but if he paid Chilvers, Harry would be no better off. Walter Pearson didn't think Harry capable of running this place, so he would either take it over himself or he would sell the assets to minimize the loss. Neither was acceptable to Harry.

If Frank knew, he would want to help. But Harry wouldn't let him. Besides, he might need the money himself soon. Frank had clashed so badly with his father that the pair were barely speaking. Harry suspected the only reason Frank still lived under Walter's roof was economic necessity. Frank's devil-may-care attitude, and his enjoyment of his playboy lifestyle, made it unlikely he could sustain a life independent of his parents. But if the argument continued, he might decide he needed to try, and then he would need every penny he could find.

Harry had offered to pay Frank, but his older brother wouldn't hear of it. That was, Harry suspected, more to tick off their father than because he was altruistic. And although Harry was grateful, because it meant he could put more into the fund to repay Chilvers, he knew it couldn't last. Sooner or later, Frank would need payment, or a proper job.

Meanwhile, Harry worked his fingers to the bone, putting everything he had into the success of the company, using every day that Chilvers delayed demanding repayment to grow it a little more, and praying it would be enough.

It still puzzled Harry that Chilvers was giving him so much time. He'd spent the last four weeks waiting for the instructions that would ruin him. Every day that passed without the demand to repay was another stay of execution, another chance to survive. The question was, why?

\*\*\*\*

Reggie entered the office building at the top of Mount Pleasant Road with less enthusiasm than she'd had on her first days of working here. Before reality had set in. It wasn't that she'd expected to be given a senior position straight away, nor had she expected deference or special treatment. But she *had* expected to do the job for which she was being paid. So far, in four weeks, she hadn't even looked at a ledger, or a receipt, or an invoice. The closest she'd come to working with figures was when her superior dumped the heavy volumes on her empty desk at the end of each day and told her to put them away on the shelves in the book room.

Other than that, she made tea and shopped for tea room provisions. She counted paper clips. Reggie shook her head in disbelief at that. She understood the need to know if stocks were low and needed replenishment, but this job had gone beyond that. Her superior wanted her to open every single carton and check there were the exact number of paper clips as stated on the label. Not one under the amount, and not one over.

"When you've done the paper clips, you can check the pencils," he'd said. She suspected after the pencils and pens, there would be staples, and after that she would be checking every sheet of paper in every ream. She wanted to scream with frustration.

Her co-workers, all men, insisted on treating her like a lady, which in some ways was nice. She wasn't quite ready to throw off all societal niceties and be "one of the lads," as James had put it in his birthday toast.

So, although she accepted it was a male-dominated office, she did not expect them to treat her as they would a man. She didn't want to be a man.

She knew the men here had made adjustments on her behalf. They had toned down their language since her first day, and she noticed they often changed the subject of their conversations when she entered the room. They doffed their hats to her in greeting each morning, and they were all unfailingly polite. That part of being the only woman here was quite nice, and she was grateful for it.

But when it came to the work, her gender meant they treated her like an imbecile. They clearly did not agree with their boss, the man who had hired her. They made it known to her that they didn't believe she had the intellectual ability to do the work. When she asked about it, asked when she would be taught to do the job, they told her to be patient, everyone had to start at the bottom, these things took time. Yet the young boy who had started on the same day as Reggie was already being shown the details in the ledgers, and had been taught how to fill them in. And he was only fourteen years old!

While Reggie made tea.

She suspected her superior in the office wanted her to quit. They couldn't fire her, not when they considered who had hired her. But they could make the job boring and unfulfilling, and hope she would walk away of her own volition. Not that Reggie would give them that satisfaction.

Even if she wanted to, she couldn't. Not until she found something else to replace this job. She'd moved into her flat now, and she had bills to pay. There was no way she was going to return to her father's house, give up her independence, and revert to his rules for her life. If that meant she had to count paper clips, put books onto shelves, and wash up teacups *ad infinitum*, that's what she would do. Eventually, they had to see she wasn't a quitter, surely? Eventually, they would give in and let her do her job.

She looked at the Situations Vacant columns in the local paper, of course. She'd even applied for a couple of jobs, although she'd known as she filled in the paperwork that she wouldn't get them. Very few businesses, it seemed, were willing to take on a woman. Not in a position of responsibility.

Worse still, she suspected that this job had not been given to her because the boss was progressive in his thinking, or because he thought she was the right candidate. Since starting here, she'd realized her boss was a friend of her father's, and she wondered, in her more cynical moments, if this whole thing had been orchestrated by William Chilvers in order to show her that working for a living wasn't as wonderful as she had thought it would be.

Well, he was right there, at least where this job was concerned. But if Father thought being unfulfilled here would make her retreat, tail between her legs, to the life he planned for her, he had another think coming. She had no intention of admitting defeat. She would stay in her flat, living on her own terms, and she would pay for it with money she had earned. Which meant working here. For now.

The office building was dark inside. Set in an old Victorian building with sturdy walls and windows that were too small, it had thick oak doors that would keep out after-hours clients and English weather alike. All of which meant the place needed the electric lights switched on all day, just so people could see to work. Even then there was a dreary, downtrodden atmosphere. Reggie thought back to the other places she'd worked in recently, and longed for their happy, refreshing air.

There'd been the tea shop, of course, with its large

windows at the front. Although the green-and-teal walls were designed to subdue the lighting in the place, it hadn't made it dreary. Besides, that was a place for dim lighting, a place for relaxing and enjoying time with friends. This place was for working. Not only that, it was for close work. She couldn't help but think the lack of light in here was bad for the workers' eyes. A glass pane in the door instead of it being solid wood, a coat of light paint on the walls, a little less masculine clutter, and these offices would be transformed.

Not that she could suggest such a thing. Not while her only acknowledged value was her ability to make a good cup of tea.

Of course, she'd made tea at Harry's warehouse, too, but that had been different. There, she had also been trusted with other jobs. He had asked her opinions, shown her his plans, made her feel she was a part of it all. She sighed, lamenting the loss.

"That's a big sigh, Miss Chilvers," said Mr. Thomas, her superior. "Something wrong?"

Reggie pasted on a smile. "No, sir. My bus was late and I had to run to get here on time," she lied. "Just getting my breath back." Hidden in the folds of her dress, she crossed her fingers.

"Good. Good," he said. "Make the tea, there's a darling girl."

She pursed her lips at the term of endearment, although she didn't suppose he meant anything by it. It was what he would call any woman. The fact that he wouldn't call a male colleague a "darling boy" wouldn't occur to him. Reggie pushed away her ire at his words, put her bag into the drawer of her empty desk, and headed for the kitchen.

*You made tea for Harry, too.* But then, Harry had made tea for her as well. And he had never metaphorically patted her head by calling her "darling girl."

"No," she muttered. "He lied to you and planned to trick you into marriage." She frowned. She couldn't say that, exactly, not if she was being honest. That he planned to marry her was an assumption she had made, not an actual confession of his. Although, she remembered his words about honeymooning in Cape Town, so maybe it wasn't such a farfetched assumption, at that.

Somehow, though, the fact that he had planned her future behind her back didn't seem so bad to her now. It was bad enough, of course. The memory of it still hurt, and she would never trust him again, but...

But what? "But nothing, that's what. He betrayed me. End of story," she told the kettle as she waited for it to boil. She reached into the cupboard and started pulling out the cups she would need to give a drink to every man in the office, then pulled out the tea canister ready to spoon tea into the pot.

"I don't need people like Harry Pearson to upend my life, thank you." In Reggie's opinion, her father was more than capable of doing that to her. He didn't need outside help.

With all of that, though, she couldn't help thinking of Harry. She wondered how he fared now. A month after the beating he'd taken from those thugs, he must, surely, be almost healed. The bruises and scrapes would be gone, the swelling disappeared. She supposed his ribs might still be a little tender. Did that impact his business? If he wasn't up to doing the physical work, would it create problems for him?

As to that, how was his business coming along? She wondered if he was getting orders, and if so, were they increasing as the weeks passed and his name became better known in the area?

Once, she'd seen his van drive past the office. It was only a fleeting glimpse through the window on the stairs. She'd stopped on her way to the upper floor with the tea for the senior staff, and she'd watched the van go along Mount Pleasant Road, until it disappeared from her limited view. As she made her way up the last of the stone steps to the upper offices, she tried to guess where Harry might have been delivering goods today. Since he drove down the hill, she assumed he had just finished, and was returning to Ramslye and his warehouse. Or perhaps he was going to the train station, to pick up more goods coming in on the train.

There had been a time when she would have known the details. He would have told her everything, about every new contract. She would have listened avidly, danced around his tiny office in celebration of each success, hugged him to commiserate every near miss, and relished being in his arms, feeling the warmth of his body close to hers, the thrill in the air around her as the flutters grew in her stomach. When their eyes met, his would be dark, unfathomable, as his breath shallowed and his lips moved nearer to hers, and…

"Stop it, Reggie Chilvers!" she whispered angrily. "You put him behind you. Leave him there!" There was nothing to be gained by constantly harking back to her time with Harry, pining for his friendship, wishing he loved her as much as she…

She froze, hand wrapped around another cup inside

the cupboard. The cold porcelain anchored her even as her breath caught and shock made her heartbeat sputter. The kettle roared louder, seeming to fill the entire kitchen with the sound, mingling with the shocked, appalled rhythm pounding in her ears.

*As much as she loved him.* That was what she'd been about to say to herself, in her head, where her private thoughts were secret, and honest.

Reggie loved Harry. She closed her eyes, but that didn't help. All she saw was him, smiling mischievously at her, eyes glittering a welcome as he gestured at her to come to him.

She shook her head, and pushed away the image. Harry did not want her to come to him. He'd had four weeks to realize he didn't need her. In that time, he'd made no attempt to contact her. He'd probably moved on by now. After all, there were plenty more fish, swimming back and forth and praying for an angler to catch them. So many fish these days. So few anglers. And, whatever he might think, Harry was a very eligible angler. Far too eligible to waste his time casting his net for one that had already got away.

With a heavy swallow and a rapid blink to rid her of the regretful tears that threatened, Reggie poured a small amount of water from the kettle into the teapot and swirled it about to warm it, then threw that water down the sink and spooned the tea leaves from the canister into the pot. This, her present job, deserved her concentration. She did not have the time to spend mourning what might have been.

Chapter Sixteen

On the fifteenth of May, Harry received a check in the post. He was not made happy by this, since it was his own check, written on the thirtieth of April to make the first scheduled repayment of his loan to William Chilvers.

His first thought was that it had bounced through lack of funds, although how that could be, he had no idea, for he'd kept his books meticulously. If there had been some error at the bank, he would set them straight, in such a way they would never make the mistake again.

A quick perusal of the letter accompanying the check showed there had, indeed, been a mistake, although not of the kind he had expected. Far from the dreaded words, "refer to drawer," the check was listed as "excess payment, monies not required."

"Oh, no," he moaned. He covered his face in his hands. This was a disaster. Not only had he missed his first repayment on the loan, but alerting William Chilvers to that would remind him that Harry's account needed dealing with. Which, in turn, meant Harry had run out of time. How could the bank have made such a mistake?

Knowing he had to at least try to put this right, Harry phoned the bank manager. The call left him even more puzzled than before. According to Hugh Burgess, the manager of the Fieldhurst branch, the loan had, indeed, been paid in full, four weeks ago.

"We received a banker's draft, with instructions to pay the monies into your account and then use them to pay Mr. Chilvers, as per your arrangement with that gentleman," said Hugh, an old school friend. He had a clerk fetch the letter from the filing room. "It's a per procurationem signature," he continued, explaining, "someone signed it with PP, on your behalf. I can't read the name of the person who signed for you, but it's on your headed paper. I can assure you, Harry, there's nothing about it that would raise an alarm in my office."

He was regretful that he could not say where the banker's draft had originated. "All I can tell you is that it is not a customer of this branch. If it was, I would have the details of the sender, although it would still be unethical of me to pass those details to you. However, if you think there is a problem with it, I can make enquiries…"

"No," said Harry. He frowned, trying to figure out what had happened. "There's no need for that. But thank you."

After he'd hung up the phone, Harry sat for a long time, staring at the check and trying to work out what had happened. How had somebody paid off his loan to Chilvers without him knowing? Where would they have found the information needed to do it?

"What is happening here?" he murmured. He twirled his ink pen through his fingers, the little fidget helping him put his thoughts in order. Several unlikely scenarios chased through his head, but after twenty minutes, he was no nearer to working out what had happened than he'd been at the start, and now his head ached as well.

There was really only one thing he could do. To be safe, and to make sure he truly didn't owe Chilvers any money, he would need to talk to him. Then, he could either clear up the misunderstanding and try to set things right, or he could investigate further, try to find out who he now owed his debt to, and how he would pay back this unknown benefactor.

He picked up the phone, intending to call Chilvers' office and make an appointment with him, then changed his mind. They had made the agreement at the man's house, so presumably, he wouldn't mind discussing it there.

A visit to the home might also allow Harry a chance of seeing Reggie again. If she still lived there. She might do. He knew she'd found a job, but that didn't mean she had moved out yet. Flats were expensive, both to buy and rent, and it wasn't always easy to find one anyway. If he went to the Chilvers home tonight, he could discuss the finances, and perhaps find an opportunity to…

"For God's sake!" he whispered. He was pathetic. He was acting exactly like his sister had when she discovered John Barrymore was playing Hamlet at the Haymarket in London last year. The minx had almost turned Father's hair white in her reckless efforts to be near her idol. She had contrived to go up to town for a week, ostensibly to stay with a school friend. Margaret and her friend had then found myriad reasons to be near not only the stage door in hopes of meeting him, but on one of the seedier streets of London, where they had discovered most of the actors had their lodgings. It didn't occur to the young ladies that Barrymore, a star from America, would not have been housed in the sort of rooms chorus players could afford. They made nuisances of themselves until Walter was forced to travel to London and bring her back, having rung a peal over her first.

Even if Margaret had managed to meet John Barrymore, Harry thought, the chances were the poor man would merely have been polite to her even as he sent her packing. Harry had no such guarantee. If Reggie was there when he turned up, she would probably cut him dead, and there'd be nothing he could do about it. She would not talk to him, and that was that.

Be that as it may, Harry needed to speak to her father. So he would go to the man's home tonight for that reason. And if he saw Reggie, he would behave according to her cues. After which, he would leave her alone and be satisfied with that.

Of course he would.

Harry waited until after Reggie should have arrived home from work before he called. He didn't see her as he was ushered into the parlor, where William Chilvers greeted him, clearly annoyed that Harry had come. He made it plain they had nothing to discuss.

"Your check was returned because it was an overpayment of the loan, which had already been repaid in full. You do not owe me anything at all. There was no interest outstanding, or anything of that ilk."

Harry frowned. "It was definitely my loan that was repaid?"

"Weeks ago." Chilvers sat down, crossed his legs and picked an imaginary piece of lint from his trousers. Harry noted he was not offered a drink this time. "Just after my daughter's birthday, to be precise. I remember being surprised that you were so prompt. I hadn't even had time to prepare the notice to repay to send to you.

You pre-empted me." The man's expression told him this had not pleased him. It seemed the least he had expected had been to watch Harry grovel for more time to pay. "I wondered how you had managed to find another source of finance so quickly. I asked myself why you would come to me in the first place, telling me I was your last hope, when you obviously had other options." Chilvers smirked. "Or was coming to me a ploy on your behalf?"

"A ploy, sir?"

"She's not an easy lady to encounter without some planning and forethought."

"No, sir, you have it all wrong…"

"You're not the first young man to inveigle his way in here, in hopes of getting to know one of my daughters. Although it's usually Florence. She's prettier. More, shall we say, welcoming of suitors."

"I did not…"

"Although you are the first to ask for finance. That was inspired. Getting me to invest in your business that way. I take my hat off to you for your initiative."

"The loan request was genuine, sir."

"I'm sure, on some level, it was. But you did agree very readily to my conditions."

"I was desperate." Harry spoke through gritted teeth. This man was making him sound like a cad. Which was exactly what he had been. "For your information, Mr. Chilvers, I really have regretted that abominable deal almost from the minute we made it. My self-revulsion has only grown with every day since. Your daughter deserved better."

"Dare say she did, my boy." Chilvers pulled a cigarette case from his pocket and offered one to Harry, who declined it. He only smoked cigars, and besides, the last thing he needed right now was a nicotine buzz interfering with his thought processes.

William lit his own cigarette and put the case away. "Had the last laugh on us both, though, wouldn't you say? Made what my son would call goofs out of us, has she not?"

She certainly had.

Harry longed to ask her father how she was, and what she was doing. Perhaps the man would tell him where she worked. He took in a deep breath, preparing himself to ask the question, plead for the information. Before he could do so, Chilvers stood.

"I wish you well in your venture, Pearson, I really do," he said, holding out his hand for Harry to shake. "But, in a way, I'm glad our plans came to nothing. Much as I wished to see her settled and behaving in a more, shall we say, ladylike manner, Regina would never have been happy if we'd succeeded. And ultimately, my daughter's happiness is what truly matters to me."

So, thought Harry, that was that.

Chilvers led Harry from the parlor into the hall, where his wife called to him, telling him he was wanted on the telephone. With a mumbled "excuse me," and a request to James that he see Harry out, Chilvers disappeared into a room at the back of the house.

James bristled at the sight of Harry. His stare was icy and he pointedly refused the offer to shake hands. He moved toward the front door, and Harry felt as if he was being forcibly ejected from the premises, rather than simply leaving politely. He still knew nothing about Reggie, how she was faring, whether she still lived with the family. He was fast running out of opportunities to find out. So he took his chance, even as James turned the doorknob.

"Is Reggie home from work yet?"

"How would I know?" The tone James used said, *And why would I tell you if I did?*

"I thought you might have seen her come in. Or do you get in later than she does?"

James glared at him. "If you've come here hoping to see her, you are out of luck. Didn't Father tell you? She moved out, weeks ago. Thank you for coming. Don't call again." He pulled open the door and stood aside for Harry to go through. As soon as Harry was outside on the doorstep, the door shut behind him. It wasn't a slam, but the snick of the lock was decided and unmistakable.

More miserable than ever, Harry made his way along the drive. His back and legs ached tonight more than they had in months. There was a dull pounding behind his eyes, and a longing for a warm bath and his soft bed, although he knew sleep would be elusive. His mind would be too busy to allow it, as it pondered the answers to the three most important questions in his life at the moment: Where was Reggie? Who did he owe the money to now? And how on earth was he going to pay them back if he didn't even know who they were?

He was almost at his car when the house door opened again, momentarily flooding the driveway and front garden with yellow light, before it closed. Quick, light footprints sounded and he turned to see a beautiful young woman running from the house toward him. Her dark hair was bobbed and her dress was scandalously short, coming to just above the knee. She looked like a flapper, the young women who were always in the newspaper for enjoying themselves raucously and horrifying their parents' generation.

As she approached him, he saw she was nothing like Reggie, although he guessed she was her sister. Her eyes were dark, and her face more fashionably pretty than Reggie's. He would bet she was never short of a beau to squire her around, but to Harry's mind, she couldn't hold a candle to her older sister.

"Florence, I'm guessing?" He held out a hand. She took it, and he was reassured to feel a firm handshake.

"And you are Harry. Or, to be more precise, 'that damn man who belongs in the last century or better yet consigned to the bowels of hell where women are in charge and men have nothing and see how they like it.' "

Harry winced. "She said that?"

Florence nodded. "She did. Question is, how do *you* feel about *her*?"

It seemed to Harry that this was one of the most important questions of his life. If he answered in the wrong way, this young woman could, and would, deprive him of every last chance of finding happiness with her sister. But if he answered the *right* way…

What did he have to lose? Reggie was already gone from him. If there was the slightest chance that he could change that, he had to grasp it with both hands. Lies and subterfuge had got him into this mess. Only complete honesty had a hope of saving him.

"I love her." It was simple, unadorned, a statement of fact. He felt the words to his very core.

"You love her?" Florence looked skeptically at him. "If you don't mind me saying, Mr. Pearson, you have a funny way of showing it."

He nodded, ashamed. "Yes."

"You hurt her, you know."

"I know."

"But then, if she didn't care for you, you couldn't have hurt her. And if you hadn't hurt her, I don't think she would be so mad at you."

Harry's heart did a strange, stuttering flip as hope captured his breath.

"Question is," continued Florence, piercing him with a very direct stare, "what do you intend to do about it?"

Harry shrugged his shoulders. This was where hope ended and reality kicked in. "What can I do? I'd like to apologize. To make it up to her, somehow. But I can't. I don't know where she is, and anyway, the last time she saw me, she wouldn't speak to me, and she sent me away with a flea in my ear."

Florence watched him carefully for another ten seconds. Under her scrutiny, it felt like an hour. Then she reached into a pocket hidden in the seam of her dress and withdrew a small piece of card. She thrust it at Harry. "That might help," she said. He took it from her, and she grasped his wrist. "But do not, and I mean it, *do not* queer it for her with them, or our next chat will not be so cozy."

Harry believed her. She looked like someone who could take care of herself, and everybody else, too.

She walked back to the house, hips swinging, the hem of her skirt swaying to and fro. He guessed she was not a woman who went ignored very often. She was certainly not one of Reggie's nine out of ten who would remain on the shelf.

Harry preferred her quieter, less flamboyant, sister.

She closed the front door behind her, cutting him off from the family in the house. Harry got into his car and read the paper in the meagre light. It was the address of an accounts firm in Mount Pleasant Road in Tunbridge Wells.

He closed his eyes. For the first time in as long as he could remember, Harry actually prayed.

The following day, with Frank's help, he raced through his deliveries, trying to finish them in record time. A policeman on traffic duty wagged a remonstrating finger at him and gestured him to slow down, although, thankfully, he didn't give him a ticket. He finished the last of his runs shortly after four o'clock, then parked his van on Church Road in Tunbridge Wells and waited.

The roads were quiet now, although they would get busier when people left their offices in an hour. Then the pavements would fill with pedestrians, dodging each other as they raced for bus queues, and the roads would be heavy with bicycles, buses, taxicabs, and private cars, whose numbers were growing year on year. He hoped Reggie would join the queue for the bus, where he was sure to see her. If she went down the hill toward the train station, or shared a taxi with friends, he might miss her. That would mean coming back and waiting for this chance another day. Already nervous about approaching her, and her likely reaction, he didn't think he could stand the delay.

He had lain awake most of last night, thinking about her sister's words, taking them apart, looking for clues to hidden meanings. As the first gray shards of dawn cracked the darkness on the horizon, he'd come to some startling conclusions.

First, Reggie cared for him. As Florence had said, she would not have been so hurt if she hadn't had feelings for him. That gave him hope that, angry though she was with him, she might still care enough to give him another chance.

His second conclusion had been the one that had really kept him from sleep, though, exercising his mind greatly. He'd realized that, if he wanted Reggie to consider giving him that second chance, he was going to have to show her exactly what she meant to him. There could be no lackluster declarations or ordinary, everyday acts of love in this. The gesture he used to prove himself to her would need to be huge, and it had to be right. Whatever he did, he had to prove, beyond doubt, she was what mattered to him, and her happiness came before everything, including his own.

It had taken all night and quite a lot of the morning to figure out exactly what he could do to show her that. He'd then spent more hours working on the details in his head while he drove around delivering his goods. His work had been done automatically, and he barely remembered any of it. If he hadn't had the paperwork signed to prove it, he might have doubted some of his jobs had actually been completed.

In what should have been his lunch break, he put his plan in motion, and now he was ready to offer it, and himself, to the woman he loved. For he did love Reggie. He loved her more than he had ever loved anyone in his life. He loved her so much, he was willing to die for her. He certainly loved her enough for this. He glanced down at the long black bag on the seat beside him. He just hoped it wasn't too little, too late.

At five o'clock, the first workers came out of their offices and headed home. Some went into the small parade of shops near where he was parked. Young men pounded each other on the back or punched each other's biceps as they walked along together or met in little groups. Women in company uniforms stood with their friends, hips cocked, shoulders back in unnatural poses they presumably thought would catch men's eyes. They coyly dipped their heads and gave secret smiles to those that took their fancy. Men in suits collected the bottoms of their trouser legs into bicycle clips and pedaled away uphill, or coasted down. A horn sounded somewhere on the road. The queue at the bus stop started to grow.

Harry got out of his van and walked to the corner of the street, so he could see the accountant's office door. He prayed he hadn't missed her.

And then, at ten past five, he saw her. She left the office, the last but one person to do so. The man following her locked the door and checked it was secure. Then he headed down the hill. Reggie walked up, toward the bus stop.

She was one of a dozen young women standing there, all of them looking tired after the working day. Harry took a moment to take in every detail of her, committing to memory the way she looked, just in case it was the last time he was allowed to come near to her. Like most of the women at the bus stop, she wore sensible black shoes with small, Louis heels. Her coat was black and the skirt pecking out from under it was gray. Her musketeer hat was black and silver and perfect, neither too frivolous nor too plain. To Harry's mind, although Reggie's outfit was similar to many of the other women there, she stood out from them, elegant in a way they could only aspire to.

Harry moved toward the queue. In the busy street, his sticks felt cumbersome and his legs clumsy. Some people muttered oaths at him, irritated that they must make way for him. Others pushed past, letting him know by their actions that he was holding them up. He ignored them all, his focus only on Reggie.

Finally, he was behind her, less than two feet from her. The woman behind her in the queue smiled at Harry, and batted her eyelashes, then pouted when it had no effect on him.

"Hello, Reggie," he said, in a voice that was mercifully clear, and a lot steadier than he had thought it would be.

She turned, startled at hearing her name. When she saw him, she tensed slightly, then nodded her head, just once. "Mr. Pearson."

At least she had acknowledged him. Her husky tone seemed to caress his name. Her eyes flitted down from his face to his chest, and back up. He felt it like a real, physical touch.

"What are you doing here?" she asked.

"I had some deliveries." It wasn't a lie. Harry was through with lies. They had cost him so much. Too much. Briefly, his conscience twinged, as he wondered whether it was as bad as lying to omit the fact that the last three of those deliveries had been some time ago.

"Oh." Was it wishful thinking on his part, or had he detected disappointment in the single word? She gave him a polite, insincere smile. "Good. I'm glad for you."

She nodded, as if to agree with herself, then looked around, awkwardly. Women in the queue turned away from them, pretending they weren't listening. Reggie gave her attention back to Harry. "I trust it's going well, then?" she asked.

He nodded. "Very well. It keeps me busy." There was a pause. He fidgeted, uncomfortable, wishing he was one of those brilliant raconteurs who always knew the right thing to say at the right moment. "How are you?"

"Fine. Absolutely fine."

He nodded in acknowledgement. They watched each other, neither one sure what to say or do next. More than one lady in the queue was paying avid attention to them now. They didn't even try to hide their interest.

"Can I give you a lift?" He congratulated himself on injecting just the right amount of insouciance.

"I'm waiting for the bus," she replied, deadpan.

"Yes. But…"

"You really don't need to trouble yourself about me, but thank you anyway." She made to turn back to her place in the queue, where, like everyone else usually did, she would no doubt stare into the middle distance and ignore her fellow passengers.

"It's no trouble," he answered. He hoped, prayed, that his tone, his expression, everything about him, conveyed the truth of that.

She turned back to him. She had the sort of look on her face that generally preceded a roll of the eyes. "It is out of your way," she said.

Harry swallowed. "No. It isn't."

Reggie's eyes narrowed and she gave him a suspicious look. "How do you know?" Which was a good question. He didn't know where she lived, so he had no idea how far out of his way it was. Except that he knew which route the bus took, and he knew it didn't matter to him. She could live on the moon and he would make certain it was on his way home.

"Do you know where I live?" she asked. Her manner suggested she was almost ready to call a constable on him for making a criminal nuisance of himself.

"I haven't a clue, actually." He gave her a half smile. "But it doesn't matter. I would go miles out of my way for you."

"Harry—"

"Brighton. London." *Cape Town.* He didn't say that last one aloud. He didn't dare. The closest he came to admitting it out loud was to say, "I'd go wherever, all around the world, if that's what it took."

"Harry…" she warned. All the other women around her were openly listening now. Which meant they were either going to see his moment of greatest triumph, or, more likely, his greatest disaster.

He needed to get her away from this audience, somewhere they could talk freely. "Come on, Reg. I can take you door to door." He winked, and pointed in the general direction of his van. "Well, corner of the road to door. No strings."

Her lips thinned. He was losing her. Then the woman behind her in the queue leaned forward and whispered, loudly, "Go on, love. It's only a lift home."

"You'll get a seat in his vehicle," said another. "We'll likely have to stand all the way home."

"And he's right handsome," added the first woman, with a wink. Reggie gave her an old-fashioned look. She didn't contradict her, though. Harry's spirits rose.

A few seconds went by before Reggie spoke. "No. It's not a good idea," she said.

The women groaned. Reggie turned away from Harry. Panic built in his chest.

"I've got the van," he said, desperately. "You never did get a ride in it."

The two women groaned again.

"Talk about an offer you can't refuse," said the first

woman, sarcastically, but Reggie half turned her head. Harry could see she was tempted.

"Please," he murmured.

Reggie glanced at him, then looked away again.

"Please," he repeated. "A lift home. And a short talk. And if, after that, you still want me to leave you alone, I will. I promise, I will never bother you again."

"Can't say fairer than that, love," said the first woman.

Reggie didn't turn to him. Long moments went by. Nobody spoke. The two women looked from Reggie to Harry, their pitying looks sinking his spirits.

She wasn't going to give him the chance he needed.

His whole being felt heavy with despair. He knew he should walk away, alone. He should respect her wishes. And he would. He would. He would see her safely onto the bus, and then he would move away. He wasn't capable of going until then. But he would be. He would go. He would keep his promise and leave her alone. And for the rest of his life, he would nurse his broken heart and think what might have been, if he hadn't been so stupid.

The bus trundled into view, its engine roaring, the bittersweet smell of diesel covering everything. The queue pushed forward as the first people clambered on.

Reggie took a step back, nearer to Harry, leaving the queue. The first woman smiled and winked at her, then moved on, taking Reggie's place. Harry's breath caught. He hardly dared hope.

"So, where's the van?" she asked as the bus pulled away from them.

He gestured toward it, offered her his arm, and they crossed the road. "Here she is. Pearson One. What do you think?"

"She's beautiful. Looks good in your colors."

He grinned, beyond pleased at her praise.

Harry helped Reggie into the van, then moved around to the front, cranked the engine, and climbed into the driver's seat. "Where to, modom?"

She gave him her address and he turned to the right direction. Reggie looked around, taking in the van's details. Finally, she nodded her approval. "It drives nicely. It's quiet."

"It is, isn't it? You can actually hear yourself think in this one." Unlike some vans he had been in. "It holds plenty of produce in the back, too." He changed gear and the engine growled. "How's your new job going?"

They went uphill and he had to raise his voice slightly so she would hear him above the laboring engine. It still wasn't particularly noisy, but it wasn't as quiet as the old-fashioned steam cars had been. Sometimes, progress left a little to be desired.

Reggie shrugged, and answered his question. "I'm still learning the ropes." There was something in her voice that alerted him, and he wondered what she was not saying.

"All that work you did at the tea shop," he went on, his own voice bright, deliberately cheerful. "It must come in really handy."

She chewed the corner of her bottom lip. "You have to start at the bottom."

He sneaked a look at her and noted her expression. She wasn't happy, but she was trying desperately not to show it. "They don't appreciate you, do they?" he asked.

She pinned a smile into place and gave a tiny shrug. "I wouldn't say that. Everybody starts at the bottom, you know. Then you move up when you're ready."

"Where's the bottom?"

Reggie hesitated. He sensed she didn't want to tell him. He stayed silent and drove, at a leisurely pace, along the road. Finally, she sighed. "I make the tea and count the paper clips. It's very important to know how many paper clips there are."

His heart broke for her. All her hopes and dreams, reduced to paper clips. Her bosses most definitely did not appreciate her.

"The van is definitely quieter than I thought it would be," she went on, and she patted the woodwork, as if congratulating the vehicle on being just right for its job. "So, business is good?"

Harry knew when she was finished with a topic of conversation. He went with her lead. "Very good. It's taken off well."

"I knew it would. I had every faith in you. It was a service that was needed around here."

Harry swallowed. "I couldn't have done it without you."

She laughed.

"No, I mean it. The way you helped me set up and get everything ready, you were worth your weight in gold."

"I wouldn't go that far…"

"Wouldn't you? I would. You were an inspiration, and a fount of wonderful ideas." Out of the corner of his eye, he could see her cheeks darkening. "You kept me going when I was ready to give up in despair."

Her blush deepened. Harry fancied he could feel its heat now, filling the cab with her perfume. "You understood what was needed," he continued.

"Sometimes before I did." He looked slyly at her and took a chance. "And then, of course, you invested a lot of money into the business as well."

She glanced at him, then looked sharply away.

"It was you, wasn't it? You're the one who paid my debt to your father."

Reggie kept her face turned from him. She seemed suddenly to be fascinated with the view on her side of the road. Her arms were folded in her lap, her fingers twisted, making her gloves taut. It was the only outward sign that she was not comfortable.

"I didn't understand why he hadn't followed through with his threat to call the loan in. I thought he would be chomping at the bit to prove he meant it. Day after day, I wondered…"

She pulled her bag higher onto her lap, so that it looked almost like a shield in front of her. She opened it and searched inside for something. He suspected she didn't know what.

"Then, when the first proper payment went out, and your father sent it back to me, that's when he told me he had already been paid."

Reggie turned back to Harry then, her eyes wide, the look on her face one of horror. "He knows, too?"

"That the debt was paid?" He nodded. "Of course he does. Though he doesn't know it was you who paid it."

There was a long, awkward silence. Harry gave all his concentration to the road. The way Reggie stared through the windscreen, it seemed she did the same. They left the town center behind and drove into the suburbs.

"How did you know it was me?" she asked, at last.

He grinned. "Process of elimination. It had to be

someone who knew of my debt to your father. There weren't many names on that list. Then, it had to be someone with enough money to cover the debt. That narrowed the field even more. For instance, my bank manager knew of the loan, but I would be surprised if he could cover it. And the bank itself wasn't going to. I had already asked them and been turned down, in no uncertain terms."

"That's their loss."

"Thank you. So, I got my list narrowed down in the end, to three people who might know about it, could do something about it, and might want to." He held up his right hand, steering only with his left while he counted them down on his fingers. "One. My father. But, believe you me, he would not have done it anonymously. He would have wanted the world to know as he swept in on a blaze of glory, saved me from my own folly, and then tried to take everything away from me and add it to his empire."

She was satisfyingly outraged on his behalf. "He has no right to do that," she stated.

"Walter would disagree. He's fond of saying that only those who pay can play. So I knew it wasn't him."

"Would you want it to be him?" she asked.

Harry laughed. "Fifty years ago, when there were still debtors' prisons in England, I might have been tempted. Any port in a storm and all that. But now, when there's no danger of going to jail just because you owe money…" He shook his head. "Can you imagine how insufferable he would be? So, no, I would not want it to be him. And besides, I knew almost immediately that it wasn't. Which brought me to my number two suspect. Your brother, James."

"James?" She stared at him, astonished. "Why would you think…James?"

"It was a fleeting suspicion. He was very interested in the business when he came to build the lift."

Reggie nodded. "I suppose he might have loaned you the money, if he had realized you needed it. He wouldn't necessarily have seen what was going on, though. Sometimes you have to really point things out to him before he notices. But then, when you do, he's always willing to help. He has a heart of gold underneath it all."

"James sees far more than you think he does. But he wouldn't have loaned me the money. If you had heard how he spoke to me… Let's say it was not how you would speak to a man in whom you had just invested a fortune."

"He spoke to you badly?"

Harry pulled a face. "He spoke to me in the way I deserved him to."

"Because of me?"

"Like I say, I deserved it. But anyway, I knew it wasn't James. Which left…" he pushed up the third finger on his hand, "you."

She gave a trill little laugh which revealed her discomfort at that. "Elementary, my dear Pearson?"

The conversation lulled as he changed gears and turned into a narrow road. Then, as he sped up again, he asked, "Why?"

Reggie stared through the windscreen. For a while, she said nothing. Harry began to think she wasn't going to. Then she sighed. "We put a lot of effort into building that business. I didn't want it all to go for nothing. And besides, Father did not deserve to win. Not with his little games. He had no right to do what he did."

"Neither did I." Harry said it softly, but the words were like a hammer beating on an anvil where his heart should be.

"No. You didn't."

"But you still bailed me out."

"There were a number of factors I took into account." It was her turn to count things down on her fingers. "One. As we have already said, a great deal of time and effort went into getting your business started. I didn't want to see all of that wasted."

He nodded. "Thank you."

"Secondly, when I stopped to think about it, you did try to tell me what you'd done. Didn't you?"

"I should have succeeded." He scoffed. "I should have said no in the first place."

"Well, I gave you points for trying to tell me. And thirdly," she pointed at him, admonishing him, "and this is in no way an exoneration of you, so don't start to feel too comfortable, but to my way of thinking, of the two of you, my father's was the greatest sin."

Harry frowned. "How do you come to that?"

"He was in possession of all the facts before he began his machinations. You were not. Which doesn't make you right, of course, and I hope you will know in future that it is not all right to try to make people into your puppets."

"You can count on it."

"But that's why I paid him off."

Harry sighed. He looked ahead, partly for safety as he drove, but mostly because he was too ashamed to meet Reggie's eyes. The traffic had thinned now they'd reached the outskirts of the town, and the road was relatively straight. The evening sun was lower in the sky than it had been just a few minutes ago. It tinted the air, the trees, the road, with a molten gold that made the black of the shadows darker and more defined. Harry was forced to squint to see very far.

Concentrating on watching where he was going, not even glancing at her now, he said, "I am sorry, Reggie. I knew what we were doing was wrong, and I should have said no. I said no to a part of it…"

"The arranged marriage bit?"

"Yes. But if I was able to say no to that, then surely I could have, and should have, said no to all of it. I was a craven coward. I thought I could—I believed I would somehow be able to make everything right further down the line. Have my cake and eat it, I suppose." He felt her gaze on him, steady, uncompromising, making him feel worse with every second. "If I'm honest—and I will be, from here on in, I give you my word—I thought it wouldn't matter if I delayed your dream to save mine. It never occurred to me that I wasn't being fair. Although," he gave a soft huff, a self-deprecating chuckle, "had it been the other way around, I would have screamed from the rooftops how unacceptable it was." He slammed the heel of his palm into the steering wheel. "I was so selfish! Full of my own self-importance. But then, I fell in love with you, and it began to matter more and more, until it mattered more than everything else put together. I wanted to get out of the deal, get as far away from it as I could, but I couldn't see how, and I didn't know how to tell you, or how to make it right, and…"

He chanced a look at her. She was staring at him, her expression unreadable. Was she disgusted with him? Would she demand he stop the van and let her out, say that she would walk home rather than be in his company, hold him to his promise never to see her again?

"I am so, so sorry, Reggie. What I did was unforgivable, I know. But if—if you could see your way to allowing me one more chance, I will try and make it up to you. Please, Reggie, just give me another chance?"

There was a long pause. When he looked at her again, he saw she was watching the road. Her brow was furrowed, and she looked deep in thought.

"Whatever you decide, I promise I will repay you every penny you gave him for me."

She turned to him then and opened her mouth to speak, probably to protest, but Harry wasn't going to let her. He would not be taking her money. A cad he may be, but he was no mountebank.

"Apart from that," he said, cutting off her protests before they could begin as he finally tried to say what he'd intended to say when he first arrived in Tunbridge Wells this afternoon hoping to see her. "I was wondering, how much do you like your present job? Because I think I have the perfect job for you, if you were interested. I've got all the details in that bag…" He gestured to the bag he had moved from the seat to the floor. "I can tell you, you would definitely be appreciated there. No counting paper clips."

She didn't move. She just continued to stare at him.

His smile faded. "You wouldn't start at the bottom. In fact, you'd start at the very top. A full and equal partnership, with equal responsibility for the work, and the decisions, and absolutely equal claim on the profits." *More than an equal claim until I have paid you back fully.* "In case you haven't guessed, there are documents in that bag. When you sign them…" He took a deep breath. "*If* you sign them, the company will become H and R Pearson. Half yours."

He looked over at her again. She didn't seem to have moved at all. He could not tell what she thought or how she felt.

"Or we could call it Chilvers and Pearson, if that suits you better, but I was sort of hoping... Reggie?"

Harry pulled over to the side of the road and cut the engine. His indicator clicked, loud in the sudden silence. She turned her head and gave him her attention. Whether that was good or bad, he couldn't say. "Reggie?" he implored her. "Say something."

She swallowed. "You love me?"

That wasn't what he had expected her to say. It took a moment to process it. "Yes," he answered. "I do."

"You honestly love me."

Harry closed his eyes in despair. He'd blown it. Why had he felt the need to declare his feelings, when he knew...? "I'm sorry," he said. "I know it's not what you want, that it's a bore and it interferes with everything you do want, but, well, I said I would be honest. So, yes, I do love you, but I promise it won't be an issue."

"You love me." She said the words as if she rolled them on her tongue, tasting them.

"Yes." It was all he could say for now.

"How much?"

Hope flickered back to life inside him.

She smiled. "I mean, I know it's enough to offer me half your business. It's like half the kingdom in a fairy tale." She smiled.

He gave a small laugh, uncertain.

"What I really want to know is, would your love get us to Cape Town and back?"

Did that mean…? Was she saying…?

"To Cape Town and back," he agreed.

Reggie nodded. "Good."

Harry frowned. The hope within him dimmed. Was this where she dashed his hopes and dreams to show him how it felt? "Good?" he asked.

"Yes. Good." She held up her hand and counted her points on her fingers. "It's good that you love me," she said, using the first finger to count that. "And two," she moved her second finger, "I love you too. To Cape Town and back."

He let go of the breath he had been holding on a half relieved, half thankful laugh.

"In fact," she went on, "if you were interested, I think that could make a wonderful, memorable, and interesting honeymoon trip. What do you think?"

Harry grinned at her, and Reggie grinned right back. Then he pulled her into his arms, and he kissed her.

## A word about the author…

Caitlyn Callery lives in Sussex, southern England, near the Regency towns of Brighton and Tunbridge Wells. She is passionate about writing and suffers withdrawal symptoms when she takes a few days away from her work.

Before becoming a full-time writer, she worked in banking, as a waitress, in the motor repair industry, in a call centre, and for a charity. As part of this last job, she helped build a school in Kenya, and drove a vanload of wheelchairs from the UK to Morocco.

She also loves reading, knitting, walking by the sea, the theatre, and spending time with her family.

Visit her at:

CaitlynCallery.com

Thank you for purchasing
this publication of The Wild Rose Press, Inc.

For questions or more information
contact us at
info@thewildrosepress.com.

The Wild Rose Press, Inc.